# THE
# FURTHER
# ADVENTURES
# OF
# HORACE
# HORRISE

## John Hemming-Clark

© Searchline Publishing 2021
First edition 2021
**ISBN:** 978 1 897864 66 1
British Library Cataloguing in Publication Data available
Published by Searchline Publishing, Searchline House
Holbrook Lane, Chislehurst, Kent, BR7 6PE, UK
**Tel:** +44 (0)20 8468 7945
**www.johnhemmingclark.com**

**Printed in England by** www.catfordprint.co.uk

The Further Adventures of Horace Horrise is a work of
fiction. Names, characters, businesses, places, events and
incidents are either the product of the author's imagination
or used in a fictitious manner. Any resemblance to actual
persons, living or dead, or actual events is purely
coincidental.

The adventures that appear in the Horace Horrise books
have been inspired by the youngsters of Chislehurst and
further afield plus other people I meet, friends, random
conversations with strangers, places I visit and so on.
There is, in fact, probably a little bit of everyone and
everything in these stories.

Have fun reading about Horace – the UK's funniest, liveliest
and naughtiest young person and his ever-so-slightly
dysfunctional family and friends!

Dedicated to Joelle
Whose fabulous deli keeps me in
coffee and carrot cake
during the writing process

# Contents                                    **Page**

Horace Horrise and the Germans              3
Horace Horrise and the Carinavirus         83
Horace Horrise and the Old Lady           121
Horace Horrise goes to Portugal           199

## IntRODUCtIOn tO THE FURtHER ADVEntURES OF HORaCE HORRISE

The nine-book "Adventures of Horace Horrise" has a distinctly scouting theme taking the reader from Horace wanting to be a scout to finally getting invested (or does he?). However, after that, I felt it was time for him to break out of this mould and focus not only on him but also his friends and his ever-so-slightly dysfunctional family as they go about causing merriment and mayhem in their daily lives.

Whereas "Adventures..." were published separately for "Further Adventures..." I have put four stories in one longer book as this seems to be what most of you would prefer.

One thing I have discovered is that many of my readers are grown-ups and of these a sizable proportion have told me that they love these stories because they can read them to their children but still enjoy them themselves without falling asleep halfway through! I have, therefore, tried to make these four new stories even more accessible to both groups although a few, a very few, sections may need to be read ahead of "Jackanory" time if the children involved are younger than eleven-year-old Horace.

Lastly, what I am most often asked is, "Where do you get your stories from?" I have put on the copyright page my source material without being entirely specific. However I thought that it might be fun to introduce each story with a bit more background. Not one adventure is complete fiction!

I hope that you enjoy the stories.

John Hemming-Clark

## Introduction to Horace Horrise and the Germans

*Karen Horrise feels that she needs to start doing her best in the community and signs up to help out with the local town twinning.*

*The Germans arrive on a week's visit but Horace and his pals are out in force with their own programme to give them a time that they will never forget.*

My father has been a member of Guildford / Freiburg town twinning for a number of years. One day he was busy matching German visitors with their English hosts for a forthcoming visit. He had little slips of paper for each member that included their likes and dislikes. "Wouldn't it be funny if a gust of wind came and mixed them all up?" he suggested. From that one question this story was written. Most people are probably aware of town twinning but have little knowledge of what benefits membership confers apart from occasional visits to and from the other country.

The Waitrose / Lidl theme had to be included due to the snob value of one and the differing perceptions of the other at home and in Germany.

The library gets a mention because it's one of those local services that many may not use but it's a vital free resource for learning, literacy and education. As I write Chislehurst library in a much-loved old building is threatened with a downsizing of space and book numbers in a shiny new building with no architectural merit whatsoever.

The trip to Uncle Bernie's pub was mostly inspired by a conversation that I had with a group of female scousers whilst working for Barclays Bank as a staff trainer in London in the 1980s. Cashiers would come for a week's residential training and one group of twenty-somethings decided to have a night out in Soho. I need say no more about their encounters with the Toronto Tornado at a less than wholesome venue in Walker's Court. One of their number told me that Wendy, wearing a white nylon blouse with gathered sleeves, went to grab a hanging strap on the tube then screamed when what appeared to her to be a giant tarantula attached itself to her elbow. "Excuse me mate!" she said to the diminutive middle-aged man, who was standing more or less underneath her outstretched arm, as she pointed to the outsized arachnid, "Is this yours?" Yes, it was indeed the now toupee-less man's hairpiece. Without saying a word he pulled it from Wendy's sleeve and stuffed it in his jacket pocket. He alighted at the next stop.

The other bits and pieces are too minor to merit space here apart from mentioning that Joelle's of Chislehurst is a real place, as is Joelle who sells a divine slice of carrot cake and who once told me that she would love to appear in a book. So here she is.

Chislehurst features in most of my stories: it's where I live and has enough of many things going on not to be included.

## Horace Horrise and the Germans

"Get the shopping in Horace," his mother demanded throwing the car keys sideways at him as she continued on her unstoppable march along the hallway from front door to kitchen. She didn't even look in his direction - a telepathic sense of his bright red t-shirt as he emerged from the sitting room was enough. A glance would have been more than was necessary, Horace surmised. In a moment of madness his mother had bought this new t-shirt for him as a special treat only a week ago and, seeing as it had the cover of Tintin's *The Blue Lotus* printed on the front, she could not have failed to identify the wearer. Furthermore Horace had worn the t-shirt every single day since he had opened the unexpected parcel that had been addressed to him and immediately put on the contents so it might have been that his mother had simply smelt his presence.

He had no hope of catching them. She had thrown fast, low and to one side. Had Alastair Cook been in Horace's place, primed and ready, he may just have got a finger to them but for Horace there was no way. He wasn't even expecting the Audi keys to be launched at him. A packet of cookies maybe but even then they would normally have been calmly placed on a table or taken into the kitchen and opened with a, "One Horace, oh go on, two then just this once," and not hurriedly thrown in his general direction. The keys shot through the door with the velocity of a cricket ball hit for six and landed clean in grandad's lap. He awoke with a start and, with a sixth sense as to the reason for their having left his daughter's hand, announced, without in any way betraying the fact that he had been in a deep sleep, that he wasn't getting the shopping in because, "It's always too heavy."

Karen Horrise, in the meantime, had reached the kitchen and deposited the one bag that she had been carrying on the breakfast, lunch, tea and sometimes also dinner table. Leaving grandad to look after the keys for a moment Horace followed his mother close behind. He thought that she looked uncharacteristically flustered and was keen to reassure himself that all was well.

"When you're done you can help yourself to some ice cream. I've bought some Belgian white chocolate flavour," she announced to the bag. Horace smiled. "Belgian white chocolate" meant one thing: Waitrose. Although he long ago realised that the choice of supermarket shouldn't be one of the more pressing decisions that one had to make on a regular basis, for Horace's mother it appeared to be a choice that was fraught with issues. The local supermarket was usually a no-no to her for all sorts of reasons that Horace mostly didn't quite understand although the main one was straightforward enough: it was a matter of privacy.

"I simply object to pushing a trolley around knowing that every neighbour that you meet may well want to stop and pretend to talk to you about some urgent business but all they're interested in is a good look at your groceries," she had once complained.

"It's just so nosey. Then you get to the checkout and Jock wants to comment on everything you're buying. 'Good morning Mrs Horrise. Oh I see you've gone for the fat-free yoghurt. Would that be because you're looking to lose a few pounds?' or, 'Weetabix this week? Such a superfood! I like the red berry version myself...'"

"Is everything okay mummy?" Horace enquired. "You look hot." Karen raised her head and gave Horace an impish smile. She recalled her husband saying to her exactly the same three words years ago, soon after they had started going out together, although his comment then was more of an exclamation of intent than concern for a patient's wellbeing.

"I'm fine thank you Horace," his mother replied. "It's just that I find supermarkets such a...." Mrs Horrise thought for a moment and then a bit longer.

"Bother, inconvenience, challenge?" Horace suggested.

"Yes, all of those," his mother replied, reaching inside the bag. "It's made me quite thirsty. That and the fact that I've still not sorted out all the stuff for the Germans' visit and time is slowly running out and now it's speeding up and I really do have to do it, like now and it's stressing me big time."

"But you haven't done anything yet mummy. Shall I get you a glass of water or try to make a cup of tea?" asked Horace brightly. He was keen to get his hands on the ice cream as soon as he could but he wanted to make sure that his mother wasn't going to pass out from dehydration in the meantime. Now that really would be a problematic situation: one-handed resuscitation with the other round the ice cream tub.

"No thank you darling," his mother replied as she pulled out a bottle of Sauvignon Blanc throwing the empty bag onto the work surface. "It's beyond tea and water right now. I need some medicine. It's worrying me *because* I haven't done anything yet." Holding the bottle tightly in one hand she gave the screw cap a firm twist then flicked at it with her thumb. The cap span off and his mother put the bottle to her lips. She took a large gulp. Horace looked at her, horrified.

"I know Horace," she said sensing his displeasure as she wiped her lips with the back of a hand. "It really should have gone in the freezer for ten minutes but this is an emergency and I can't think straight. The problem is Horace I never know where to shop. The supermarket down the road is convenient but full of nosey neighbours as you know. I can never stock up on France's finest without murmurings of, 'Look how many bottles she's got in her trolley' when they don't know that I'm buying for the next six months..."

"It's usually six days mummy."

"That's enough Horace. The one on the bypass is far too big. If I want some exercise I'll go for a walk in the woods with your father not round a load of shopping aisles that have to be as wide as dual carriageways so that they can accommodate their outsize customers pushing outsize trolleys piled high with outsize food items. The one over the hill doesn't have a human till and I can't be doing with d-i-y scanning. I know I have to drive a bit further and pay a little more but Waitrose is such a pleasant shopping experience and now they've been sending me money-off vouchers so if I spend over seventy pounds it's become no more expensive than down the road..." Karen Horrise pondered for a moment before adding,

"...apart from today."

"What happened today mummy?" Horace asked, quickly picking up his cue. Slowly he felt he was getting to the heart of the matter and that his mother was about to announce that she had been accosted, robbed or worse. Had someone beaten her to the last hot garlic and pomegranate-roasted chicken with wild sage and onion stuffing?

"Today, Horace," his mother sighed, "I had put all my shopping on the conveyor belt thing and then was perfectly content chatting to the cashier whilst packing my purchases. I had everything sorted, you know - freezer, fridge, cupboards on so on, when I looked up and saw who was behind me, next in the queue, with a great big grin on their face. I froze."

"Who was it mummy? Bear Grylls?"

"No you stupid boy. It was Susie from next door," his mother disclosed with a look of horror.

"Is that such a bad thing mummy?" Horace enquired. "After all, you were in the right place."

"Yes, it most certainly is and I will tell you why. It's not just one reason, it's a multiple. Firstly I wasn't using any Waitrose bags for life, I was using all manner of other bags for life and single use ones, even Sports Direct and Lidl. I was just using what was in the boot. So I then had to grab a load of Waitrose ones from the packing area, unfold them, which isn't easy with one hand - thus giving Susie time to stare at my purchases - put them in my trolley then put the other bags inside so Susie couldn't see that I was a sometime less than loyal Waitrose customer. My packing system had gone to pot and I was by now just chucking everything all in together. Secondly I had a few bottles of wine, well a dozen plus this one and Susie was staring at them also and..."

"And why couldn't you have opened the bags with both hands?"

"Because I was holding my voucher of course."

"And why couldn't you have put your voucher down for a moment?" His mother grimaced.

"Because Susie would, not could - would have seen."

"And?"

"And I was not going to be seen dead holding a voucher with Susie staring at me. I wasn't going to hand it over with her gawking. She would have thought that the only reason that I was at Waitrose was because I had a voucher and that I had to use it because I couldn't afford not to and so..."

"What did you do with the voucher mummy?"

"I put it back in my purse of course. And it expires today and so I bought a load of stuff that I didn't really need but I could hardly say to the cashier 'Oh silly me I've put all this stuff in my trolley by mistake.' I got it because I thought that with the voucher it was effectively all but free and then she appeared and..."

"So many 'ands' mummy."

"And to cap it all, once I had finished packing and I had paid I was getting my own back by staring at Susie's shopping, although she didn't seem the least bit concerned. Then when she went to pay she handed over a frigging voucher. I gave her a disdainful look and do you know what she said? She said with her stupid little smile, 'I'm surprised

**10**

you don't have vouchers Karen given that you're always telling me about how you're always in Waitrose. Once you start visiting regularly, at least once a week, you will start receiving vouchers. I discovered this quite a while ago. It's like a loyalty programme for their best customers.'"

"And?"

"And so I told her. Actually I let rip. And I let rip good and proper I'm afraid on so many levels although I guess it's been a long time stewing inside of me. I looked her up and down but mostly down as I was wearing my Jimmy Choo heels and said, more accurately spat, 'That's odd Susie, because I was under the impression that they sent vouchers to people who couldn't otherwise afford to shop here - people like YOU! - to give them a bit of encouragement or to help them to shop above their social station.' Then I marched off leaving her to fiddle with her silly bits of paper. But I didn't get very far. I realised that I had forgotten to pay for the extra bags but I wasn't going to go back so I crossed my fingers and headed for the exit. As I went through the fssshhing doors I prayed that nothing would happen but something did. Big time. The stupid alarm started ringing and a huge red light was flashing and I froze for a second time inside ten minutes. A security man in a peaked cap came over and asked me if I had paid for everything in the sort of voice that suggested that both he and I knew the answer. I patiently explained that I had and then he asked to see my till receipt. It must be a common occurrence because the first thing he said was, 'You don't appear to have paid for any of your bags for life.' So just as Susie appeared back at my side I had to explain, 'Oh dear I was distracted, yes I'm sorry.' Then he pulled one of the bags out of my trolley but it was the inner bag and there he was with, oh the shame, a Sports Direct bag in his hand, asking me why I needed to double bag toilet rolls. By this time another security guard had appeared with a bottle of whisky in his hand and it still had one of those white tag things on it. It transpired that it wasn't me that had set off the alarm but some ruffian who had gone through the scanners at exactly the same time. So there's a lesson for you."

"Don't stop unless you're stopped."

"Exactly. So by the time that I reached the car I was actually shaking."

"Because it was past wine o'clock?"

"No, because of the shame, the embarrassment and the fact that I haven't saved a penny but spent a pretty one instead." Horace looked at his mother and frowned. Sometimes he wondered what on earth it was that she was talking about.

"I'll go and get the shopping in mummy and then I'll find you a glass." Horace knew that his mother would not be starting her serious evening imbibing just yet as if there were but one thing she detested it was warm white wine. He thought that if he moved slowly, by the time he had retrieved all the shopping his mother would have calmed down a bit and he could make her a cup of something. Maybe a fruit tea, that wasn't too hard. He was immediately thwarted in his plan when he found that grandad was outside by the car, boot open, and was unpacking the bags from the car and onto the drive.

"What are you doing grandad?" Horace demanded. "I thought you said they would be too heavy for you."

"I can manage toilet rolls; there's a couple that are a bit heavy but I would like to think that the Belgian white chocolate ice cream offer is open to me as well. I'm feeling peckish after all that, um..."

"Sleeping grandad?"

"You can lose a lot of weight whilst you're asleep Horace. Your body's burning energy and you're not eating. Now come on, let's get these bags inside and then we can have your treat."

\*\*\*

Soon six pristine Waitrose bags for life were lined up on the kitchen floor. Horace peered inside each one in turn. The double bags' contents were as expected. One had wine, one freezer items, one fridge items and the fourth miscellaneous tins and jars. Horace stuck a finger in the freezer bag and gently moved things around. There were plenty of frozen vegetables but no ice cream. "No ice cream mummy," he announced looking at grandad who was standing ready holding two dessert bowls and spoons.

Mrs Horrise did not reply. She was sitting with a large glass of wine in her hand. The opened bottle was in front of her on the table now wrapped in what to Horace looked like a mini silver duvet. "Mummy?" Horace asked. "I know I sometimes ask silly questions but Miss said that I shouldn't worry 'cos it's the quickest way to learn those extra little facts that make life so interesting, so why are you trying to warm the wine up?" His mother put down her glass and smiled. She loved her younger son dearly, especially when he came out with unexpected nuggets. This was one such nugget.

"Miss is quite correct darling. Never be afraid to ask. This is a rapid wine cooler," she said, poking at the metal sleeve. "I bought it the other day and it's fantastic. It fact I bought two, the second as a backup. They have some sort of liquid in them and you put them or rather keep them in the freezer. When you need to chill a bottle of white wine quickly you put one over the bottle and leave it on. It only takes a couple of minutes. It's a bit like putting a bottle of wine in the freezer but this sleeve doesn't keep freezing it just chills the wine whereas, well, you know what happens when you put bottles of wine in the freezer and forget about them don't you Horace?"

Indeed Horace did. The previous Christmas he had taken it upon himself to chill a bottle of Champagne in readiness for his parents' return from an evening out. "Put the Champagne on ice," his mother had instructed Horace's older brother Sam with a giggle before they left but Sam wasn't sure if they were joking; in any case he had forgotten. Horace decided that drastic action was needed. Sam was not to know that a bowl of ice, water and salt would have worked better than the freezer and, with the bottle nestling amongst the frozen peas, Horace went back to scouring the upstairs cupboards for a feel of secreted wrapped presents and had himself then forgotten about the Champagne. When his parents returned in a particularly jovial mood and had plonked themselves down on the sofa far too close together for their offsprings' comfort and Horace's father had asked him to, "Fetch the Champagne my good man and two flutes," Horace scurried into the kitchen returning with two glasses and a cracked glass bottle containing a very expensive block of Champagne ice. "Given the number of glass shards in the freezer daddy, I wouldn't even like to suggest that you lick it," said Horace forlornly. David Horrise eased himself to his feet and went into the kitchen on a rarely-seen mission - to prepare a pot of tea for himself and his wife, such was his keenness for what Mary Wesley described in *The Camomile Lawn* as "comforts." When he returned a few minutes later with a tray laden with the tea, two cups and assorted festive goodies he found his wife sprawled across the sofa, fast asleep and snoring like a malfunctioning chainsaw. He put down the tray and carried / pulled / dragged her to her bed. The cold tea was still in its pot in the morning. The goodies had all gone.

Horace moved on to the last two bags, single bags. He scrutinised the contents firstly with his eyes and then his nose but no fingers. Horace knew that these two bags were the last to be packed. It was as his mother had intimated. It was as if someone had grabbed random items from the supermarket shelves, chiller and freezer cabinets, thrown them in a shopping basket and when it was full tipped the purchases straight into a bag for life. Horace noticed a hot herb-roasted chicken in its own bag, carelessly thrown on top of the other groceries instead of being assiduously placed in its own coolbag that was normally taken along for this sole and specific duty. "Are we having hot herb-roasted chicken tonight mummy?" Horace asked. He knew the answer. A cooked chicken was always bought when shopping at Waitrose for no other reason than his mother would invariably complain that supermarket shopping always wore her out and so wanted something simple to prepare in the evening. When Horace occasionally accompanied his mother on such trips he had noticed that she would go a little bit "soppy," is how he would describe it, if Alphonse was serving. "A chicken for you Mrs Horrise? Herb, garlic or lemon or maybe a couple of guinea fowl?" "Ohhh, I just can't decide Alphonse, what do you think?

Which is fresh out of the oven? Which looks like it has 'eat me' all over it?" "Mrs Horrise, I can only see one thing that has 'eat me' all over it and it hasn't been roasted..." "Ohhh Alphonse, you are so naughty!"

"Mummy, mummy!" Horace protested.

"Yes, yes darling," his mother eventually replied with a sickly grin. "Can you fish it out and put it in the microwave? I can then zap it in a minute once I've prepared the salad. Then you can go and play in the evening sunshine."

Horace lifted the warm bag from its irregular place and noticed that the underside was somewhat cooler than the rest. Handing the chicken to grandad, who had by now put down the bowls and spoons, he peered back into the bag. "Found it!" he announced as he grabbed the large tub of Belgian white chocolate ice cream. Something didn't feel quite right however. Horace put the tub to his ear and shook it.

"Everything okay Horace?" his mother enquired. Grandad looked nervously on.

"The ice cream's sloshing about," he advised. "I think it's melted."

"Quick. Got the other of those rapid wine cooler duvet things Karen?" grandad asked his daughter with an expression that suggested that he felt that the collapse of civilisation as he knew it was upon him, as he made for the freezer at a speed not often seen in octogenarians. "I think we're going to need it."

But Karen now had moved on to other things - the impending arrival of the Germans.

\*\*\*

Although she would never admit it, Karen Horrise was mostly a genuine lady of leisure. In fact she would go further than that, she would fully deny it. She would say that running a household with three children, her father and a cat was enough work for anyone. She would say that such work was full-time, that it needn't be if one were to throw creased-up clothes and ready-meals at her family but she took a pride in making sure that everyone at least started the day looking as if they cared about their appearance and ended the day with a properly prepared meal (apart from Alphonse chicken days) and that this was a time-consuming business. That said, although she was not quite ready to own up to it, she had started to become just a little ever-so-slightly bored. One day not so long ago she had put down her cup of coffee that she had been nestling in her hand, closed up the magazine that she had bought on the strength of a cover line that read, "Do something worthwhile every day!" and began quietly to ponder. Eventually her father broke the silence. He had fallen into a catnap and had awoken to find his daughter in the same position that he had left her in for his few minutes' battery recharge - sitting back in the sofa, arms folded and staring blankly at the ceiling. So much of the article was completely irrelevant to her life. She was not going to get a job, she was not going to find a(nother) husband, she was not going to take up a dangerous sport but the suggestion that did strike a chord was the one that focused on dynamic community involvement.

"It doesn't matter where you live in the country, there is always a number of organisations looking for volunteers. Don't panic! Often you do not necessarily need any special skills, just a desire to give something back. Don't be put off thinking that there is someone better qualified than you or that someone else could do a better job - if we all thought that then nothing would get done. Don't think that no one needs help either. They're not always visible but they're out there. Scratch beneath the surface and you'll find all sorts of concerns desperate for people like you. Don't forget, there is never a right time! If we all waited for that then nothing would definitely ever get done," Karen read.

"A penny for your thoughts Karen," her father eventually commented, if only to bring his daughter back to the present. Karen smiled.

"I need to get out more," she said vaguely.

"You don't do too badly at present," grandad snorted. "There's the coffee meetings, the lunches, the afternoon teas without starting on the shopping and the taxi service. If anyone could justifiably mention getting out more I would dare to suggest that you start with me. How often do I get out? I was thinking just the other day, when I was a boy..."

"I don't mean out doing vital things like socialising," she replied having taken in not a word of her father's. "I mean doing stuff, helping out, making the area a better place to live."

"It's not a bad place to live."

"And that's my thinking. But it's only a not bad place to live because people put themselves out. I think it's fair to say that I don't particularly put myself out."

"You don't."

"You don't have to agree."

"But I do."

"In that case, how do I start? I don't know what invisible people need my help. What surface do I scratch? I haven't a clue where to start but I like the idea of someone who's desperate. I might as well do something where people are going to appreciate me and not just take me for granted but I'm not going to walk up and down the High Street with a placard that says, 'Can I be of service?' Goodness knows what I'll end up doing."

"And you'd probably get paid for it with a placard like that," said grandad with a grin. "In all seriousness I would suggest you consult someone who has their finger on the pulse of what's going on around here, certainly more than we can ever hope to have. And that would be..."

"Horace," they said in unison.

When Horace finally decided to return home from school after he was delayed by a visit to Miss Humbug's for one hundred grams of gobstoppers and he was immediately confronted by his mother in the hallway saying that she needed his urgent advice, Horace's first instinct was to run. He couldn't imagine for one moment what pressing matter it could be that his mother felt compelled to bring her son into it and that probably the most accurate conclusion was that she had once more gone momentarily slightly mad. But he could see that there was a large slice of Victoria sponge on the kitchen table and so Horace decided that he could run after he had scoffed it if need be. He threw down his rucksack, kicked off his shoes and made a beeline for the kitchen. Once he had sat down and had taken his first mouthful his mother, who had followed behind, asked simply, too simply, "Who needs help around here?"

Without looking up Horace chomped some more on the cake before uttering, "You by the sound of it."

It took grandad to come the rescue. "What your mother is looking for Horace, is someone, or something that could make use of her various skills like, um..."

"Wine tasting? How about a smelly-air?" Horace suggested as he unsuccessfully grappled with one of the more crackjaw French words to enter the English language.

"No. I'm thinking more of empathy and understanding or maybe something of an administrative nature."

"The thing is Horace," his mother continued. "I feel that I need a bit of meaning in my life. I don't need to find my mojo because I haven't actually lost it. But I need to get out some more and do some more fun things, some useful things..."

"Sounds like the Ravings mum," said Horace, thinking about his tight-knit group of pals and the adventures that they always seemed to be having, "but I think you're probably a bit old. But if you're wanting to join a club or something I can make a suggestion of where to start. How about the library? They always have loads of leaflets in the entrance porch. You could go there and have a look." His mother eyed him suspiciously.

"The library? Are you sure? I don't remember when I last went to the library. Probably when you were in the infants."

"No mummy," Horace corrected. "You never took me to the library. I used to have to take myself to the library and tell the librarian lady, you know although you don't - the one with the glasses and the thick woolly jumper although thinking about it that describes all librarians as far as I can make out - that you were waiting outside which was almost true 'cos more often than not you were in the café nearly next door with one of your friends. You never took the slightest bit of interest in what I was taking out. In fact I still have a library book somewhere in my bedroom that I never took back."

"How long have you had it?" asked grandad.

"About three years," Horace replied. "The trouble is, I don't know where it is. I seem to have mislaid it and I can't take any more books out until I've found it."

"In that case Karen, you can take me to the library because I have some books to return and you had better wait in the porch in case they recognise you."

"I don't think mummy knows any librarians grandad," Horace suggested, "and in any case any outstanding fines incurred by a minor are unenforceable debts."

"Hark at you top-shot lawyer!" grandad exclaimed. "How come you're so up on finance law?"

"Sonny told me," said Horace as if to fully answer the question. And it did.

"Do you think that you could take my books back by any chance in that case Horace?" grandad asked obsequiously. "Because I've had them out for twenty-seven years and any outstanding fines incurred by an octogenarian are unenforceable."

"Oh yes they are," said his daughter. "Old people should know better and you can come with me."

"I'll leave my books for another time," said grandad promptly. "I'm not even sure if the library I borrowed them from is still there. I think most people just look at pictures these days."

"They'll take them dad. They have the name of the library on them and they'll just send them back for you. The fine won't be very much and in any case I think it's limited to the cost of the books."

\*\*\*

It was pouring with rain the following day but Mrs Horrise was not to be put off from beginning her quest to be of use to the community with dynamic involvement. She bundled her father into the car and drove down to the local library. Fortunately there was a car park behind the building so grandad did not have far to walk. She had convinced him that he needed to own up for his twenty-seven year oversight himself but no sooner had they reached the lobby, with two large notice boards that had so many posters pinned to them it looked more like a doctors' surgery waiting room, grandad sat down having picked out a leaflet from one of the freestanding racks under the notice boards. "I can't go in," he declared obstinately.

"Well you're jolly well going to," his daughter commanded. "I'm not doing all your dirty work by myself."

"You know I would come in if I could, but look," he replied, nodding his head. Between the lobby and the main library through a double door there were a pair of imposing white scanners standing like a couple of opened French window shutters that had been set in concrete. "I can't go through them! They'll interfere with my pacemaker."

Mrs Horrise wasn't convinced but she thought that the entrance to a library was not the most suitable of places in which to have a heated argument. She held out her hands. "There's no sign but just give me the books and I'll take them," she said. "I can't believe people would want to steal books but if they do I would suggest that it's in some ways a good thing. Now you sit there quietly and find a leaflet for me. I want something that will challenge me a little bit."

"Shouldn't be difficult," grandad muttered.

Karen walked boldly through the automatic doors and up to the scanners then passed between them. "Nothing doing," she muttered to herself as the double door closed behind her. To her front stood a welcoming receptionist with a happy, smiling face. Mrs Horrise hadn't noticed that the red lights on top of the scanners had started flashing but she was certainly aware of an alarm, a short but loud wail, so loud that she almost jumped out of her skin.

"I'm sorry about that," said the librarian pressing on some buttons on a pad under the counter top. "It really doesn't have to be that loud. We're not deaf. Let me just reset the scanner lights. I'll get the doors unlocked in a second."

"Is there a fire?" asked Mrs Horrise innocently. "And if there is the last thing that should be happening is that the doors are locked. Surely they should be flinging themselves open?" The librarian laughed.

"Oh no, no fire, nothing like that. Now let me have a look at your books." She held out a hand. Mrs Horrise sensed that it was twitching. She placed the books on the counter. "Who set it off then?" The librarian gave a little squeak.

"You."

"Me?"

"Yes you. The reason why I'm sure that you won't be surprised to learn is that it's a warning that the national library service has been informed that a book or books that have been reported as effectively stolen have just made their way back into the system. So let me just have a look at these books and..." The librarian placed the books side by side, lifted the front covers fully open so that each rested on the title page of its neighbour to form a neat and continuous line, and picked up a black infra-red zapper. She hmmed quietly as if she was already more than aware that something wasn't quite right, despite the audible warning, and began to zap the bar codes. She hmmed some more as she, otherwise silently, worked her way along the row. Karen stood quietly with her hand in her pocket fondling the edge of her debit card. Whatever the fine she wanted this over and done with as quickly as possible. She was looking straight ahead, praying that she would soon be told the amount - she could tap her card without being asked to insert and enter her PIN and be off with words of apology still hanging in the air. This was not the place to be lingering, in the middle of Chislehurst, with friends and neighbours all around like soldiers waiting to ambush. Her fear was well founded. She didn't turn her head when a familiar voice beside her said,

"Hallo Karen. I haven't seen you in the library before. What a surprise! But what is it with you and red lights?" Karen knew in an instant that this wasn't a real friend and neighbour, it was not-much-of a friend and not-much-of a next-door neighbour either.

"Hallo Susie," she replied without moving. "I'm, er, just sorting out some books..."

"I can see," said Susie. "What have you been reading?" she asked but Karen didn't move to let her see over her shoulder so Susie walked around to her other side and looked over the counter.

"Well, well, well, that's interesting!" Susie exclaimed. "'How to Satisfy a Woman Every Time... and have her beg for more!' Interesting! And, 'The Frugal Gourmet.' Okayyya. And, 'Iron John: A Book About Men.'" Susie looked up at her neighbour but their eyes did not meet.

"Have you, er, learnt anything from the books?" Susie asked. "And I hope you had them wrapped up in a Waitrose bag for life or maybe Sports Direct?" Before Karen could respond the librarian informed Mrs Horrise that the books were overdue by twenty-five years.

"My goodness Karen!" Susie exclaimed. "Did it take you that long to get everything to sink in? You must have started when you were a teenager or, thinking about it, maybe a little bit older."

"They're d...dad's," Mrs Horrise spluttered. "He's in the lobby waiting for me. He didn't want the scanners to put his pacemaker into spasm."

"Oh they won't do that," said the librarian brightly. "They're very weak. They just pick up the electronic bar codes on the books, that's all."

"I didn't see your father outside," said Susie. "I'm sure if he were there I would have seen him." Mrs Horrise turned round and looked back through the double door. Grandad was indeed nowhere in sight.

"So, madam, the total due with the fines and the reminder letters and the debt collectors is..."

"Debt collectors?!" Mrs Horrise screamed. "I've not had any debt collectors..."

"Ssssh. With all due respect madam, that's what everyone says. Now if you could be a little bit more ssssh. This is a library after all. The total amount outstanding is three hundred and fifty-two pounds and twenty-seven pence."

"Keep your voice down! I only have a debit card," said Mrs Horrise wafting her piece of plastic gently in the air.

"Cash only I'm sorry," said the librarian.

"For goodness sake!" Mrs Horrise bellowed. "Who carries that amount of cash around to pay overdue library book fines?"

"Most fine aren't more than a pound or two," said the librarian soothingly.

"I do!" said Susie cheerfully as she reached into her handbag. "You can pay me back, or rather Harry can."

"Thank you," Mrs Horrise muttered. "Very kind. Now if you'll excuse me I need to go and find dad. Please ensure that the doors are unlocked before I reach them." She turned and walked out of the library leaving Susie to pay her neighbour's or her neighbour's father's dues and have her latest borrowing, "Murder Thy Neighbour," stamped. She was glad Karen hadn't looked over *her* shoulder.

Back in the lobby Karen found her father with a cup of coffee in his hand. "Where have you been?" she demanded. "You'll never guess how much I've just had to shell out!"

"I think I'm just about to find out," grandad muttered as he took a sip on his Americano.

"I've just paid a three hundred and something pound debt for you." She scrunched up her eyes and stared at him. She hadn't finished.

"Have you ever had debt collectors round for your unpaid library fines?" she asked.

"Oh yes, several times," said her father cheerfully, "when I was at home. But I told them that Harry Harris had moved and I thought once I actually did move they wouldn't be able to catch up with me. And they haven't."

"That is no reason to avoid your debts dad. Now they've sort of caught up with *me* and here comes Susie so you can tell her yourself that you're to blame."

"I shall do no such thing. You should have just dumped the books on the counter and ran." Grandad watched Susie emerge past the scanners and through the door. Seeing grandad she smiled mischievously.

"Hallo Harry. Read any good books recently?" she asked.

"Certainly not," he replied gravely. "I wouldn't be seen dead with my daughter with what she had tucked under her arm. I think it's disgusting. I was so embarrassed I've been sitting out here reading leaflets with a nice cup of coffee that I purchased from Joe..., er, nearby."

"I'll be off then," said Susie with an even wider smile as she walked out onto the pavement. "Don't forget to pop round to settle up!" Mrs Horrise turned to her father.

"Drink up and we'll go. I'm not having you spilling that down your trousers. When Horace finds his book you can bring him here yourself."

While grandad drank his coffee Mrs Horrise leafed through the leaflets in the racks. There were plenty of flyers for events and activities but nothing that was asking for volunteer help. "It's hopeless," she announced despondently as her father slurped the coffee from the bottom of his paper cup. "I come to a place where Horace thinks I'll get some inspiration and I end up with a huge debt that you probably won't pay and to a neighbour who now thinks I'm a bisexual cheapskate cook who desires Zeus-like levels of energy."

"Come on Karen," grandad said with a grin as he rose slowly to his feet. "Let me buy you a cake and coffee from Joelle's before we drive back so that I can start to knock a few quid off that bill."

"It's a bit of a trek dad; do you think you can make it?"

"Just about," he replied.

The pair wandered slowly up the high street whereupon Mrs Horrise decided that she was going to have a sit down drink and eat for she adored the sights and smells of this her favourite deli and it was almost elevenses. Plus the fact that her father looked exhausted. And it was still raining a little. She loved Joelle's. She couldn't quite put her finger on it but it was always full of interesting and unusual items. There was the grocery side with tins and jars of exotic foods as well as ice cream, pastries, cakes, cold meats and of course coffee. "Would you like anything with that?" Joelle would invariably ask with the result that whatever you went in for you would normally exit with a multiple. Go in for a coffee and wait for, "Would you like anything with that?" "Oh, go on then, I'll take a slice of panettone." "I can recommend the classic. It's great toasted with a spoonful of organic raisin jam. I have a couple of jars left." They entered and settled themselves at the one free table. Joelle herself came bustling over with a pen and pad in her hand. "Hallo again Harry. Back for more?"

"'Back for more' what?" asked his daughter.

"Oh no, better not. Prostrate and all that. Coffee goes straight through me." Joelle tittered.

"Not that straight I hope or you'll be outside behind that tree and probably lying down!" Grandad frowned. He wasn't too sure what Joelle was talking about but it sounded like a joke at his expense.

"I'll have a piece of carrot and nut with orange zest cake and whatever Karen wants."

"I'll have an Americano and a slice of lemon drizzle..."

"Would you like anything with that although I'll throw in a chocolate titbit for free if you pour your heart out?" said Joelle looking slightly concerned. She felt that her job was more than deli owner. She was a friend to all, a shoulder to cry on and a port in a storm. As far as she was able she would make sure that every customer left her shop, like the hairdressers', in a better place mentally if not physically than when they entered, but she thought she might have some work to do with Karen Horrise. She signalled for her assistant to prepare the refreshments. She pulled up a chair and looked expectantly at her friend. She didn't need to coerce her, she knew that whatever it was it had made its way to the surface and was ready to bubble out and over. To grandad's surprise his daughter suddenly burst into tears.

"I'm such a failure!" she sobbed. "I just need to do *something* with my life. I want to give freely of my time to help someone or something but I can't get started. Oh Joelle, what can I do?" Joelle immediately nodded towards the table where sat a couple of females looking similarly distraught, although there were no tears. "What timing! Those two over there," she said quietly, "They need some help and quite urgently. They have some problems with organising a visit from a bunch of Germans." Grandad's ears pricked up.

"Germans? I'm having nothing to do with Germans. I thought you said 'Shermans' Joelle. I thought we were going to get a visit from a tank regiment. I'm having no Germans staying in my house. When I was a boy..."

"You, I reckon, Karen would be just the person," said Joelle as she stood up, ignoring grandad's little rant.

"Shut up dad," said Karen with a weak smile, "whatever you're talking about. Come on. Let's push the tables together. There will be no Germans staying in our house."

The apparently chance meeting in Joelle's delicatessen was just the fillip that Karen Horace needed. Over her coffee and cake with grandad listening in, not daring to scowl but feeling that he had been ever-so-slightly set up, Karen listened to the tale of woe.

"We're a not particularly large group in the area and you may not find us that interesting," said the elder of the two ladies who had introduced herself as Janet, "but what we do is ensure that our great nation, represented by Chislehurst, is able to extend hospitality to the German people in the town of Nochalt where we have established contact through the Town Twinning Association. This twinning enables friendship, understanding and cultural pursuits to be advanced. Several years ago a number of us went to Nochalt and enjoyed legendary German hospitality. We ate and drank our way through a local beer festival, we visited museums and parks. We had a tour of the local dyke and attended its annual flower festival."

"Sounds like great fun," said Mrs Horrise. "What do you offer the Germans when they come here?" When Janet gave

31

Karen a frosty stare she wondered what on earth she had said wrong.

"Nothing," she replied. "That's not to say they've turned up and we have had nothing to offer them. We just haven't had them to visit us yet. No one feels suitably qualified to put a programme together and we two certainly don't have the time what with all our social engagements and so they have never been invited. But now we've been told by the Town Twinning Association that if we don't invite the Germans over here this year then we're going to lose our holidays in Nochalt and we don't want that to happen; we have such a lovely time. So we've invited them. It seems like the whole town wants to come but we've agreed on eighteen. That's a decent number without going over the top. To make it fair we're taking new people, that is to say they'll be Germans with whom we haven't stayed before. The idea is that in that way the links can grow. They're coming in a little over a month's time, on the twenty-first. We just need someone to put a programme together for a week's visit. You don't know anyone who has a flair for community projects and a teensy bit of spare time that might get involved do you? There's really not much work to do. They're all ages and I would imagine a bit fussy and they like things to be organised and we're a bit stuck in our own era with our own rather dull ideas so we could do with someone who has a bit of insight into what the young enjoy."

"She'll do it," said grandad, pointing to his daughter.

"There's really not much to do," said Janet's companion Mary. "Just a little outing or activity each day to showcase Chislehurst and beyond. It's up to you. What do you think? We would be most grateful. Is that a yes?" Karen looked at her expectant father who said nothing but who was nodding

- small nods of anticipatory encouragement. She considered that it would only be for a short while and there didn't seem to be an awful lot to it.

"Oh, okay then. By coincidence I have been looking for some voluntary work and it must be that this meeting was written in the stars," Mrs Horrise said finally.

"Oh thank you Mrs Horrise," said Janet beaming. "We'll be in touch very soon."

"My pleasure," she replied. "But one thing - how do you know my name and why's Joelle just slipped dad a cherry brandy?"

\*\*\*

"I love the summer!" Horace dreamily exclaimed. He was lying in a prone position looking up at the sky, beautifully blue even though the evening was wearing on, with tiny wisps of cloud far, far away. He was on the cricket ground with his pals, the Ravens, for once not doing an awful lot apart from chatting. Horace was happy with this activity at any time but today especially due to his having consumed one quarter of a hot herb-roasted chicken, no salad, and drunk more than eaten half a tub of Belgian white chocolate ice cream.

"It's all so... kind of peaceful this part of the day. People calm down a bit," Emily added from the same position. "I think it's because there's less to do this time of year especially for parents and by the evening they're quite chilled..."

"You're right," said Edward. My parents have calmed right down. I think it's 'cos the sun's warmed them up a bit and they've had a vitamin D boost."

"How can you get a vitamin D boost unless you eat something?" scoffed Archie. "Don't you have to eat stuff like fish?"

"You can vitamin D from sunshine and that's why it's so good for you and that's why lying in the sun's so good for you," said Melanie.

"Unless you get burnt. Then it's not good for you. I wonder how long you have to lie in the sun to get enough vitamin D?" said Charlie. "I wonder if you can get vitamin D from walking? I don't eat much fish so I wonder if..."

"My parents are a bit more chilled Ed," interrupted Emily who had quickly had enough of Charlie's wonderings. "Has everyone else got chilled parents?" They mostly agreed that they had to a greater or lesser extent. Even Sonny concurred with a nod which was enough for the Ravens as they didn't want to press him further, even indirectly, on his absent father. However he then offered, somewhat obliquely, "I have interesting parents." Horace remained silent.

"Persons of interest more like," said Archie looking very serious. Only Melanie understood that he had made quite a good joke but realised that the beauty of the moment would be magnified by not responding.

"What about you Horace?" she asked. Melanie was also staring at the sky. She had lifted her head slightly and was waving her blond hair that was now hanging down and barely touching the grass. "I didn't hear you say anything." Horace turned to look at this prepubescent beauty. He felt that Melanie was the one that most deserved a response.

"That's because it's not particularly peaceful at home at present and that's why I'm having a very pleasant time out here," Horace confessed.

"Nothing horrid I hope?" said Emily not sure how else to encourage Horace to elucidate. "I hope..."

"Mummy is looking for meaning in life and has apparently found the answer in being dragged into planning a programme for a bunch of Germans who are visiting Chislehurst next month on a twin towning or something a bit weird like that," Horace blurted out. "She hasn't a clue what to do. I think they're all a bit old so they will want to do stuff like visit National Trust places and tea rooms and churches. I suggested bingo but I reckon what she should be doing is giving them a taste of the area and maybe London 'cos that's where all foreign people want to go."

"Is she gettin' paid?" asked Sonny who had been quietly listening to Horace's report of Horrise-household strife. He had been mostly silent due to his suffering from a touch of hay fever that meant that he was continually in the act of trying to stifle a sneeze.

"It's like takin' snuff," he had told the Ravens a short while earlier, although none was any the wiser. "All I want to do is atishoo the whole time but nothing comes out."

"No. For some reason she wants to do it for nothing but Germans will have plenty of spending money 'cos if they're old they will have loads to get rid of," replied Horace.

"If they're old they'll have paid off their mortgages," Emily added.

"I don't think they have mortgages in Germany," said Melanie assuredly. "Dad says that German people all rent."

"Well, someone must own the properties," said Archie.

"The fing is," said Sonny. "They 'ave loads of money an' they'll probably bring cash so I'm sure that we can fink up a programme then we can get tips. Let's go an' give yer mum the good news. How long they comin' for 'Orace? Ahhhh-choo!"

"A week."

"That's easy then. We'll have a day each. I'll go first."

"In that case," said Horace, surprised but also delighted at the way that Sonny dealt with other people's problems - listening for not very long, thinking for a few seconds and then coming up with a solution that involved everyone even without asking, "I shall inform mummy that we have it all sorted. We need to make sure that our programme enables friendship, understanding and cultural pursuits to be advanced." Horace sat up and rubbed his face.

"I'll be getting off home now. I don't want to get sunburn."

"I don't think you can get sunburn at half past nine in the evening Horace," said Emily.

"Well I think that you can Em," said Horace pointing. "Just think how far the sun has moved since the middle of the day. It's only gone from there to there. It's not any further away it's just sort of down a bit. I don't think we're safe from sunburn until it's gone round to Australia."

"And then you're still not safe," said Archie getting to his feet, "'cos then you could get moonburn."

\*\*\*

Although it was very near to ten o'clock by the time Horace reached home, for some reason with Sonny in tow, it was sufficiently light for the pair to feel that bedtime was still some time away. "Come on Sonny," said Horace as they walked up the side path to the back door. "Mummy will make you a hot chocolate if you like then you won't have to get your mummy to make you one when you get home."

"As yer like," said Sonny.

But Karen Horrise was nowhere to be seen. Sam was sitting at the kitchen table nursing a hot chocolate - by himself. "There's loads in the pan. Help yourself. And you Sonny. There's also some Waitrose pear, ginger and blond white chocolate cake if you want a slice." Sonny most certainly did want a slice. He was never one to complain but Waitrose to his mind was a supermarket that his mother could only ever aspire to frequenting.

"Jus' goin' for a pee." What Sonny didn't say was that he was going to look for Mrs Horrise to let her know that it was his idea that the Ravens would do some programme planning. He put his head round the sitting room door but there was no Mrs Horrise, just grandad asleep and the television on. Sonny thought that he would do a good deed and turn it off but he wasn't going to go anywhere near grandad even though he had the remote control in his lap. He looked across the room at the TV but couldn't see any buttons unlike the one in his house. He didn't want to wake grandad just as he was reaching for the control and give him such a fright that he had a heart attack or think that he was about to have his person or personal space invaded and give Sonny an involuntary slap round the face. He tiptoed past the coffee table noticing a large number of sheets of paper, neatly lined up in eighteen pairs down the table each with a transparent plastic bag on top. He ran his hand along the bottom of the television and found one, a small protruding button, which he pressed. The Ten O'Clock News had just started. As the news reader disappeared from view and all went quiet grandad awoke.

"I was watching that!" he exclaimed.

"What was you watchin'?" asked Sonny.

"The Six O'Clock News," grandad protested.

"See outside mate. Don't look like six o'clock to me." Sonny turned to walk back out of the sitting room. As he passed the coffee table he once more let out an enormous sneeze.

"Ahhh-tish-OOOO!" The sheets of paper and accompanying bags flew off the table and onto the floor in a jumbled mess.

"Oh dear," said grandad.

"Can't be that important," said Sonny snappily as he quickly got down on all fours, picked up and replaced the sheets back into pairs. "All sorted. No damage done. No one'll know. No 'arm done so keep yer 'air on. See ya mate." Sonny got back up, marched out of the sitting room without looking back. He returned to the kitchen to claim his hot chocolate and the rest of the cake.

"Can't find yer mum 'Orace," said Sonny as he sat down.

"I don't think you'll find her in the toilet," Horace replied. "Sam was just saying that she's gone to bed exhausted by the Germans..."

"'an they're not even 'ere yet. Did ya tell Sam that we would do the programme?"

"He did, thank you Sonny," Sam responded. "But it seems that that's now not all. Unbelievably no one's organised homes for the Germans to stay in. What I mean is, they have the town twinning people but you can't just stick people together at random what with everyone having likes and dislikes and that's before we even start on the food. In the past the English have been put in a hotel but the Germans have asked for some home hospitality but, apparently, they're extremely fussy about these sorts of things. Janet's just given mum a load of completed forms to match everyone up. Then there's something called 'GDPR'. I think that's something to do with old Germany but it's been making mum sweat. I said I would sort it and I have but it was a bit of an effort."

"And no one has organised the transportation Sonny so mummy's had to hire a coach to go and pick them up from the ferry at Dover," said Horace.

"In that case," said Sonny totally unfazed by what was being shared with him, "to make it easy fer ya mum, let's us Ravings hop on the coach down to Dover and give them a proper welcome. That means big tips from the start. Then on the way back to Chislehurst we can 'ave a good chat wiv 'em and tell 'em that us lot 'ave organised a week that they'll never forget."

Sonny could never have imagined how prescient his words would soon turn out to be.

\*\*\*

Early on the twenty-first of July the Ravens were to be found sitting at the back of a large minibus going to Dover down the A2. Propped up against the back seat facing out of the window was a sign that the Ravens had made. It read

CHISLEHURST ♥ NOCHALT
TOWN TWINNING
WELCOME

"It's a Roman road," said Melanie.

"Feels like it," Emily replied.

"Have we got enough seats Horace?" asked Edward suddenly. "Has anyone thought of that?

"Yes, yes, yes!" replied Horace. "Everyone's thought of everything. Mummy says that there are eighteen of them and with us seven that makes twenty-five and that's how many seats there are and their luggage can go underneath somewhere like a boot but like on an aeroplane. So here's the plan. The driver's going to get as near to the port as he can and then Charlie and I are going to meet the Germans once they get though passports and have been searched and all that stuff. Then we'll get them on the bus and we're going to St Saviour's to the car park so that they can see what a church looks like where Sam's going to be waiting to give everyone their pairings. Then they're going to their hosts and in the morning we're going to meet back up at St Saviour's for Sonny's programme for the day 'cos he's doing day one or day two if you don't count today. Any questions?"

"No," said Emily, "but we mustn't mention the war."

"Which war?" asked Melanie.

"Any war I think," said Edward. "We used to fight the Germans quite a lot in the old days and the Germans used to lose so it's a bit of a sore subject for them."

"Yes," said Archie, forgetting for one moment where he was and putting his hand up. "I have a question. What are we doing tomorrow Sonny? We need to know to avoid any clashes."

"It's a surprise," Sonny replied, "but I think that they're goin' to enjoy it." Then he added, "I don't fink there'll be any clashes wiv what cultural pursuits I 'ave planned."

Arriving in Dover the minibus driver parked by the entrance to the port as instructed and Horace and Charlie made to jump off the bus. "And the rest of you," the driver commanded.

"Oh, no," said Horace confidently. "They're waiting here unless we lose someone. The two of us are getting off to go and find the Germans and then we're going back to Chislehurst."

"Oh no we're not," said the driver shaking his head. "I'm off now. This booking was for one way. It was from a Mrs Karen Horrise."

"That's right," said Horace, "that's my mummy. She would have wanted a return."

"She may have *wanted* a return sunshine, but she's not *asked* for a return. Now off you all jump and get on with it."

"But we're picking up some Germans," Charlie protested.

"I don't care if you're picking up the Queen of Sheeba," the driver replied. "The station's only a mile away..."

"I think you'll find that Sheeba is a cat food;" said Melanie sniffily, "I think you may be wishing to refer to the Queen of Sheba." Having suitably deflated the driver Melanie continued.

"Now just give me a moment." She reached into her dainty orange clutch bag that she had slung over her shoulder. She pulled out her debit card and waved it at the driver.

"Will this do?" The driver smiled benignly. Normally it would.

"I'm sorry love, but I have another job to go to in Margate," he replied almost apologetically. "I've got to pick up a party of pensioners that I dropped off yesterday."

"What's goes on in Margate?" asked Emily.

"It's the centre of Kent entertainment love..."

"It sticks out on the east coast. Hardly the centre," Melanie interrupted.

"It's the centre metaphorically love. If you want to give your visitors a bit of cultural pursuits I can recommend it. You could take them to the Turner gallery. That would be a good start. Then there's the old town but for now off you get or I'm going to be late."

"Um, could you hang on for a few minutes and take us all to Margate?" asked Melanie who was still waving her debit card in the air.

"More than me job's worth sadly. Now hop it love and take the others with you."

The seven Ravens shuffled off the bus, through the car park and into the passenger terminal. "So much for a proper welcome," said Edward with a scowl. "Welcome to England but we don't know how we're going to get you to Chislehurst. It's just so embarrassing. I don't know why I said that I would come down here today. We're going to be a laughing stock."

"No we ain't," said Sonny holding onto the sign. "We're going to give the Germans a great time even though I fink they're quite serious people and it looks as though it starts now 'cos Horace is just about to make contact."

The Ravens turned to watch Sonny running towards Horace who was slowly approaching a crocodile line of travellers who had appeared from round a corner all pulling suitcases on wheels. Charlie was soon following on behind. Sonny ran past the two of them waving the "Chislehurst ♥ Nochalt

Town Twinning Welcome" sign in the air. "Over 'ere Germans!" he shouted.

"Look at that!" exclaimed Emily. "All different shapes, sizes and colours!"

"The luggage is also quite varied," said Archie and everyone laughed.

"The Germans look a bit old mostly," whispered Emily. "What are they going to make of us?"

Sonny waited until Horace and Charlie had caught up with him but when the pair failed to utter a word Sonny hissed, "Speak to them!"

"I don't know what to say," Horace replied. "Do you think they speak English?" Charlie cleared his throat.

"Ahem. Welcome to Dover! We are to get you to Chislehurst where you will meet your hosts. Unfortunately we don't have any transport due to a bit of a mix up. Do you understand what I'm saying?" The Germans all nodded. One stepped forward and said,

"Doess anyvun speak ze German here?" Sonny put up his hand as the other Ravens stared in disbelief.

"Oh gott," said the man. "Ask me mine name." Sonny gave a little cough whilst he, it appeared, thought of what to say. He lifted his head up and announced,

"Vot iz your nim?" The Germans all laughed.

"Was ist mein Name? Ich heisse Max." Sonny look slightly alarmed before regaining his composure and replying,

"Zat is gut then but now can ve spick in English?" The Germans nodded.

"In that case, wot we need a do is sort art 'ow we're goin' git ya up the A2," said Sonny.

"And zat is Engleesh?" asked the man.

"It's Sonny English," Melanie explained.

"Zounds a bit lik German Engleesh," said the man.

"I think we need to get a train so you need to walk to the station. It's about a mile. Is that okay?" Horace asked.

"A mile? What is this in metres? And you hef spelt our name wong on the sign. It's N-O-C-H-I-L-T. No A."

"Quite a few," said Melanie.

One of the other Germans pushed forward to the front of the small throng. "It zat case," he said, "as vee are in no urry I vant to zee the Dover Castle. Can vee go zere?"

"Er, yes," said Charlie, "but I don't know where it is."

"It iz up on top ov zee cliffs," said the German pointing to the ceiling. "We can zee it from zee boat but 'ow do vee get up zere?"

"We 'ave to walk," said Sonny, "but it's okay 'cos you can leave your bags on the way at me uncle's. 'e 'as a pub along the road outside 'ere an' 'e 'as plenty of space in 'is garage."

The Ravens shrugged their shoulders and sighed. Was there any place where Sonny had no friends or relatives? It seemed not.

Sonny led the way out and along Marine Parade. Soon the Ravens and the unladen Germans were climbing Castle Hill Road to the great medieval castle. Not many words had been exchanged since the terminal meeting due to a degree of apprehension between the parties. However this was just about to change.

"Don't mention the war," Emily whispered to her friends.

"Tell them about the old Roman lighthouse," said Melanie.

"Did you want to see the old Roman lighthouse?" Archie asked loudly in a tone of voice that suggested that he knew all about it whereas, in reality, he didn't even know if it existed, but if Melanie mentioned something, it was usually accurate. The Germans chortled.

"No, zat iz not our reaason," said the one who had requested the visit. "Vee vant to see vere Hitler vonted to live."

"Hitler didn't live at Dover Castle," Melanie replied.

"No, but he vonted to and zat iz vy he didn't not bomb it. 'e vonted to make it iz H Q ven he von the var!"

"But he didn't vin the var!" said Melanie.

"No! So now vee can go and zee if it vos vorth not to be bombed!" The Germans all laughed and this time so did the Ravens.

After an hour or so of looking round the castle the Germans decided that it was time to move on. "Iz all gutt but vee vont to have zum fun!" the man said. "Vere can you take uz? Dover does not zeem too gott. Ve sink it oz full of foreigners!"

"I 'ave an idea," said Sonny. "Let's go t' Margate!" The Germans all nodded enthusiastically in agreement. The only person not to nod was Edward but no one took any notice. The unlikely party walked back down the hill, retrieved the Germans' bags from the garage and went in search of the railway station. They arrived hot and bothered, the Ravens that is. The Germans had collectively hardly broken sweat. Once they arrived they were informed that it was possible to get to Margate with one change. Soon they were chugging along the coast to Kent's answer to Blackpool.

"Vot is gott here?" asked the man when they arrived.

"Um, we can take you to the Turner gallery?" suggested Melanie and although no one knew quite what to expect no one ever found out for once the party was walking along the seafront towards the architecturally bland white building that jutted out across the sand one of the Germans pointed over the road and announced,

"Vee vont to go zere! To Dreamland! To 'ave zee lunch and to 'ave zum fun!" No one was going to say, "No! I want to go to the Turner gallery," and so, with their luggage once more safely stashed away in a store room that Sonny had managed to arrange despite having no relative to assist, the Ravens and Germans went on the scenic railway, the chair-o-plane, the big wheel, the dodgems, the hurricane jets...

When Horace eventually suggested that they unquestionably should be making their way back to Chislehurst no one disagreed. "It's six o'clock and we need to find out if we can get a train."

"We can," said Melanie. "I checked at the station when we arrived. We just have to go up to London and then down again to Chislehurst."

"Down again?" said Max. "To tschüss du hast? We are going to London nein?"

"Sort of," said Melanie. "Chislehurst is in London but only administratively. Chislehurst is in a London borough and we have London buses - red buses - and we have a London mayor but postally we're in Kent because we have a Kent postcode. The first bit is B R which means Bromley and Bromley is in Kent. If it wasn't we would have a London postcode like S E but we don't. However Royal Mail doesn't use counties now but it's not wrong to put Chislehurst, Kent but Chislehurst, London is wrong. It's always been wrong. Prior to nineteen sixty-five we were in an urban district - in Kent. Understand?"

"Nein," said Max.

"Cool," said Melanie.

This journey was finally a time for discovery about each other. Horace explained that he and his friends had planned the programme for the week and that they would do something exciting every day that would encompass friendship, understanding and cultural pursuits. "We 'ave started vell," the man said. "We sort our trip voz to be quite boring wiv zee lectures and zings."

"No lectures," Horace assured him, "but just one thing: How many are you here? Mummy said that you were to be eighteen and I haven't thought to count."

"Zat iz not correct," said the man. "Vee are twenty-five."

"This should be interesting," thought Horace but he said nothing, he merely nodded gently.

As the train drew into London Bridge station the Germans began talking animatedly to each other. Then one of them said, "If it is gott with you vee would like a beer in a auzentic Britisssh pup."

"I don't think there are many authentic British pubs at London Bridge," said Melanie. "Dad says they're full of City boys round here who seem to think it's cool to drink weak lager straight out of a bottle and then spill most of it down their shirt 'cos it's fizzed up."

"No. You must never drink zee beer from zee bottle. Zat is the way of zee people who are wiv zee two short planks, you understand? You need to zee zee beer, to smell it and to get zee gott taste. You cannot do zis ven you go straight from zee bottle. We vant pleeze a real pup wiv zee crafty beer!"

"But we don't know a real..." said Emily.

"I can take you to a real pub," Sonny interrupted pushing to the front. "It's a proper East End pub where you can drink proper drinks and 'ave a sing-a-long. We can teach ya some Cockney songs. D'ya fancy that?" Sonny didn't wait for a reply.

"Good. We 'ave to get a tube to Shoreditch..."

"Zee 'tube'?"

"Oh never mind."

Before long the party found themselves walking down Shoreditch High Street, the Germans pulling their bags behind them, when suddenly Sonny, who was leading, darted into an unlit narrow road.

"He iz going for a piz!" one of the Germans exclaimed and they all laughed.

"Maybe ve are going to be mugged!" said another and they laughed some more.

"Follow me!" ordered Sonny.

"This should be interesting," Melanie muttered but soon realised that they had all mistaken Sonny's intentions for, at the end of the blind alley was a pub. The Rose and Crown had a huge England flag draped from one of the upstairs windows. There were oversize hanging baskets full of colourful annuals everywhere that there was a spare space. If there wasn't a door or a window or a sign there was a hanging basket.

"Oh my goodness!" exclaimed Melanie as she stopped to take in the scene. "How on earth did you know this place existed? It looks like something from out of a floral Charles Dickens novel!"

"It's owned by me uncle. C'mon in, he's expecting us," Sonny replied. "Well, actually not until tomorra but I don't 'spect it will make much difference."

The party made its way past a large sandwich board sign on the pavement. Under TONIGHT! on one side was a poster promoting, "TORONTO TOORNEDO - back by popular demand!" On the other side Sonny read, "SILICON CINDY - BIGGER THAN EVER!" with the 'B' having been rotated about ninety degrees. Puzzled, Sonny pushed at the door and walked in, followed by the Ravens and the Germans. Inside there were a few drinkers but it was quiet, more akin to Chislehurst library than an east London pub.

"Hi Uncle Bernie!" Sonny called to the man who appeared to be in the middle of changing some optics behind the bar. He turned and gave Sonny a huge grin.

"Hallo Sonny, me old china!" Then his smile turned to a look of concern. "What are all these kids doin' 'ere an' I thought you was comin' tomorra? We was goin' do a Cockney sing-a-long for yer German friends. I got it all sorted. Cindy was goin' to exercise 'er lungs in an altogether more, 'ow shall I put this, 'olesome way."

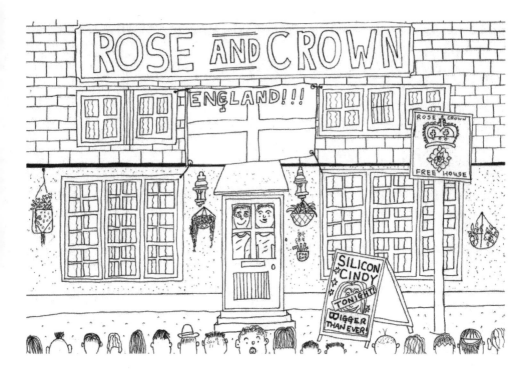

"It's a long story Uncle, but they wanted a drink in an authentic pub."

"Most welcome for a kitchen sink Sonny but we 'aven't got no sing-a-long for this evening." Uncle Bernie lowered his voice and beckoned Sonny forward. "We 'ave got a load of strippers in though."

Uncle Bernie may have lowered his voice but Horace had elephant ears. "If I can say something as my mummy's sort of in charge I don't think the Germans want to watch you do decorating even though it looks like it could do with a bit of lick of paint if you don't mind me saying. I think they want a taste of real London with cultural pursuits."

"An' they're goin' to get cultural pursuits young man, I can guarantee you that!" Uncle Bernie replied showing a full set of over-white teeth. "Sonny, you take the kids upstairs and put on a film and put an order in at the kitchen for some grub on your way up an' I'll look after the Germans, believe you me. I know what wets their whistle. They like a sherbet an' I'm sure the entertainment will make their day. They look to me like they can handle a bit of adult London. Now shift yourself an' put their bags in the front room an' look lively 'cos me Jack the Ripper's appearin' in two minutes! C'mon ladies and gents, get yer drinks in. We take Deutschmarks and Dollars. American Express will nicely thank you! But we also do bangers and mash - parnd notes, Euros if you must but we'll do you a good rate..."

"'Jack the Ripper?'" thought Horace. "Isn't he dead?" But Horace wasn't taking any chances and the grown-ups could look after themselves.

"Come on Ravings, follow me and Sonny! The Germans are going to do some wallpapering though goodness knows how they're going to manage with all these people that are now pouring in through the door."

"I expect the women will do most of the work and the men will just drink and watch," said Emily innocently.

\*\*\*

After two hours had passed that seemed like a half that time to the upstairs customers (and a fraction of that for those on the ground floor), scampi and chips and soft drinks all round with a showing of *Bend it like Beckham,* Uncle Bernie came upstairs to usher the Ravens down and out through the back door. "I've rung yer muvver an' she's tellin' the others yer on yer way. Now meet the Germans out the front and no peepin'. Cindy's just doin' an encore with a pastin' brush."

Once round the corner the Ravens found the Germans in high spirits, all of them. "Zat was marrrrrvelous! We have learned zee gott English vords, 'pints und chasers!'" screamed one of the older ladies who until then hadn't much uttered a word since disembarking.

"Sonny, why's Max got lipstick all over his face?" Horace asked.

"No idea 'Orace. Why don't you ask?" But Horace didn't like to and Max wasn't telling.

\*\*\*

The party eventually arrived at Chislehurst station after eleven o'clock. It was only a short walk to St Saviour's so didn't take much more time and add to Horace's mother's trauma. Horace's partial explanation took a smidgen longer. "Anyway you're here now and it sounds like you've had a bit of an adventure. So let's get you to your host homes. Sam you read out the names," said Karen.

"Vot is going on?" asked Max. "We sink you meant 'hostel.' We sort vee ver going to hotel."

"Oh no," said Horace. "We are a very hospitable and friendly country. You will be staying in our homes."

"Zat zounds like fun."

Sam picked up the first transparent plastic bag and pulled out two sheets of paper. "Mrs Ives, you have Hans Schneider; David Jones you have Fräulein Weber..."

"Ve love your accents Zam but my name is Karl and Fräulein Weber is Fräulein Wegner."

"Near enough," said Sam. "I don't do much German at school."

The Germans did their best to understand Sam's pronunciation; as they slowly paired off and made their way out of the church hall Mrs Horrise began to notice that something wasn't quite right. She remained silent for a while but when there was one host left and eight Germans she knew that she had to speak and it wasn't to say, "Sorry, we've overbooked, we'll have to take you back down to Dover - now!"

"Horace, we're going to have seven Germans left over. What's gone wrong?"

"In a nutshell mummy, your administration. But don't worry 'cos all the Ravings are here and we want to do our best and each Raving has at least one parent here so they can all take one - and us. I'm sure we all have room or tents."

"Firstly, there is no way that I am having a German in my house: Grandad will have a heart attack. Secondly I can't have a German going to Sonny's. They'll end up in prison," she hissed.

"Judging by Sonny's efforts this evening mummy, I think Sonny's German's going to have the best time of all. Now, quickly, take your pick; you don't want to be left with the dreg. Max has gone; he's with Sonny 'cos they seem to have hit it off."

\*\*\*

Fräulein Marie Muller was up and dressed and tucking into a full English breakfast when grandad appeared. She had already consumed a bowl of cornflakes and a glass of orange juice. A mug of tea was in front of her and a rack of toast had been prepared and was sitting waiting to be eaten. "Good morgen sir," said Fräulein Muller when she saw grandad.

"You're in my chair," he responded.

"Oh I am so sorry, I shall move," said Marie. She put down her knife and fork and made to stand.

"You will do nothing of the sort Marie," said Mrs Horrise. "Stay there. Now then dad, come and sit next to Marie and tell her about your life, some of it at least. What would you like for breakfast?"

"I'll have what she's having," said grandad grumpily as he sat down in an unfamiliar seat. "Most of my young life I was being shot at and bombed by you lot."

"I didn't ask to stay here," said Marie gently.

"I didn't know you were staying here," muttered grandad.

"I don't think so grandad," said Sam chuckling. "You were only five when the war ended.

56

"Was I?" he replied. "I don't remember exactly. It was a long time ago."

"Yes, it was. Now I hef brought a present for you. I voz going to giv it to Karen when I found we are not in otel but she said that you might like it. So just one moment." Marie left the table and returned a minute later holding a bottle. Grandad had momentarily unmagnanimously thought about taking the opportunity to regain his seat but stayed put.

"Zis is for you."

"What is it?" asked grandad suspiciously, taking hold of the bottle as he spoke.

"It's Black Forest Cherry Schnapps. Iz been aged for ten years. I sink you vill like it. I voz going to dvink it myself but you can have it."

"And so do I," said grandad, his eyes suddenly lighting up. "Can I try some now?"

"Is very strong so maybe later. But now hef some breakfast and zen we can go and zit down and hef a chat over coffee. I will just hef to remove my clothes..."

"Er, I don't think that will be necessary," said grandad, his face reddening. "But I know what you Germans are like. I once had to go to the doctors' for a check up. The nice German lady asked me to strip to my slippers so I did. When she returned she took one look at me and screamed."

"I wonder why," said Sam.

"Seems like she got a bit muddled. Pants in German are slips. It's only a short trip from slips to slippers and there I was standing in my shoes and not much else with my trousers and pants around my ankles. Well nothing else actually. So please don't remove your clothes on my part although it would make it one-all as far as my life is concerned."

"But zey are all offer the sitting room where I was sleeping."

"Oh, I see what you mean. But I don't think it's right that a lady should be sleeping in the sitting room. You could have had my room."

"Oh come now dad," said Mrs Horrise. "You know perfectly well that you were asleep when we returned. I could hardly have woken you up and chucked you out of your bed could I?"

"You could've if I knew that there was a bottle of cherry schnapps on offer."

"Oh for goodness sake dad, eat your breakfast. I have to go to the church hall with Marie for a welcome chat and to get everybody on Sonny's programme for the day. Fingers crossed. Fingers very, very crossed."

"I'm coming too," said grandad. "This could be fun!"

However when they arrived at St Saviour's Mrs Horrise wondered why they had bothered. The Horrises walked in to be greeted by some loud voices and some very loud voices. Janet was surrounded by a number of hosts as the Germans mostly looked on. Seeing Karen Horrise she pointed a trembling finger over the complainants' heads

58

towards her. "There she is! Mrs Karen Horrise. H-O-R-R-I-S-E. That's who you want to see!"

The mob turned round and advanced towards Karen. She remained rooted to the spot although her instinct was to run. The first to reach her was Ray whom the Ravens recalled from when they helped in the churchyard. Horace remembered that he was a man who liked to make the most of the hospitality that he was meant to be showing, helping himself to a couple of cakes before offering them round, but he wasn't being very hospitable today. "I put on my form CHRISTIAN!" he thundered in a very unchristian-like manner. "And what have I ended up with? THAT!" Mrs Horrise followed Ray's out-stretched, shaking finger. A young lady, extremely attractive Sam thought, but with a very sad face sat quietly on her own. He took an immediate fancy to her bright purple hair so decided that the least he could do was go over and introduce himself to her.

"Hi," I'm Sam.

"Heidi."

"I love your hair."

"Zank you."

"I'm sorry that it doesn't seem to be working with Ray. I seem to think it might somehow be my fault."

"Oh no, don't vurry. His family iz very nice but he vonted to say grace for ze breakfast and that is okay but I didn't shut my eyez but neither did he and he vent cross and zed that Christians always shut zee eyez for grace but I am not Christian. I am Druid."

"Cool," said Sam.

Meanwhile Mrs Horrise was being accosted by Mrs Ives. Mrs Ives, Karen decided, was looking drabber by the day, and felt that, with her hair put up, her mouth drooping and black clothing dressed down it wouldn't be long before she would be able to have a reasonable stab at a widowed Queen Victoria impersonation. "Mrs Horrise," she barked. "I specifically requested to have someone who was comfortable with chickens. I was expecting someone with means who was used to living in the country, maybe a gentleman farmer or suchlike if it had to be a man. However my first preference was for a female as I am not properly over the passing of my husband five years ago so maybe a gentle lady farmer. Look, I am still wearing the wedding ring that he gave me on that wonderful day in nineteen, er, whenever it was." Mrs Ives shook her hand so vigorously in Karen Horrise's face that she thought that there was a good chance of it flying off.

"Instead you have paired me up with a Mr Schneider. Mr Schneider lives in a town penthouse flat. He is not a female. He has never been married and has been giving me a lot of unwelcome attention. Very unwelcome attention. Most of it extremely unwelcome. I would have thought that he would have been much better suited to Mr Jones..."

"No he would not!" Mr Jones screamed. "I do not want a man staying with me! I asked for a woman..."

"But you have a woman," Mrs Horrise reminded him. "You have Fräulein Wegner."

"You are quite correct madam, that is most observant of you. But Fraulein Wegner is about half my age..."

"Does that matter?" asked Mrs Horrise.

"Yes it does! When I asked for a woman I presumed to have someone around my own age. I can tell you I've totally freaked out Fraulein Wegner. It was most important that my guest likes bees. I put that on my form. When I picked her up last night she was a bit giggly but I didn't take any notice. All I did was tell her that I like having bees whereupon she screamed and told me to stop the car because she wanted to get out. I didn't of course but when I reached my house she jumped out and ran into my back garden. Unfortunately she ran straight into my hives and knocked two over and that's why she had to go to hospital last night and that's why she's covered in bandages and I have yet to work out what I've said wrong."

"I tell you vat you said vong Herr Jones," said Heidi who had wandered over to see what all the fuss was about. "Ingrid zought zat you said zat you like having babiesss."

"Oh," said Mr Jones quietly. "That explains a lot. I can see why that might have caused her some distress. Even so..."

"Mrs Horrise, if I may have a word? My name is Edgar Fripp. You may remember my name." Above the melee Karen spotted a man, tall and lanky, smart floppy hair, dressed in an ornate shirt and casual jacket sporting a red with large white spots silk handkerchief in the breast pocket. On his feet he wore a pair of hand-crafted brown leather brogues. His attire demanded attention. She recognised the name as belonging to a member of the group who had played at her husband's birthday party or to be more accurate, had attended her husband's birthday party having been booked to play with Chislehurst String Quartet but left without sounding a note.

"Yes Edgar..."

"MR Fripp."

"Mr Fripp. We meet at last. Have you come to give us a recital?" she asked with a grin.

"No I most certainly have not Mrs Horrise. But I can tell you one thing Mrs Horrise, you are here to face the music. I had volunteered to be a host in order that I might discuss the narratives of the great quasi-German Mozart that were bound up in the worlds he lived in. If the individual was to bring their violin or viola we could have practised some Vivaldi, Beethoven and, of course, Haydn. I especially wrote on my form that I wanted, in fact needed, a serious musician. However, when I asked Anna what instrument she had in her misshapen case, she brought out a Fender Stratocaster and asked me if I had any requests that I would like her to play. I was speechless! She then told me that she covered many genres including country, folk, soul, blues, rock, pop, and R and B. Fortunately I had my smelling salts to hand but I inhaled so deeply that I thought that I was going to ingest them! Thank goodness she hadn't brought any amplification but then I awoke this morning to find that she had located a suitable cable and had plugged her guitar into my Bang and Olufsen sound system and was trotting out, to use her over-familiar expertise with the English language, *Paranoid*. Poor Sagwa, my precious Siamese was meouwing so loudly that I thought she was going to split her vocal cords." Mr Fripp pulled out his spotted handkerchief and waved it theatrically across his forehead.

"Maybe she was singing along," suggested Mrs Horrise. "Any more complaints?"

There were many. Eighteen in total to be precise. The butcher had been paired up with a vegan, a couch potato with a rock climber, a carpenter with a university lecturer, a beer-drinker who watched, but never played, darts and football with a teetotal opera lover who enjoyed opera, ballet and performing with her local choir, a capitalist with a communist, a paedophobic was placed with a family that had three small children. Then there was the untidiest person in the country who was paired with a lady who loved a tidy house. "She's a 'neat freak,'" Miss Lamb complained. "Although we arrived at my house well after bedtime she insisted in hoovering her room. He's too polite to mention it but you've paired Mike the vicar with Mia who's an atheist. This is quite the most shambolic town twinning hospitality that I've ever been involved with. And another thing..."

Mrs Horrise had had enough. She raised her hands in the air to try to quell the crowd. "WILL YOU ALL JUST SHUT THE FRIG UP! I'll tell you 'another thing' Miss Lamb. There has never been town twinning hospitality this way round before and do you know what, there probably won't be again as far as I'm concerned, you miserable sods. So stuff your town twinning and stuff the programme that our lovely local children have prepared. You've got your guests so just swap them round among yourselves or can't you even organise that? Who's going first? What about the kids? Mel, Em, Archie, Ed, Charlie, Sonny, how are you getting on?"

"If it's all the same to you Mrs Horrise," said Melanie quietly, my family has so far quite enjoyed having our visitor and there's no reason to think it won't continue. I think she finds us a bit odd but we've been getting on just fine. And, if you would allow me to speak for the other Ravings, it appears, apart from a minor issue with Sonny that has now been resolved, everyone has made sure that they extend the hand of friendship and love."

"So Mrs 'orrise, can I just say that I 'ave everyfing sorted for today for my programme," said Sonny sounding as if he had not ever suffered from a minor issue in his life, "so d'you fink we can just get on?"

"Over to you Sonny," said Mrs Horrise as she went and sat in the corner. Sonny stood on a chair and raised his hands in the air.

"My nom is Sonny und I vould like to speak to you in German..."

"Please don't!" Karl shouted and the Germans all laughed.

"In that case," said Sonny, "I would like to continue my programme for today. We are all goin' ta walk down the road to Chislehurst caves where you can go on a guided tour of some ancient manmade tunnels and stuff from the Druids onwards. You can see a church, a 'ospital, a munitions store an' a mushroom farm and other stuff. An' I would like you all to behave like grown-ups which the Germans are doing already but not the English so ya need to pull ya socks up. Any questions? Yes Max?"

"Can you tell us vhy zere is a hospital in zee caves and a church az well?"

"Yes, the reason is because durin' the war people round here had to shelter from you lot down there so a sort of village set itself up. After all it was better ta live down there in the cold and dark than up 'ere in the light and warm and be bombed by you Germans."

Karen Horrise sighed.

"Ya, that is true. We were very good at dropping bombs!" and the Germans all laughed.

"Yeah, but not good enough," said Sonny, "otherwise we would all be speaking German!"

"Ya. Like you Sonny, ha, ha, ha!" and the Germans all laughed some more.

"C'mon," said Sonny with a huge grin, "follow me!"

\*\*\*

The Germans and their hosts disappeared into the caves on their guided tour. Sonny stayed in the cafe with Horace's mother who had asked if he could stay behind. He was happy to do so when he found out that he was going to be treated to a hot chocolate and a slice of cake which he was beginning to think were Horrise staples that went together like peaches and cream. Sonny made sure that he had a slice from the largest cake he could see behind the counter. "You're probably wondering why I wanted to have a quiet word with you Sonny and the reason is this. I'll come straight to the point. I need to ask you a question and that is..."

"Hold up love," said Sonny with a mouth full of cake. "You wanted me to stay behind and for that you got me a 'ot choc an' a slice of Sexton. I fort it woz 'cos you was scared with the Druids an' stuff and wanted someone t' sit wiv ya. If ya now tryin' to pump me for some info then that's another slice."

"It's not really information I'm after Sonny; I was just a little concerned when Melanie said that you had a minor issue presumably with your German," said Mrs Horrise lowering her voice and speaking more gently than she had in a while. I just wondered if everything was okay." She reached out and touched Sonny's arm. "I had a quick word with Melanie on the way down and she said that they had plenty of room at their house and that she could take your German if it was too much for your mum." Sonny looked shocked at the suggestion.

"Nuffin' of the sort love. It's just that there was a little misunderstandin' to start with. That's all. Nuffin' big. Tiny in fact."

"Would you care to elucidate?"

"We was sittin' down at the kitchen table after our evenin' at Uncle Bernie's place in Shoreditch an' mum asked Max what 'e was into like what did he like back 'ome. An' you'll never guess what 'e said well 'e said, 'stolen bikes.' Well me ears pricked up straightaway and there's me finkin' we could get a little cross-border arrangement goin', you know to sort of make the trail go a bit cold either way. So I asked 'im how many did 'e 'ave an' e said, 'a couple a day' and there was me finkin' I was made for life. Then 'e said he 'ad some in his suitcase that was in the sittin' room and I thought somefing wasn't quite right 'cos they must be very special fold up ones and then 'e said 'e brought them as a present for anyone at the 'otel who 'e met which was a bit odd. Anyway 'e disappeared off into the front room and when 'e came back 'e 'ad a box of little cakes in 'is 'and which 'e gave to mum and she said, 'Thank you but what are they?' and 'e pointed to the box an' it said 'Stollenbisse' an' 'e said, 'It translates as 'stollen bites'' and we said, 'Oooooh' and mum looked like she was suffocatin'. Then he asked what we thought 'e said and we said 'stolen bikes' and then 'e laughed a lot and then 'e said a bit weirdly, 'I 'ope not 'cos I'm a part-time policeman when I'm not extruding vulcanised rubber!' and then he laughed some more and so mum asked him why he 'ad lipstick all over 'is face an' while he was tryin' to tell mum about the decorators in Uncle Bernie's pub she was up out of 'er chair quicker than you can say 'Jack Robinson' an' hidin' stuff."

"I see," said Mrs Horrise finally. "So would you like me to move Max to Melanie's so that your mum can breathe again?"

"No fanks love. Mum says it was quite nice 'avin' a bloke around. We ain't complainin' unlike all the others."

"In that case you keep Max and let's just hope that our other hosts grow up a bit." Sonny nodded.

"I know. Bunch of kids if you ask me love."

\*\*\*

Fräulein Marie Muller was more than happy with Karen Horrise's suggestion that they do their own thing for much of the week without "the whinging others, well most of them."

"It is fine," she said the following day over breakfast. "I am appy to immerse myself in English culture for my stay however unexpected," and as a result Marie was treated like an old friend who had come to stay for a few days. She was shown all that was good in Horace's part of the country, not that there was too much bad to find even if they had wanted to search for it. To Mrs Horrise's horror, one day when they drove past a Lidl she asked if they could stop so that she could go in for a look around.

"I'm afraid Marie that I do not normally allow myself in Lidl in case I see my neighbour Susie who's a bit of a snob," she said, "but Horace will accompany you." Then Mrs Horrise gave him "a small list" of items that she needed, "while you're in there." Unfortunately for Mrs Horrise Susie was in Lidl and when Horace said, "Hello Susie," and Susie looked his companion up and down with a quizzical look Marie volunteered that she was staying with the Horrise family and they were doing some shopping for Karen who was waiting in the car park. "I expect she is," said Susie who then left by the other door and waited until they had gone before going back into the car park with her shopping.

"I don't understand Karen," said Marie once they were back on the road. "In Germany Lidl is very popular and we are pleased to be seen in there."

"It's not my problem, it's Susie's," said Mrs Horrise but later that evening, when they were alone, Horace told Marie about his mother hiding her Lidl bags and any other bags for that matter inside her Waitrose ones and then taught her to say, "I shop at Waitrose," in an almost perfect home counties' accent.

Too soon the week was up and Marie was taken down to St Saviour's church hall to meet up with her fellow Germans to get on the minibus back to Dover. "I am dreading going in," said Mrs Horrise once they had reached the car park but when she saw Sonny emerge with a huge grin on his face she thought that maybe nothing too dreadful was going to happen that hadn't already. "Is everything okay in there Sonny?" she asked nervously.

"It's a bit tense love, but you'll be okay," he replied. Mrs Horrise, her sons and Marie went into the church hall with their heads down.

"Hold the door Horace, just in case I need to run out again," she instructed. She was waiting for Janet's voice, "There she is! Mrs Karen Horrise. That's who you want to see! To hang, draw and quarter," but there was no Janet and no Mary anywhere to be seen.

"Hiding probably mum," Sam suggested.

Mrs Horrise looked up and all she could see were smiling, happy faces. "Drei cheers for Mrs Horrise!" Max called out. "Hip hip hurra!"

"Max," said Horace beckoning. "Come over here please whilst mummy waits near the door 'cos I think she's momentarily stuck to the floor. What on earth is going on?"

"Oh it is zimple Horace. The English have fallen under zee spell of the German freundlichkeit. We have made zem not so uptight and we have some stories to tell. Would you like to hear them? First we hef Ray."

"I think I'm about to whatever I say," replied Horace.

Ray walked over to Karen with Heidi on his arm. "Oh my goodness, Ray," said Horace, "what has happened to your hair?"

"It's quite simple Horace," said Ray. "I decided that I have been a bit of a prickly old plonker for a while and I needed to loosen up a bit. I think that Heidi has helped me in this endeavour. My hair was losing quite a bit of its colour so I thought to myself, 'Let's try purple.' It suits me don't you think?"

"It's the mark of a spiritual person," said Melanie who had joined them.

"It makes you look more like a wrinkly prune mate in my 'umble opinion," said Sonny in his usual honest way.

"Thank you Sonny," said Ray with a grin.

"I'm glad to hear that you're getting on much better now Ray," said Karen felling somewhat relieved. She took a step further into the church. "And what of you Heidi? Are you okay with Ray's Christianity?"

"Oh course I am," she replied. "Druids and Christians are not so different."

"'What if Merlin's Afallen and Jesus' Rood are the same Tree? One rides it to his destiny, One sits beneath to prophesy,' so says a poem I've learned," said Ray as the couple turned to wander around the church with its magnificent stained glass windows.

Mrs Horrise looked around her. No one else seemed to be paying her any attention at all. She took a further step into the church. Then she stopped.

"Horace, is that Mrs Ives over there with Herr Schneider and what is she doing? Oh my goodness, Horace, avert your gaze!" she commanded all the time staring with an intensity that bordered on voyeurism.

"I think they're kissing mummy," said Horace. "Are they allowed to do that in a church?"

"It's not that!" said Mrs Horrise. "It's more the case that her husband's only just died."

"He died over five years ago mummy. I think that she's allowed to kiss someone else after what's probably over two thousand days."

"It looks like she's making up for lost time then," said Horace's mother wincing.

"Ssh," said Horace quietly, "she's coming over."

"Mrs Horrise," said Mrs Ives with a smile, "I just wanted to say 'thank you' for all your hard work in arranging this town twinning..."

"It's my pleasure," said Karen beaming. She looked down and noticed that Mrs Ives had moved her wedding ring to her other hand.

"I feel like a new woman."

"If you don't mind my saying, you look like a new woman. Your hair, your smile..."

"I am liking the country life," said Herr Schenider. "Und the chickens are growing on me so I'm sure I will be returning bevor too long."

Karen Horrise turned to see Fraulein Wegner and David Jones deep in conversation. "Looks like they're okay," she said nodding in the direction of bee-keeper and his twinning partner. Mr Jones and his friend saw them looking and started to walk over.

"Oh yes," replied Mrs Ives. "They are getting on just fine."

"It's true," said Mr Jones. "Ingrid has been making me feel all young again since her return from hospital." Mrs Horrise raised an eyebrow.

"Ingrid has been ringing the changes. I used to go to bed early and get up early, now I keep younger person hours. I go to bed late and get up late. I used to tend to my bees in the morning, now I tend to them in the evening. I still do the same things but at different times of the day. It's all so refreshing. Thank you so much Mrs Horrise."

Karen was beginning to think that everything had been going rather well after all. She approached another of the hosts. "Good morning Mr Fripp. Dress down day today is it?"

Mr Fripp turned to face her. He was sporting a red t-shirt with "ROCK ON!" printed in vivid yellow in a sort of zigzag fashion across the front. His jacket had gone, there was no silk handkerchief and brown brogues had turned into trainers and quite dirty ones at that.

"Stepped in a puddle Mr Fripp?"

"Please, call me 'Edgar'. Or 'Ed'. And no, I haven't. They're made like this. Made to look not new. What a great idea baby!" he smirked.

"And what's that in your hand?"

"Oh this fine instrument?" he asked lifting it high in the air. It's an axe. Actually it's Anna's strat. but we call them axes. I've been laying down some cool vibes and knocking off a few licks. Haydn's so eighteenth century! I'm bashing out some new rockin' riffs. Even Sagwa's been joinin' in. It's so far out! Cheers Karen!"

"Er, my pleasure Ed."

The story was the same wherever Mrs Horrise went. The butcher had started to sell vegan products having taken down a notice in his window that read, "VEGANATARIAN? GO CHEW ON A CARROT!" the couch potato had been to The Rock at the local country park and had had his first climbing lesson, the carpenter had taught the university lecturer how to build a proper bookcase for all her books, a beer-drinker had started a dry day every week when he would engage in a cultural activity, the banker had made a huge financial donation to a food bank with a pledge to continue to give regularly to worthy causes, the paedophobic had overcome his irrational fear and had been taking the three small children on regular trips to the playground. Miss Lamb was learning to be a little more relaxed with a bit of excess tidiness.

So convivial was the atmosphere in the church that Mrs Horrise decided to tackle what she thought was probably the most difficult pairing, that of the vicar and Mia the atheist. Spotting him on his own for a moment Karen ambled up to the priest and said,

"I hardly dare to mention this but could you let me know if you've been getting on okay with the, um, Mia?" Mike let out a hearty chuckle.

"Ha, ha, ha!" he chortled. "It's been great! I even said a prayer with her this morning. It's what I do, well on God's behalf of course. It was William Temple who said something along the lines of the Church of England being the only organisation that exists solely for the benefit of its non-members. You can't prove the existence of God but if you strive to be pure in heart you can see him. I have given her my own personal testimony which I believe is as powerful as anything. The whole week has been one of immense satisfaction. Ask her."

"Jah, it's been great," said Mia. "Mike has been telling me about an astronomer called Carl Sagar. He once commented zat an atheist is someone who is zertain zat God does not exist, someone who has compelling evidenze against zee existence of God but he knows of no such compelling evidenze. So now I am aving to zink some more about vot I do believe."

As the Germans climbed into what was now more of a coach than a minibus for the return trip to Dover everyone was in high spirits. Marie was waving through the window at grandad who was in floods of tears. "We won the war but she's won my heart!" he sobbed.

"'Scuse me love!"

Mrs Horrise turned round to find Sonny looking particularly sheepish, not an adjective that she would have used for him very often.

"What's the matter Sonny?" she asked.

"The fing is, Max has told me that the one thing to do in life is always tell the truth. So although I'm not telling you this 'cos I've told a lie it's a sort of lie 'cos I 'aven't said anfing and sort of let people just like...assume."

"Oh spit it out Sonny for goodness sake," Karen Horrise implored. Sonny dropped his head.

"When I was round your house a while ago I sneezed on loads of papers an' I was only in yer sittin' room lookin' fer ya to tell ya 'ow we would be doin' the programme 'cos it was my idea and I sneezed on the papers and I put them back but prob'bly not quite right but I don't need payin' much or nuffin' and I just wanted to say..."

"Yes?"

"Sorry."

"Oh Sonny, come here and let me give you a hug. Look, what you did was fabulous and all I can say is that the Germans have had a great time so why not put a container at the front of the coach and tell the Germans that it's for tips for the main organisers, that's to say you and the Ravens?"

"Mostly me Karen love."

"Mostly you Sonny," then she gave him his hug before he freed himself and jumped on the coach having gone as red as an overripe tomato.

"What are you up to with Horace's mum Sonny?" asked Emily who went and sat down beside him. She had been watching him through the window and wondering what had been going on between them.

"I woz just givin' 'er a hug 'cos she said that I could collect tips for all me hard work," replied Sonny. He sat down and pulled out a large sick bag from the rack in front of him, borrowed a pen from the driver and wrote

SPENDEN
VIELEN DANK

"Now all you have to do Emily is pass the bag up an' across an' down an' across an' back up to me," said Sonny.

"Fine," said Emily, "but what does it say?"

"It says, 'Tips for Ravens." I've bin takin' lessons from Max.

All seven Ravens were allowed to go on the journey as a special treat, Mrs Horrise having first made sure that they would also be brought back. Once they were back on the A2 Melanie walked to the front of the coach and asked for the Ravens to be left in Dover for the rest of the day. "We can find our own way back," she confidently asserted but just like the driver from a week ago this one was having none of it, only this time the other way round.

"It's more than my job's worth," he said as Melanie flashed her debit card in his rear view mirror in her desperate attempt for a one way trip only.

"I'm paying you to leave us in Dover," she implored but it was no use.

"You're just like the other driver we had, useless!" she shouted as she returned to her seat.

"What's the point in having money if you can't spend it doing useful stuff like, er, bribing people?" she demanded of her friends.

"We could let down his tyres," suggested Emily.

"Then he would be stuck with us," said Edward, "and I thought the whole idea was that he wasn't."

"Anyone got their passport with them?" Charlie asked with a grin. "No, no, no, not you lot!" he added when twenty-five Germans waved theirs in the air.

As the coach descended the steep road that curled over the top of the ferry port Sonny took delivery of the sick bag and plonked it and its sizable contents straight into his rucksack with only the briefest of glimpses inside. He stood up, walked to the front and over the Tannoy thanked the Germans and then asked them what they wanted to do. "We have a spare hour or so 'cos we've made good time."

"Ve vont to go to your uncle's pub!" someone shouted.

"To do some wallpapering!" bellowed Max.

The driver was instructed to drive along the front to The Jolly Sailor and the travellers alighted.

Uncle Tom greeted Sonny and his friends, old and new, warmly. "Stayin' for a drink this time Sonny boy?"

"Yes uncle, we 'ave 'alf an hour and the first drinks on me! Pints and chasers for all!" Sonny declared as he reached inside his rucksack and pulled out a small handful of notes.

"It may be just a coincidence but there's another group of Germans at the far end of the bar and I must say they look nothing like as happy as your lot with their forlorn faces and halves of lager."

"Maybe they're sad because they're going home. C'mon Max, let's go and say 'hi.'"

Max marched off in search of his fellow countryman with Sonny on his tail. The other group wasn't hard to find in the busy pub. They were just as described. Sonny fancied that they had collectively lost a shilling and found a penny but wasn't sure how that translated so left the talking to Max. Max spoke to them in German. He introduced himself then asked the glum group if they had had a good holiday.

"Sicherlich nicht!" said one of the Germans. "Es war schrecklich. Wir sollten bei Familien in einem Dorf namens 'Chislehurst' in Kent auf einer Städtepartnerschaft wohnen. Stattdessen brachte uns der Bus zu einem schrecklichen, billigen Hotel im Süden Londons und jeden Tag wurden wir in den Sinn gebracht- betäubend langweilige Konferenz über die Extrusion von vulkanisiertem Kautschuk. Workshops, Vorträge, Diskussionen. Es war schrecklich.

Wir haben versucht, uns zu beschweren, aber niemand hat es bemerkt. Wir sind froh, wieder zu Hause zu sein."

[Translation: "Certainly not! It was dreadful. We were supposed to be staying with families in a village in Kent called 'Chislehurst' on a town twinning. Instead the coach took us to a dreadful, cheap hotel in south London and every day we were taken to a mind-numbingly boring conference on vulcanised rubber extrusion. Workshops, lectures, discussions. It was awful. We tried to complain but no one took any notice. We'll be glad to be back home."]

"And where is home?"

"Nochalt. And you?"

"München," said Max. "Good to meet you."

Walking back to their friends Sonny said, "Slow darn a sec. Max. Did I understand that right?"

"Probably," said Max. "And I do not sink that they are going to forget in a urry. Town twinning may be receiving a letter or two soon. You better warn Orace's mum."

"Oh dear, oh dear, oh dear!" thought Sonny.

"But 'Munich' me 'arris! Whatever 'appened to always tellin' the truth? An' I confessed to 'Orace's mum when I didn't need to," complained Sonny.

"I did live in Munich when I was a boy."

"Oh friggin' 'eck, now you sound like 'Orace's grandad."

"Come on Sonny, let's join ze others. You can tell them what has happened on your vay home."

"So you know all about vulcanised rubber extrusion? What's that like?" asked Sonny.

"Mind-numbingly boring," said Max with a grin. "Unlike the vantastic past week that ve hef had. So thank you. We are all so very, very happy to haf met you all. It vos such vun!"

Sonny only realised how fantastic the Germans had considered the week to have been when he arrived home and went up to his bedroom where he worked out that he would be able to take his mother shopping in Waitrose not just for cake but for the rest of the family's groceries every week for at least the next year.

As Karen Horrise tucked Horace into bed she remarked on how well the week had turned out after the initial difficulties.

"In some ways mummy I think that the difficulties have only just begun," he said sleepily as he closed his eyes.

"What do you mean Horace?" she demanded softly.

"Let's put it this way mummy," he replied, "I think that your dynamic community involvement is right back to where it was a couple of months ago."

"Like at zero?"

"And possibly beyond. Goodnight!"

## Introduction to Horace Horrise and the Carinavirus

*What Horace anticipated was going to be a pleasant few hours in the sole company of one of his best friends takes an unexpected turn when the pair bump into another of the gang. Over lunch Melanie's behaviour shows signs of a certain lack of maturity which is brought to a head when Sonny takes the three of them on an errand.*

*Inadvertently they add to tensions surrounding a global health emergency but they soon realise that they are able to use it to their advantage.*

*However the day does not end well for all concerned with coronavirus at large.*

We're probably all fed up with Coronavirus but it was too good a subject to pass by.

The pandemic started in the United Kingdom in around March 2020. Before we knew it we were in lockdown. I was struck by the contrast between those who used the difficulties to do their best, not only those who always do so such as our wonderful NHS staff but also those who selflessly volunteered to help in the community with the delivery of food and other essentials to the housebound and those self-isolating, and those who used the situation for personal, mostly, financial gain. Sonny invokes the spirit of the wartime spiv who provides goods / services but unfortunately uses the circumstances to profiteer.

I keep chickens. When I visit my local feed store based at a stables I always think about what a wonderful melting pot of society it is. There's the designer horsey set with all their posh gear and immaculately groomed nags rubbing shoulders with the manure turners and scruffy jobbing smallholders: a great location for Melanie and Sonny.

Mr Lillie's Workshed is the link. There was a shop in Chislehurst, The Workshop, that stocked everything hardware. You could buy one washer if you needed it and not a sealed pack of one hundred. It had a window display that spilled out onto the pavement a bit like Arkwright's shop in *Open All Hours* on the BBC. The Workshop has now closed and is much missed. Coronavirus isn't.

I was in a great gastro pub, The Seahorse, in Shalford, near Guildford where they had a pudding - Passion Fruit Martini Eton Mess - "for over eighteens" only. "A great marketing ploy," I thought. And another very useful story device for the                oh-not-so-grown-up-and-certainly-not-over-18 Melanie.

## Horace Horrise and the Carinavirus

In many respects Horace was like any other eleven-year-old. He had his good days and he had his bad days although they were not of the sort that grown-ups would be thinking. It seemed to Horace that if an adult spoke of having a "good day" it would be in the context of relative freedom from worry - that they were getting through without having to resort to medication or alcohol, maybe both. A "bad day" would be one in which they would succumb to - rather than enjoy - a glass of wine. It might also be described as such if there was a hospital appointment or a large bill to be paid. No, Horace's days were measured as good or bad on nothing more complicated than whether he had mostly done things that were to his (long or short-term) advantage, such as completing his homework on time or helping his parents with an errand or two but more likely to be finding a ten-pound note in the woods, or to his disadvantage which would mostly be things that if caught in the act would lead to his being justifiably sent to his room. However, such bad things could also be to his advantage, but maybe his alone. Ever the philosopher, Horace realised that he could be having a good day but having it doing something bad but this was so often much more preferable to having a bad day doing something good although he realised that it was perfectly possible to have a good day doing something good. It was just that there didn't appear to be many of these in his life however hard he tried. Today however was hopefully going to be a good day doing good and he wasn't even going to have to do very much to make it so. As ever the *actualité* didn't turn out as expected.

Horace looked up from his Weetabix to find neither his mother, Karen Horrise, fussing around him, as was usual, taking his order for his cooked breakfast, it being a

Saturday, nor his father, David Horrise, sitting at the table attempting *The Times* cryptic crossword. Horace wondered why his father ever bothered with the cryptic; he hardly ever managed to start it let alone finish. "I can only manage the junior quick," he once lamented, "but anyone can do that." Yet when Horace once decided to help him out whilst his father was in the toilet and filled in some of the squares, when he returned he was not best pleased to say the least. Mr Horrise had reappeared and picked up the paper, then his head had jolted slightly as he processed what he was seeing. He stared at the crossword for a few seconds then said in a tone of voice that was totally unsuited to a Saturday morning, "Who's been mucking up my cryptic crossword?"

"I thought you needed a bit of help daddy, that's all," said Horace dismissively.

"But your answers are all wrong," his father replied shortly.

"I'm not sure how you can say that daddy," Horace countered, "when you don't know what the answers are yourself." Mr Horrise put down his paper and sighed.

"I don't know the *correct* answer..."

"*Any* correct *answersssss* daddy."

"I don't know *any correct answersssssss* YET Horace," said his father testily, "but I will know some of them later and the correct answers are not what you've put in."

"I can't see why it matters though, daddy," said Horace brightly, "whether the answers I've put in are actually right or not. After all, who's going to know? I would've thought the important thing is that you've filled it in. Otherwise you're just going to stare at it like chess players do on a board when they're playing a game and even then you might not come up with the answer. At least chess players eventually do something."

"This is not 'a game' Horace," said his father jabbing at the paper in front of him. "And you are going to 'do something' Horace and wrap up whilst I finish my breakfast quietly cogitating." His father's tone of voice had changed to one that signalled the end of the conversation whether Horace liked it or not. Getting the last word in was simply not worth it at times like these. Horace's father was getting closer to "the edge" and it was time to back off even though Horace still felt he had done nothing wrong.

"Mummy," said Horace finally as the smoke from the frying pan went from sizzling blue to acrid black. "Mummy," he repeated when he received no response. "Any chance of my cooked breakfast?" What was wrong with her this morning? Mrs Horrise slowly stood up and turned round. She had been leaning on the work surface listening to the radio that she had turned down low, not appearing to do anything much with the egg that she was holding in one hand.

"If mum holds that egg for much longer it'll hatch!" said Horace's older brother Sam with a chuckle.

"Sshhh," she said as she turned back round.

"Mummy, where's daddy?" Horace used as few words as he could to ask his question. "Sshhh" to Horace didn't mean what it did to most children; to Horace it simply meant keep speaking but in shorter sentences and a lower voice. His mother's response was even shorter and lower.

"Study." Horace sighed.

"Mummy, what *is* going on?" Horace was already getting a little tired of having a virtually one way conversation but eventually Sam came to his rescue.

"Mum's listening to the radio and dad's in his study looking at the TV. And the reason is - we're soon going to succumb to the blood-sucking killer that is already on our shores. It's a virulent virus with no known cure and it's called, it's called...um..."

"Carinavirus," said Horace's younger sister Olivia without missing a beat.

"It's not 'blood-sucking' Sam,'" said their mother without moving. "It's a virulent virus for sure but that's all. Nothing to be worried about if you don't stick your dirty hands in your mouth, if you wash them before eating and sneeze into a hankie and bin it." Then she stood up, walked over to the frying pan and cracked the egg on the side with one hand. She squeezed and the yolk and white plopped into the pan sending off a loud "SSSSSS!" The egg was already being subjected to a heat so intense that it was unlikely to survive looking like a fried egg after only a few seconds in the pan. Horace got up and walked over to the hob. His mother forced a spatula under the egg and flipped it over. The underside was pitted black with burnt oil.

"I'll think I'll just have toast today mummy," said Horace as he returned to his seat leaving his mother to the bread and knife. "She should be able to manage that," he thought as his father walked in, sat down and stared distractedly at the crossword.

"Not good news," he finally announced to the paper. No one said anything. There was more on its way.

"I've just been catching up with the latest developments in my study and it's not looking at all good. The number of coronavirus cases has doubled in the UK from three days ago and if it goes on like this for much longer we're going to have to get some serious shopping in and batten down the hatches for quite a while. I am actually getting fairly worried and we need to start taking some serious precautions."

"Mummy says it's okay if we wash our hankies, sneeze into our mouths and stick our dirty hands into our food and bin it," said Olivia assuredly. Her father glanced up, looking only slightly perplexed. She was his daughter after all.

"It's not what *you* do Olivia," he said, "it's what all the other people do. If you're outside in that big wide world," Mr Horrise waved his right hand expansively across his chest as if perfecting a backhand lob, "and some poisoned person death sneezes into the air as you walk past them then no amount of washing or wiping is going to stop the virus attaching itself to a cell lining and bringing you down big time."

"So what's the answer if we want to go out into the big wide world today?" asked Horace, his voice quavering almost imperceptibly. He was expecting to go shopping at any moment but the thought of someone sneezing a death sneeze was reducing the level of excitement and anticipation that he had been feeling the night before to almost nil. Not that Horace's anticipation of going shopping was ever anything other than nil unless it was he who was doing the shopping. "Know what you want, know where to go and get it, go and get it, get it, pay and return." That was Horace's idea of shopping whereas it seemed that everyone else's idea, especially the female members of his family, was to go shopping not knowing what they wanted, not knowing where to go and get what they didn't know they wanted to get, go and look for it and anything else that took their fancy on the way, maybe get it, pay and return. Horace fondly recalled his mother and sister going to Tunbridge Wells for a day's shopping with one of his mother's friends who lived down that way and coming back with precisely nothing.

"We had a great day, didn't we Olivia?" Mrs Horrise enthused and Olivia nodded in agreement. But what did they actually do? Horace wondered.

"Well we shopped. But just didn't buy anything."

"I don't understand mummy," said Horace. "That's like going camping and staying in your tent all weekend. Do you understand daddy?"

His father shrugged his shoulders. "I don't understand Horace, but I don't think that we're meant to understand. What I do know is that your mother and her friend had a great day out and it cost precisely nothing."

"That's where you're wrong daddy," said Olivia, who hadn't realised that her mother was staring at her with pursed lips and frowning, "'cos we had lunch in Le Petit Fleur and we had Champagne and then we had tea and then we..." Olivia finally looked up at her mother. "Oh sorry mummy," she spluttered, "have I said something wrong?"

Today, however, was different. Horace was going to be shopping with a female, that much was similar but other than that he was not expecting the outing to be anything like that which he had ever experienced with his mother.

He was to be shopping with his friend Melanie from the big house up the road. And just as he asked his question the doorbell rang. "I'll get it," he said as he leapt up out of his chair and went to answer the door.

"The obvious answer is, don't go out into the big wide world. Stay indoors," said Horace's father as he picked up his pen and stared a little less distractedly at the crossword. "But if you do have to go out, keep away from crowds or sick-looking people. If we're not careful we'll all be wearing surgical face masks and self-isolating before the month's out."

"I thought that Horace was going out with his friends when he said yesterday that he was going shopping, but it looks like he's going with just one of them," said Mrs Horrise as she peered round the kitchen door just in time to see Melanie walk through and Horace shut the front door behind.

"Come and say 'hello' to everyone," said Horace as he led Melanie into the kitchen. Sam looked up at this vision of loveliness as she walked over and gave him a slightly-embarrassed hug as her mother seemed to do to everyone. Mrs Horrise thought that Melanie looked as though she was dressed as if she had just gone shopping not just about to with the addition of a Fjällräven Kånken rucksack that was just the right colour and shade that she gently slipped off her back and dropped on the floor in the manner of a child coming in from school and divesting themselves of bag and

91

jacket. Sam hadn't really noticed her before but her countenance that morning was giving off an air of maturity and sophistication. She smelt good too.

Mrs Horrise had been warming to Melanie recently. She was all for Horace having a wide circle of friends but she was beginning to think that Horace's was more of a line than a circle with Sonny at one end and Melanie at the other. Horace seemed to have been spending just a bit too much time at what she considered the "wrong end," an end that was almost exclusively the preserve of Sonny Christie, an individual that she tolerated but felt was mostly a bad influence on her son. Now, however, things looked as though they were starting to balance up a bit and she was all for that and would do whatever she could to encourage it. She knew that Horace was only eleven but there was nothing wrong with a little bit of encouragement to help things along. Her husband wasn't averse to doing his bit either. If Horace could find a girlfriend as charming and delightful as Sam's Tanya then they were two-thirds of their way to smugness personified.

"Come in Melanie and have a seat. I'm sure someone will move or you can have grandad's chair as he's in the sitting room. Would you like something to eat?" Mrs Horrise detected a very expensive perfume wafting around the room. At least it was countering the rather noxious smell that had greeted Melanie's arrival she thought, trying hard to hide her jealousy. Sam stared at Melanie as she walked over and stared into the frying pan. It was at this point that Sam decided that his was by far the better view as Melanie then turned and stood with her back to the work surface, rested the palms of her hands on the edge and hauled herself up and onto the work surface in one fell swoop. "Oh I don't think we're that short of space Melanie," said

Horace's mother slightly disapprovingly but trying her hardest not to say anything more than that for more would mean a bit of a moan at the very least but more likely a great big steaming rant. Horace smiled. The last time he had done what Melanie just had he was told to, "Jump down immediately and go and get a cloth and wipe where you've parked your bottom with some Dettol: that is a hygienic work space that you're sitting on not a park bench."

"I'm okay Mrs Horrise, I'm not that hungry unless it's cake," Melanie replied sweetly without moving. "You can't have too much cake. Anyway I don't really like black pudding."

"Despite appearances to the contrary, it's not actually black pudding Mel, it's an egg," said Horace.

"Blimey," said Melanie with a chuckle, not the least bit embarrassed. "It's like being on scout camp with Charlie. Do you remember Horace when he had to do the bacon and he put it in that enormous frying pan and then the pan got so hot and he couldn't get near the bacon to turn it over 'cos the fire was scorching and he couldn't get the pan off the fire 'cos the handle had turned red with the heat and he didn't know where the oven glove was and the bacon went black and I told Skip that they were charcoal slices and that they were very good for the digestion and so..."

"Thank you Melanie, but we're not on camp in my kitchen," said Mrs Horrise shortly, "whatever the apparent, but actually very distorted, similarities. Now what are you up to today? I understand Horace is going shopping. That will be an experience for him. He's not very good with shops."

"We'll we're not going near proper shops. Dad's not in favour of too much interaction with the masses at the moment what with the Carinavirus thing." Horace's father nodded without looking up. His mother beamed. "I said to Horace that he could come down to the saddlery at the stables to pick up a bridle that I've had repaired and then we're going to muck out Pitkin and after that we're going to lunch - Horace and me that is not Pitkin..." Melanie let out a little giggle and Horace's father sniggered, "...in the Coach House and after that who knows?"

"Who knows indeed," said Horace's father without appearing to move a muscle. His wife went and stood behind him and poked him in the back.

"It's either going to be oiling the tack or going straight into tea with Anthea. I never say 'no' to a piece of cake."

"And who's 'Anthea?'" asked Mrs Horrise. She was already well-versed in Horace and his friends' love of cake.

"Anthea Wykenshawe-Jones of course silly," said Melanie wrinkling her nose. I thought everyone round here knew Anthea. She owns the stables. Well her dad does really but it's some sort of tax dodge. He has to be careful these days with his work and his enterprises what with the knighthood and stuff."

"Of course," said Horace's mother feeling ever-so-slightly deflated but still more than keen that this early-stage coupling should be given every encouragement to progress. Money, breeding, horses, lunch, knighthoods - it was all sounding just perfect apart from the "tax dodge" bit which she decided not to dwell upon. She was curious to hear the reason for her son's being chosen for this trip though out of all the other possible suitors. "So why do you need Horace on this endeavour today Melanie?"

"Well I don't particularly," Melanie replied with brutal honesty, "but mum was getting a bit concerned that outside of school and scouts I was hanging out with too many of my posh horsey friends and she felt that it would do me good if I had a day or two with someone my own age who came from a family that was a little less cultured and Horace came to mind."

It was the way that she said it that made Mrs Horrise almost choke on her cup of tea. No "I'm not sure how to say this" or "Don't take this the wrong way but..." or straightforward lie or maybe a bit of diplomacy or just "I like him." She came straight out with it as if she was fully aware of what she was saying and that the intention was to give maximum offence. Melanie had certainly succeeded in that endeavour however innocently she had in reality spoken.

"Do you normally sit on work surfaces at home?" Mrs Horrise asked by way of reply now that she was a little less concerned at offending their Saturday morning visitor. At this Melanie slid off onto the floor.

"No," she replied. "Mum doesn't let me. 'Go and do it round Horace's if you want to do something like that,' she once told me. 'They won't care.'"

Mrs Horrise had heard enough. "Well *they* most certainly do," she said crossly. "Horace, go and get ready to go out. I think Melanie's waiting." But Melanie wasn't particularly waiting. She had spotted that Mr Horrise was pondering *The Times* crossword. Up to that moment she had been thinking that he had been feeling sick. Actually he was. He couldn't discharge one single clue. He had looked at the small answers, the ones with three or four letters, but couldn't manage those; he couldn't bear to look at the eight letter clues because he had yet to get any helping letters - no useful consonants to start the word off or words with a less popular letter in the middle to help things along. He couldn't even solve a three, two, three answer.

"Give me a clue Mr Horrise," Melanie demanded. Mrs Horrise scowled.

"David's doing the cryptic, not the junior quick," she informed Melanie whilst scraping her burnt offering into the bin.

"That's fine by me," said Melanie as she peered over Mr Horrise's shoulder. "I can't do the junior quick. It's sort of too simple if you know what I mean. There was a clue the other day which was, 'Container for cereal' and the answer was four letters. And I'm thinking, 'Packet, box, probably sack,' so I put in sack and then nothing else worked..."

"Bowl," Mr Horrise interrupted triumphantly. "The answer was 'bowl.'"

"Exactly. Too simple. So now I've moved on to something more intellectually stimulating. Oh look, Mr Horrise, you haven't put any of the answers in. Do you do that to make it more of a challenge; to make you remember in your head the answers you've done already then put them all in at the end?"

"Something like that," he murmured.

"Which ones are you stuck on?" Melanie asked, now leaning far too closely over Mr Horrise for both his and his wife's comfort.

"Try one across," said Sam biting into a slice of toast. "He always has trouble at one across."

"Yeah, that's where his trouble starts..." confirmed Horace.

"...and continues with two across, three across then one down, two down..." said Sam.

"Let's look at one across then," said Melanie. Oh fab, it's an easy one - a three, two, three. Have you done that one David?"

"Mr Horrise," corrected Mrs Horrise. Melanie said nothing. She merely wondered why her friend's mother was being so formal in addressing her husband.

"I...err..."

"I know what it is," said Melanie standing triumphantly back up giving both Horace's parents a moment to catch their breaths.

"And..?" enquired Mr Horrise.

"Write it in," Melanie commanded.

"You tell me what you think it is first," said Mr Horrise, "whilst I look for my pen."

"It's in your hand David silly!" Melanie giggled again. Mr Horrise looked surprised. Mrs Horrise sighed.

"Let's write the answer down on a bit of paper each and then compare," Melanie suggested.

"We're not a school now Melanie dear. Let's you write in the answer and then you go off shopping with Horace," Mr Horrise countered. Melanie took the pen and wrote in, "ALL AT SEA."

"There you are David," she said as she handed the pen back. "'Everyone on boats needing directional assistance,' Answer 'all at sea.' It's because when it says 'everyone' it means..."

"Off you go Melanie," said Mrs Horrise, "or you may find the saddlery's shut. Don't forget your rucksack." Melanie looked up at the clock on the wall. It was ten o'clock.

"It's only just opened Mrs Horrise. We'll be fine. Shall I help you with another clue David?"

"No you won't and that clock's slow," said Mrs Horrise as she started to clear up the plates.

"Unless it's seven hours slow we'll be okay."

"Goodbye Melanie; see you later Horace."

As the front door shut behind them Mrs Horrise let out yet another sigh. Mr Horrise looked up and spoke in a sympathetic tone. "The course of true love and all that goes for the implications for the wider family darling," he said. "You were rightly getting a little bit concerned about Sonny and Melanie brings what he can't: culture, a bit of breeding, money..."

"You'd better fill that crossword in before they get back," said Mrs Horrise, "otherwise you'll be adding 'smarmy' to the list."

"Still at least she won't be likely to pick up the coronavirus very easily if she makes human contact whilst they're out after I sprayed the work surface with Dettol first thing this morning because now it's all over her hands," said Mr Horrise.

"And bum," Sam added.

"No one's going near that," said Mrs Horrise hurriedly. Sam merely smiled.

"Talking of hands, need a hand with one down now father?" Sam asked.

"Let's get ourselves ready and go and get some face masks before there's a mad rush and we end up paying five pounds each," said Mr Horrise studiously ignoring his older son as he put down his pen.

\*\*\*

The unlikely pairing strolled down the road without a care in the world: Horace dressed for action and Melanie dressed to kill although neither was conscious of any subtle undertones in their little trip to the saddlery. They were, after all, both part of the close-knit Ravens scout patrol, it was just that they were a pair on this occasion and not the usual full complement. Seven, in any case, would have been a bit difficult, as several (but not all) of the other members were occupied in "family activities" that morning. Those so summoned would have responded with the lowering of the shoulders and a heavy groan.

As soon as they had arrived at the stables and walked in through the front gate Melanie loudly exhaled, almost whistling. "I so love it here Horace!" she exclaimed as she absent-mindedly took his hand and led him up the narrow path and into the saddlery. Once inside Melanie exhaled again as Horace inhaled. It smelt of new leather and horsey people he decided - Land Rovers, point-to-points and stirrup cups - mostly things that Melanie had talked about but Horace didn't understand but he thought that he would recognise the smells if they ever came his way.

"Melanie, hello!" Horace turned as a maxi-me version of Melanie came bounding over with her arms out at full stretch. Horace later would tell his brother that she cantered over – a description that pleased him greatly. For now he was preoccupied with Isabella, to whom he was soon introduced, before being totally ignored whilst the two females had a discussion that Horace would describe as equine in nature. He had nothing to add to the conversation as he had not the faintest idea what was being talked about. After a few minutes of staring at his feet he wandered off round the shop to see if he could find anything he recognised amongst the jodhpurs, chaps, bits, girths and whips. He was subconsciously taking in a world that had so far escaped him; a world that his mother was keen for him to ascend rapidly into and Melanie's mother for her to descend fairly slowly from, but only with regard to the amount of time spent within as this would always be her societal home.

Horace imagined himself in all the gear that he was seeing before his eyes. He had started to touch, to feel, to stroke and to caress but when he plucked up enough courage to look at a price tag he let go very quickly as if he had just received an electric shock. Nevertheless he was immersing himself more consciously now. This was *the* place to be. That said, this was not the place to be if you were someone of what his parents would refer to as, "the lower order." "We welcome Miss Melanie Smith, daughter of Sir James of Smith and Co Investment Bank and her companion Mister Horace Horrise, son of, er, whoever..." "First place in the dressage Mister Horace Horrise of Chislehurst!" "The Randolph Christopher award for services to eventing this year goes to... Mister 'Orice..."

"'Orice! 'Orice! 'ORRRR....IIIICE!" "The name's Horace with an 'H.' 'Horace Horrise,'" Horace corrected with a smile.

"Yeah, alright you daft twot. What you doin' here?" Horace shook his head gently from side to side as he emerged from his mini reverie and turned round.

"Look who I've found!" said Melanie with a huge grin on her face. She was holding in her hand a collection of leather straps that resembled a Victorian hammock for babies, Horace decided. Isabella had gone and had been replaced by...

"Oh hello Sonny," Horace said sounding far less enthusiastic than he would normally have. "What are you doing here?" Sonny held up his hands with fingers pointing like a big cat about to strike.

"GRRRR!" he growled before pulling up a blue surgical face mask to cover his nose and mouth.

"Alright 'Orice?"

"Yes I am very well thank you Sonny," said Horace trying to sound the part of a *bona fide* saddlery customer, "but why are you here? Are you trying to pass yourself off as a vet?"

"It's true that that could be one explanation 'cos they do earn a bit of dosh but if I'm gonna do somefing daft like that then I ain't going to eurinate on my own doorstep am I? I ain't that stoopid."

"So have you contracted Carinavirus? 'Cos if you have you should be in hospital. Or are you afraid of catching it from the horses? I thought that it was supposed to have started with bats." Sonny shook his head.

"Nuffin' like that. I've bin 'elpin' out in the stables that's all. I've got a Saturday mornin' job. I came over 'ere for me elevenses an' bumped into Mel who said that you were 'ere an' you're gonna 'elp wiv Pitkin."

"That is correct Sonny. And then we're going to lunch in the Coach House..."

"And you must come too Sonny," said Melanie brightly. Horace smiled and nodded in agreement but inwardly he was feeling just a little deflated although he wasn't sure why.

"I've got another hour then I'm off so that'ld be great. You go an' sort Pitkin out. I'll oil 'is bridle an' then we can meet up..."

"Sonny - why the mask...?" But Sonny had gone.

"The stables recommend them as a sensible precaution when dealing with dry straw," Melanie told Horace as they walked over to the stables together. "You might be sensitive to the dust and you can get Farmers' Lung if it's a bit mouldy. It's up to you. I normally wear one. Now I'll just go and get changed whilst you go over and give Pitkin a pat and a carrot."

"And where do I get a carrot from?" asked Horace sarcastically. "This is a stables not a greengrocers."

Melanie slipped off her rucksack once more and unzipped the top. "Here they are on top of everything." She handed Horace a small bag as Horace peered into the rucksack. "It's only my change of clothes." Horace looked puzzled.

"Why have you brought a change of clothes when you knew that we were going to do the mucking out?"

"Well it's perfectly obvious," Melanie answered. "I could hardly walk down to yours and then to the stables dressed like I was a farmhand so I wore my posh clothes. Now we're here I can get changed into clothes for Pitkin stuff. Then, once we've finished, I can get changed back into posh for when we do lunch and possibly tea and then we can go for a walk if you like. You, on the other hand, have what I would call 'all-day clothes' so it doesn't really matter what you're doing in them. Anything really."

"So why couldn't you have dressed in all-day clothes?"

"I could've apart from I felt that I needed to look a little bit more respectable for lunch and tea plus Anthea will be all dressed up plus it's all about being prepared 'cos if you're scruffy and you're out somewhere it's difficult to make yourself smart whereas if you're smart to start with you can always go and make yourself scruffy and also..." Melanie paused wondering if she should continue. "...I thought that you would like it."

Horace immediately stared fixatedly at the ground. He bobbled and babbled, burbled and blurted but nothing meaningful would come out – just some strange disjointed noises. "Look at me!" Melanie commanded. Slowly Horace lifted his head and stared, for the first time shyly, at his friend. "Oh my goodness!" she exclaimed. "Go near Pitkin that colour and he'll think you're a carrot! Wait here. I won't be a moment."

Horace stood in the middle of the yard looking extremely ill at ease but not daring to move an inch as his face slowly resumed its normal pinkish colour. When Melanie finally reappeared Horace wondered quite what discernible difference there was between posh clothes and Pitkin clothes but he didn't say anything. He did however notice that she was now wearing wellies on her feet but even they looked brand new – and a surgical face mask. Melanie waved a mask at him that he put on at her insistence.

Pitkin stood chomping on his carrots whilst Melanie did most of the hard work shovelling and sweeping. After half an hour Pitkin's stable looked good as new. The only adverse incident had been when a man saw Horace in his mask feeding Pitkin and asked, "What's the matter - radioactive carrots?!" before marching off chortling to himself. Melanie disappeared again to get changed back leaving Horace talking to Pitkin. As soon as she was out of sight Horace went into Pitkin's stable and closed the door. He wasn't going to be accosted a second time. "Melanie will know where to find me," he thought with more assuredness than was wise. All of a sudden it was very dark. Pitkin was restless and was shuffling around pawing at the straw. At one point he heard a very strange noise coming but a couple of feet away from him and his leg soon felt very, very wet. Did the stable leak or had he been stabbed by an alien hiding in a corner? He hoped against hope that Sonny may have forgotten his lunchtime invitation or may only make a cursory inspection of the grounds to find them but he had done neither. In fact it was Horace who was nearly the one who was absent at the meal for when he had waited far longer than was necessary for Melanie to return before eventually deciding to chance it and went to look for her he found her in the Coach House, tucked away in a secluded corner talking animatedly with Sonny about the merits of different types of horse bedding.

"Oh there you are," said Melanie with a big smile on her face. "He's with us," she said to the advancing waiter. "Come and sit down. Where have you been? I thought that you had gone home and what's that on your leg?" Horace glanced down and breathed a sigh of relief. There was no sign of blood but then he wished that there had been because at least blood didn't have much of a smell.

"I was talking to Pitkin and didn't realise the time," Horace said lamely.

"I walked past but his door was shut so I thought that you had left him and someone fancied that he needed a sleep. I'll go and open it after lunch. In the meantime, given what I think is down your trousers I would go and get changed into something less smelly."

"But I don't have a change of clothes. I think I'll have to go home," said Horace pathetically. The thought of Melanie and Sonny lunching together filled him with dread on so many levels but sometimes one's choices were mostly made for one. Melanie, however, was having none of it.

"We've no time for that. Go and find Isabella and say that I sent you. She'll sort you out. Tell her I'll pay." Horace didn't need telling twice. He turned around and shuffled off but as soon as he was outside he ran. There was no way that he was going to leave Melanie alone with Sonny any longer that he had to. He was soon back. He re-entered the restaurant to be met by a loud wolf whistle from the corner and it wasn't Sonny.

"They're a bit tight," Horace complained as he sat down.

"They're hunting breeches. They're supposed to be like that. They look fine and they smell a whole lot better for sure," said Melanie who couldn't stop smiling. "Now what are you having for lunch? I'm having everything with alcohol in it and so's Sonny."

"Is that allowed?" asked Horace cautiously.

"No, certainly not unless it's in the cooking. But if you're in the know you can work your way round that. So we're having an appetiser plate of black olives steeped in orange-infused gin, for starters we're having French onion soup 'cos they bring you a little pot of brandy on the side which you're supposed to pour in which I don't, then we're having the beer burgers but you don't get a glass of beer with them, then it's the lemon vodka sorbet but they pour the vodka over at the table so if you're lucky we'll get extra. What do you fancy?" Horace took a deep breath.

"I'll have all that also please."

If Horace and Melanie had made an unlikely pairing as they walked down the road earlier in the day, with the addition of a pair of riding breeches and Sonny the somewhat bizarre sight had exponentially worsened. One diner who walked past their table was heard to remark that the three of them together looked like the protagonists from a junior version of *Lady Chatterley's Lover*.

The lunch was mostly a success once Horace had successfully steered the conversation away from matters horse. Sonny had decided that he didn't like brandy and so Melanie helped herself to his and then he didn't fancy the vodka on his lemon sorbet so Melanie had Sonny's portion of that also. Horace had had a sip of both then passed the remainder over.

As Sonny and Horace were waiting for Melanie to stand up and stay up a faint murmur moved around the restaurant like an audible Mexican wave, as a large suited gentleman appeared at the door. "Who's that?" Horace hissed at Melanie but she didn't have time to turn around before Sir Jack Wykenshawe-Jones was behind her.

"Melanie!" he exclaimed and as she shuffled around he gave her a large, avuncular hug. "Anthea said that I might find you in here. She sends her apologies but she's had to go off in search of some essential supplies. Face masks! We've run completely out for some reason and need to get some more in at the double. Our usual supplier is being rather dilatory and the more tender customers are getting twitchy. I did suggest they tie a tea towel round their noses but one of them told me this was Chislehurst not the Wild West though sometimes I wonder if there's any difference. So she says, 'Sorry,' and she'll be in touch about a..."

"I can get yer face masks mate," Sonny interrupted having listened quietly to this exchange. Horace grimaced at the reaction that he was anticipating from Sir Jack but it wasn't forthcoming.

"Can you Sonny? That would be first class. Can you get them for me like, er, now?"

"I can 'ave a go mate. Leave it wiv me. I'll be back in an hour. 'Ow many d'ya want?"

"Could we say a hundred for now?"

"'Ow much do you want to spend?" Sir Jack leant down on the table and beckoned Sonny towards him. "Get me a hundred and lunch is on the house."

"Deal," said Sonny. "Come on you two. We've got work to do."

"I feel sick," said Melanie weakly.

"Put yer face mask back on then 'cos you don't want yer lunch to go all down your frock do ya?"

As the trio left the stables and started on the short walk down to the high street Sonny confidently predicted that the chemists opposite The Workshed would have face masks in stock. "When I walked past yesterday there was a big sign in the window saying, 'Surgical face masks in stock! Two for one pound.' I can't think why they suddenly wanted to promote face masks but I reckon that we've spent a whole lot more that fifty quid on lunch so if you pay fifty quid on face masks Mel then we've saved you a few bob and if you can bung a bit of the difference my way we can say that we're all quits. What d'ya think 'Orice?"

"I think I have no idea what you're talking about Sonny but I'm sure it's all mostly okay."

"You alright Mel?" Sonny stopped his route march and looked into her eyes.

"I feel very sick!" she wailed.

"Keep yer mask on Mel," he commanded, "an' you and I better do ours as well 'Orice just in case we breath in 'er sick fumes."

Once Melanie had advised them that she could manage a few more steps the three of them completed their journey to the chemists at a slower pace. As they walked down the high street Horace noticed that pedestrians coming towards them were stopping in their tracks when they were within sight. Some were crossing over the road, several without even looking, the rest were turning round and going back the way they had been coming from. No one screamed, no one shouted but no one, not one single person, passed them. Arriving at the chemists Sonny pointed at the window and sighed. "Oh dear. Oh dear, oh dear, oh dear." The three of them looked up at the sign that Sonny told them that he had seen just the day before. The wording had been crossed out and underneath had been scrawled in thick black ink, "SOLD OUT!" Sonny pulled down his mask and Horace and Melanie followed.

"I feel extremely sick!" Melanie complained. "I need some water Horace."

"In a minute," said Sonny. "Right now I fink we may be on to a nice little earner." Sonny pulled his face musk back up and signalled to the others to do the same.

"C'mon," he said, "let's go over the road to The Workshed an' 'ave a word with Mr Lillie."

As they walked inside Mr Lillie was waiting with a jug of squash, a plate of biscuits and a fulsome welcome. "Hello Horace, hello children. I say, you playing highwaymen or should I say 'highwaypeople' and have you heard the news?"

"Somfing like some of that mate but no we ain't heard the news for a while," said Sonny. "We've bin doin' lunch," he added in an attempt to emulate the sayings of Melanie.

"Well if I were you I would get yourselves home pretty sharpish. This Coronavirus thing sounds like it's getting a bit out of hand."

"Alright mate but first I've got a bit of work to do. Do you happen to 'ave any dust masks? I've got a bit of a rush job on. An' can Mel sit down?"

"I'll just go and have a look out the back. I won't be a moment." Mr Lillie did indeed return in a moment. He had a large cardboard box in his hands which he dropped on the counter with a dull thud. "There you are. One thousand dust masks. Out of date, these are. I can't believe you have to have date marks on face masks. When I was a boy..."

"Yeah, yeah. Later Mr Lillie. 'Ow much for the box?"

"You can have them young man. I can't sell them. Get rid of them for me. You'll be doing me a favour." Mr Lillie looked at Sonny suspiciously. "What exactly do you have in mind young man? I'll tell you this for free: I can't sell them and if you're thinking what I'm thinking they're neither sterile nor medical grade." Sonny fished in his pocket and pulled out a ten pound note.

"'Orice, whip inta the supermarket and get ten quid's worth of anti bac. spray. Put your mask on and then wing it back 'ere. Me and me mate 'ere 'ave to 'ave a little chat. Understand?"

"I think so," said Horace. At least he understood the purchasing requirement. He returned five minutes later waving two cans of spray that he hadn't had to pay for. He found Melanie outside on the pavement slouched on one of Mr Lillie's chairs. She looked, as far as he could make out, unconscious, and wondered if he should put her in the recovery position. "There were loads of people in the supermarket," he explained to Sonny, "But when they saw me they just ran off. I went to the 'Five Items or Less' till that was empty. The cashier just waved me through. Most people were buying trolley-loads of groceries and the shelves were looking decidedly bare in places." Sonny had heard enough.

"Gimme, gimme!" Sonny grabbed the cans; in silence he opened up the flaps of the box that was by now on the floor and emptied the contents of one whole can over the dust masks. Then he closed up the box and Mr Lillie taped it shut. He turned the box upside down and repeated the procedure with the other can. Finally he picked up the box and tipped the contents into a metal refuse bin onto which had been stuck a sign that had written on it, patently not by Sonny:

STERILE MEDICALLY-TREATED FACE MASKS
£5 EACH

Only then did Sonny speak once more. He gave a small paper bag to Horace with the instruction to, "Run these masks up to the stables and then get back 'ere, quick as you can." Horace didn't need telling twice; he would rather not be around at the start of one of Sonny's ventures especially one so audacious in its planning and therefore probably as much so in its execution. He would return once everything was successfully underway and sneak back in under the cover of others.

Even so, Horace was only gone twenty minutes. He found Sir Jack, handed over the dust masks, Sir Jack cursorily checked them and declared them, "even better than what we were giving out before," and wandered back to The Workshed. As he went past the bank he noticed that there was a long queue at the cash machine. He peered through the window and saw that there were dozens of customers jostling for position in a non-existent line; it was more akin to a rugby scrum than a bank queue. He was slightly surprised that the bank was still open as it usually closed at lunchtime on a Saturday. As he continued down the high street he came across the back of another long queue with more and more people continually joining on, mostly looking very anxious. "I wonder what this is for?" he asked himself not wishing to ask anyone in the line. He couldn't see the start but he could see roughly where it was coming from. He was not at all keen to acknowledge the most likely answer to his own question.

"There's a queue son," was said to him by more than one person in the line as he walked past but Horace continued on. Reaching The Workshed that now had a CLOSED sign hanging in the window even though it was only early afternoon, Mr Lillie was nowhere to be seen. A police car was parked outside with its blue lights flashing like a crazed Christmas display. Two police officers were standing nearby wearing dust masks. There was a strong smell of antiseptic in the air. Sonny was standing behind a table from which was hanging the sign, unchanged from when Horace had first seen it apart from the "£5" had been crossed off, "£10" had been written in and crossed off and in its place there was written "£20 - NOTES ONLY." Edward and Archie were standing guard over the dustbin, Emily and Charlie were handing out the quantities of dust masks that Sonny was telling them to as customers stood in front of the "counter" pressing twenty pound notes into Sonny's hands. At the far end of the table sat Melanie with her eyes shut, head drooping and looking very pale. She had her mask on, as did all the Ravens, but only she had a sign on her lap and propped up against her tummy that read, in Sonny's hand,

DO KNOT YOU END UP LIK THIS!
AVOID KARINERVIRUS NOW!
STOP THE SPRED!

Horace went over and knelt down beside Melanie. "Put your mask on son!" ordered one of the police officers. Horace did as he was told.

"Are you okay Mel?" he asked. In response she lugubriously opened one eye, winked, then shut it again. Horace went over to Mr Lillie who had emerged from his shop. He had locked the door and walked down the ramp. He was grinning from ear to ear.

"Mr Lillie!" Horace hissed. "What are you up to?"

"I'm keeping the takings secure," he whispered as Sonny handed him a huge wodge of notes.

"What about the police?"

"They appeared a few minutes ago. There was a bit of a scrum to begin with but Sonny called up for reinforcements and Mel managed to get the round robin going for your pals so now things have calmed down somewhat."

"I'm not asking about maintaining law and order for the customers, I'm asking about the legitimacy of what Sonny's up to."

"Have you not heard? A national state of emergency has been declared and so Sonny spearheading making a few bob in doing his bit to protect the health of at least nine hundred locals is not high up on their list of priorities. What I don't know the answer to is what's this ambulance doing coming down here?"

Horace looked over to where the emergency siren was emanating as an ambulance appeared over the brow of the hill. It screamed down the road and came to a sudden stop behind the police car. Two paramedics immediately jumped out of the back. They were dressed from head to toe in full hazard suits. Without speaking they followed the pointing finger of the police officers and came to a halt in front of Melanie. One produced what resembled a liquid shoe polish tube and, lifting Melanie's head up, pressed the sponge end against her forehead for several seconds. When they removed it to look at the reading Horace half expected Melanie to have gained a large black ibble dibble mark. Without warning a third fully hazard suited paramedic appeared; this one was pushing a large wheeled stretcher with a huge yellow and black HAZARD sign stuck on the headboard. The metal frame was painted bright red. The paramedic pushed the stretcher over toward Melanie and applied the brake. Melanie was then picked up and laid carefully on the stretcher in one smooth and unbroken operation before wheeling her away. As Horace stood by watching helplessly, not knowing quite what to do, if anything, he heard Melanie shout from inside the ambulance, "I'M NOT SICK! IT'S JUST A HANGOVER!!"

before the police officers stood in the road, stopped the traffic and gave priority to the ambulance that turned round so quickly that it left tyre marks on the road and went speeding back up the hill. They looked at each other and chuckled. One said to the other,

"'Hangover!' At her age? Why can't people let the doctors take care of them? Don't they realise how serious the situation is?"

"Where are they taking her?" Horace asked feebly.

"Isolation," said the other police officer as they resumed their positions on the pavement. "Newcastle, Wirral, maybe north London if she's lucky."

"'Orice!" Horace's thoughts were interrupted as he looked over to his summoner.

"'Orice! C'mon over 'ere. All 'ands on deck! This bloke wants a hundred! Can yer 'elp count 'em out? That'll be two grand please mate. Cash only."

\*\*\*

Horace was home before nightfall. As he walked up the garden path the door mysteriously opened in front of him. He walked in as his mother appeared from behind a curtain and shut the door quicker than he had ever seen her do before in his life apart from when it had been slammed shut but those were usually completely different situations to what was being faced today. "Oh darling. I'm so glad you're home!" His mother gave him a big hug and held him tightly for longer than Horace felt comfortable with. "We were *so* worried! Where's Melanie? What have you been doing? Did you have a nice time? What did you have for lunch? Did you meet Anthea? Did you meet her father? Were they nice? And where did that mask come from? Is that from the stables?"

"Mummy, I think you ought to come and sit down. Let's go into the kitchen. Is there any cake?"

"Oh yes darling, there's plenty of cake. That's one thing we did manage. Daddy's been shopping. He went out to get some face masks but was unsuccessful. However he's been a bit more successful with stocking up on provisions although he couldn't get everything that I suggested. I see you were more successful on the mask front. But why are you wearing one?" Horace walked into the kitchen and his mouth opened so wide he could at that moment have swallowed a whale.

"'Stocking up on provisions?' How much food do we need mummy?"

"Just enough to keep us through this little emergency our nation seems to have got itself into. Now then, would you like to hear daddy's news?" Horace noticed that his father had resumed his place and position that he had left him in some hours earlier. The crossword was once more in front of him; his pen was in his hand.

"Where's Melanie?" he asked. "I have something to show her. I've done one down!"

"And?"

"Just one down," said his father bashfully.

Horace was just about to sit down when Sam appeared and immediately burst into fits of laughter. "What on earth are you wearing on your legs? Where's Mel?" he asked. Horace shoved a mouthful of cake into his mouth before replying.

"I'll answer just one of those questions if you don't mind." Sam rubbed his chin and patted his mouth.

"Where's Mel?" he asked.

"Why's everyone so concerned about Mel? I'm wearing a mask 'cos I was instructed to by her. At this precise moment she's in hospital with a hangover and suspected Carinavirus," he replied through another mouthful of Victoria sponge.

Horace's father was first through the kitchen door. He almost jumped clean over the table, followed by his wife and finally Sam. "You can come out in fourteen days," Sam shouted through the glass as his father turned the key in the lock, "if you don't show any symptoms!"

Horace smiled and sat down at the table. He had a sizable portion of nearly two thousand pounds in his breeches, enough cake and other groceries to keep him happy for a year, a radio and an all but virgin cryptic crossword in front of him.

Today had been a good day he surmised. In some respects a bad day but mostly good. A very good day indeed actually. And hopefully Melanie would appear very soon when the hospital realised that there wasn't very much wrong with her that a glass of water and a bit of sleep wouldn't cure and they could sit in the kitchen and eat cake - as much as they wanted, just the two of them.

## Introduction to Horace Horrise and the Old Lady

*Horace is dismayed that he hasn't been able to do any good deeds of late when, like buses, three opportunities come along almost at once - a cat stuck up a tree, an injured pigeon and a disorientated old lady.*

*Horace and his friends are more than up for the restitutive challenges but their attempts to do their best are somewhat thrown off course by the wayward Sonny who, as ever, seeks to look after himself first.*

My son, Charles, and I were walking down Chislehurst High Street when we came across a frail and very elderly lady who looked in need of some assistance. It was a hot summer's day but there were storm clouds gathering. She was wearing a thick overcoat and had pink slippers on her feet. Something wasn't right. As we approached her she let go of the rail outside the Post Office that she had been holding onto and grabbed Charles' arm. She said in a whisper that her name was Betty and that she thought that she had bitten off more than she could chew and would we mind taking her home? Naturally we were happy to oblige and we started off in the supposed direction of her house.

Then the heavens opened.

We sheltered in the lychgate of the Church of the Annunciation and used the unavoidable interruption to try to work out exactly where Betty lived. "My son is looking for me," is all she kept saying.

Once the rain had subsided we continued our task of trying to locate Betty's home. With a bit of help we eventually found it, tracked down a neighbour with a key and managed to get her back indoors. "That good deed should last you until the end of the year," she said as she thanked us profusely and indicated for us to leave.

On the walk back up the hill Charles suddenly turned to me and remarked, "You're quiet." By the time that we had reached home the main part of the story was almost finished in my head. All I had to add were the characters and the incidental stories with an assortment of side characters, human, feline and Columbidae.

## Horace Horrise and the Old Lady

"I haven't done a good deed once yet this month," Horace moped, in a tone of voice that was as far from his usual upbeat sound as it was possible to get without someone thinking that they should call for an ambulance, "and today is no exception." Despite the fact that he was in the company of his favourite friends, the Ravens, he kept his accompanying expressionless gaze fixed on the ground; not once did he look up to gauge reaction. However, albeit subconsciously, he wanted reaction. It was often such a one-way affair with Horace. He sighed then he sniffed then he vigorously rubbed his forehead with all available fingers as if trying to erase what little he had of a furrowed brow. Such was the level of angst in his voice that his fellow Ravens did actually look up, immediately and altogether, although not one of them stopped what they were doing which they would have to have done if they were to give Horace their full and undivided attention. But they didn't because they weren't going to.

The Ravens had gathered under their favourite large oak climbing tree on the common mostly to seek shade from the afternoon summer sun, despite the threat of a torrential downpour later on, and had been spending a very pleasant hour or so with their penknives, stripping bark from walking-stick-sized branches and whittling them into nothing more demanding than crooked spears when Horace made his startling admission. They mostly had full or partial family events to attend to later in the afternoon but had sneaked out from their respective homes knowing full well that nothing would happen for some time after each parent or guardian had said that they would be ready, "in a minute," which never meant sixty seconds, more likely a couple of hours at least.

123

That wasn't to say that no one was prepared. They were a motley crew of mostly washed and partially showered, casually smart and smartly casual. And then there was Horace.

Archie was the first to reply. As patrol leader he felt that it was his duty to reply although he wasn't at all sure quite what to say. It was just that if he were to keep his leader position, both in (appointed) and out (unappointed) of scout meetings then he needed to exercise some form of leadership and this meant leading the response, however slight or inappropriate. He put down his large bag of sweets and pushed it under his outstretched legs, opened his mouth and managed a long and drawn out, "Welllllll..." before he was interrupted. He didn't mind though. In fact he was grateful. He hadn't even thought beyond that one word but he knew that in that one word he had given notice that he was going to respond with at least a sentence and not just a "true" or other one word answer, and that was good enough for him, even if he didn't know what the sentence was actually going to be. He could hardly say not doing a good deed for a month was okay but neither did he want to disagree as he could then lay himself wide open to a charge of hypocrisy although no one need necessarily know what good deeds he had, or hadn't, done recently. It was all so difficult being a leader.

"I wouldn't be too concerned Horace and look after my camera up there Em; it's new and cost a load of money," said Archie's interrupter. Melanie, who was for once sounding more magnanimous in her response than was usual, had inadvertently and unknowingly come to Archie's rescue but Archie knew that an assistant patrol leader was a patrol leader-in-waiting and needed to be kept under tight

124

control at all times. And the present situation was no exception. "Well I would be," he said more firmly than was necessary, having at last found a more active tongue and a way of disagreeing whilst partially avoiding a potential hypocrite charge. "It is vital that you do a good deed every day otherwise, to start with, you will get out of the habit and once you've got out of it, it will be very hard to get back into it. I would imagine. A bit like missing school and playing truant. I would imagine too."

"That depends entirely on whether doing a good deed a day is a necessity," said Edward with his serious voice, which was how he normally sounded so no one took much notice of what he had to say. It was just too much like school. "After all," he continued to the air and Horace, "you can't spend a load of time looking for good deeds to do, especially if there aren't any to be done. You can't make opportunities for good deeds. You would be better off just waiting for a very good deed situation to come along and do that and that would be worth a week of not-very-good deeds, or things that are vital like, um, whatever..."

"But I haven't even done any not-very-good deeds either Ed," said Horace forlornly. "At this rate I'm going to have to do an exceptionally plus good deed, like rescuing someone from something or someone or saving a life or helping a damsel in distress or..."

"Helping a damsel in distress is not a good deed," said Charlie with a grin. "It's a necessity, like walking on the outside of the pavement or opening a door or..."

"I don't need anyone to open a door for me," said Emily rather too aggressively, Charlie thought, as she started to whittle her spear to an even more acute point from her vantage point of halfway up the oak tree from where she could be heard but not seen. She was getting to quite like being up the tree looking down on the others, especially as she had found a black cat with a bright red collar up there - stretched out purring on a bough. She had climbed up the tree with Melanie's new camera slung around her neck and had been busy taking shots of not much in particular having been told by its owner that it could hold more than two hundred thousand shots, that Edward was quick to point out meant that if one picture was taken every day by the time that the snapper had reached such a number they would be over five hundred years old.

"But you ain't a damson Em," said Sonny, who was beginning to wonder whether he had ever done a good deed in his life. "I fink to 'ave a door opened for ya ya 'ave to 'ave a flowin' dress and flowers in yer 'air, somefing like that."

"Well I don't think that I'm a damsel Sonny," said Melanie jumping to her feet. "Look," she said, running her fingernails down her sternum, "I know I'm in a dress today but that's only 'cos I have to go out with mum later for shopping and tea. Normally I'm just shorts, t-shirt and nothing in my hair apart from a scrunchie unless I'm going to the saddlery but I wouldn't complain if someone opened a door for me, so long as he was being chivalrous and not just doing it 'cos he needed to get a few good deeds under his belt."

"What if it was a she?" asked Sonny.

"She's don't open doors for other shes," Melanie replied dismissively; "they just all pile through together in my experience."

"I'ld like to see you all pile through into a car," said Sonny but unsurprisingly received no further response.

"But does it matter what the motive is?" asked Edward, who was by now wondering if the conversation was getting a bit too serious even for his liking. In any case it was only Horace's problem as far as he was concerned although no one else had yet volunteered when their own last good deed was. "After all, it's the fact that you've done it that's important, not the reason. You don't need a motive. Like if I was in hospital 'cos I had broken my leg all I'm concerned about is whether the surgeon can plaster me up so that my leg gets better; I'm not concerned as to why he wants to make me better which could be probably only something simple like 'cos he wants to get paid and he gets a bonus for each job well done or he wants to please his wife or God or just show off. So your knight in shining armour may open a door for you but you don't know why he's doing it. It might be 'cos he's short on a few good deeds or 'cos it's a necessity 'cos he's a chivalrous knight and it's expected of him but it doesn't matter. What matters is the door has been opened for you so that, um..."

"So that you don't walk into it Mel," said Charlie. "Which you wouldn't do if your knight in shiny amour was around 'cos you would be waiting for him to dedistress you so you would be standing by the door and not going through it unless you were Em."

"Which I'm not," said Melanie firmly, "although she is usually my best friend."

"I think what's important," said Edward conclusively, "is that we should encourage Horace to do a good deed every day if he can."

"Whoa, hang on a minute," said Horace, finally looking up from his pool of dejection. "I was only just saying; I wasn't suggesting that I needed any help. And I certainly don't feel that I need any help from you lot. After all," Horace looked directly at Edward who felt that he ought to avoid Horace's gaze before it became too fixed but couldn't as he decided that it would imply embarrassment at least and guilt at worst, "when did you last do a good deed?" Edward opened his mouth but only managed a very short, "Well..." before Melanie announced that she had done a good deed earlier in the day, "although it wasn't a very good one. Anyone else?"

It soon became apparent that, apart from Melanie's minor effort which she had managed to put into the public domain for instant approval whilst skilfully avoiding elucidating further so that no one was any the wiser as to what it actually was, not one of the Ravens had done anything approaching a good deed either so far that day or the day before or even within the past week for it was for sure that had they done so they would have mentioned it. "Mummy gave me some money to go and get some lamb chops from the supermarket so let's all go for a walk down to the high street and see if we can each do a good deed on the way. We can mark them out of ten and the Raving with the highest score can get, um, something," suggested Horace waving one of his mother's large supermarket bags for life around his head like a manic mixologist. "And if we can use our spears to kill a rabbit or something on the way like we're wild Sumerians then I can use the chop money for something else."

"And what's your mum going to say when you get home with no chops but a rabbit?" asked Mel.

"And," added Emily, "with its fur still on. At least with a chop it's been defurred and cleaned and chopped and stuff..."

"I'm up for getting somefing," said Sonny showing an early interest in finding an alternative purchase with Horace's mother's cash as the Ravens slowly got to their collective feet and headed for the footpath through the woods down to the village, spears in hand, but not before Edward had climbed the oak tree to rescue Emily ("I'm coming Em!") despite the fact that Emily had neither asked to be rescued nor had needed to be rescued who then himself had to be rescued - by Emily.

"If you hadn't said it wasn't possible Ed," said Emily, as she led Edward down a particularly tricky section of the trunk, "I would've suggested that you've just made an opportunity for a good deed."

"And even if that's not the case," added Melanie. "Emily has now done her good deed for the day."

"I would further suggest," replied Emily with a smirk, "that as a life-saving deed that should fall into the category of a very good deed and so I am off the hook for a week."

"I wasn't that stuck," said Edward defiantly.

"Then climb back up and rescue yourself and bring down the black cat with a red collar while you're at it," demanded Emily, determined to show that hers was a deed worthy of the highest of scores.

"He can't," said Melanie scowling as she took back possession of her camera, "'cos Ed doesn't believe that you can make opportunities for good deeds, do you Ed?" But there was no reply; Edward was already over the stream and on his way.

\*\*\*

The trees on the well-worn route through the woods were usually witnesses to much laughter and horseplay whenever Horace was around but this afternoon was strangely silent - to begin with. It was as if the Ravens had suddenly morphed into adulthood and a world where no one says much to each other apart from the occasional grunt or groan around the dinner table. The *actualité* of the present silence was that the individuals were each quietly plotting a very good deed, at least something better than Emily's; the kudos that came with the goodest good deed, was not to be underestimated.

The small but muddy stream that ran across the path at the start of the woods normally claimed as a victim at least one Raven, if not all; it was too easy to use the bridge and so they would invariably end up mostly with very wet feet. However this was usually no longer Sonny after his response to the inaugural shove that he received in his back just as he was preparing to hop over the minor stretch of water, and it was not today either. All of the Ravens had made it safely over with their minds on greater matters when Horace and Melanie, who were bringing up the rear, approached. "After you Mel," Horace said quietly to Melanie as he held out his hand to encourage her across. Melanie feared an imminent shove but it wasn't forthcoming. Once she had hopped safely over she turned to Horace and suggested that although she had no objections she wasn't a damsel in distress at that particular moment but when she was she would let him know. "And I'm not being chivalrous," said Horace, "but I was just giving you the opportunity to ask for help if you needed it, as you may well at some point. Good deeds and all that."

"Well thank you very much Horace," said Melanie with a glint in her eye. She looked all around but mainly down the path and when she was sure that no one else was looking she turned back and gave Horace the briefest yet sweetest of smiles but it was enough. Horace blushed, not for the first time, and Melanie tittered nervously, putting a hand over her mouth. This was enough to attract the attention of the others who collectively turned round just in time to witness Melanie jump back over the stream and announce that she was now, "no longer a damsel in distress but a damsel in a dress and a wicked one at that," before shoving Horace so violently that his torso took off before his feet had even moved with the result that he went hands and head first down into the mucky morass.

"I thought you were going to jump," said Melanie sounding almost apologetic. Horace said nothing. He stood up, trudged out of the stream still holding his bag for life, but maybe for less of a life than had been the case a few moments earlier, and continued his walk without either looking up at Melanie's smiling face or down at the veneer of mud that covered his front, literally from head to toe. He made a mental note to beware whenever, if ever, Melanie next gave him one of her sweet smiles.

The Ravens continued their journey in silence and were nearly out of the woods and back onto the road when they became aware of what sounded like a person calling out with a high pitched voice from what appeared to be the undergrowth. They slowed their pace and looked all about. "Sshhh!" exclaimed Sonny. "Someone's bein' murdered! That's a whole lifetime of good deeds if I can stop it!" Edwards's eyes were nearly popping out of their sockets. "What is it?" he demanded of no one in particular.

"Prepare to do a good deed Ed," said Sonny with a chuckle as Edward suddenly and unexpectedly began to retreat from the direction of the noise.

"I am prepared to execute a good deed, even if that means just running away," replied Edward, articulating Sonny's thoughts. He thought he could make out a female voice calling out what sounded like, "Flicks! Flicks!" The Ravens looked at each other, no one admitting to ever having been known by such a name when, without warning, a lady emerged from behind a large oak tree as a fat tabby cat with a half-chewed ear appeared from nowhere. Sonny only managed a glimpse of him for in an instant the cat had shot up the tree on the lady's blind side. Such was the lady's attire - comprising in the main a large blue woollen baggy cardigan and a pair of thick and very loosely-fitted slacks, even though it was a reasonably warm afternoon, with her feet in a pair of dirty wellington boots - and with dishevelled grey hair that fell randomly around her face as if she had just emerged, Horace imagined, from the spin-cycle of a washing-machine, that Horace decided that in his experience she was an archetypal cat lover and that she was calling for her feline friend.

"Oh thank goodness you're here children!" the lady exclaimed as she clapped her hands together and then rubbed them enthusiastically, as if she was washing them in the way a surgeon would before a major operation. "I'm sure that you can help." (Not that the Ravens had yet offered their services.) "My beloved cat Felix has escaped from the house which is most unlike him. I live over there," said the lady, waving her hands behind her and in the general direction of the road on the far side of the woods. "He usually stays in, but when he does go out he only ever goes out into the back garden for a wander and a little sniff before returning. However today when I opened the front door in order to take delivery of a parcel he shot straight out, down the garden path, across the pavement, across the verge, across the road and into these woods. I screamed but I didn't think that that would help bring him back so I went into the kitchen to bake a Victoria sponge but once I had finished, which took a good couple of hours I can tell you, I went to see if Felix had returned although I'm sure that had he he would have made a beeline for the kitchen so I don't know why I searched the house but I did and he was nowhere to be found so I thought it was time to cast my net a little wider and hence why I'm now in the woods looking for him. Oh dear, I do hope he's alright and hasn't come to any harm. He's my sole companion you see since my husband died and all my children are grown up and have left home. I used to have a daily which was a great help as well as a friend and confidante. She used to do everything for me but she's recently retired and I've yet to find someone of sufficient calibre to replace her. I'm very particular you know. I don't leave the house very often myself and I don't have many friends so Felix is the only human, I say 'human' although I know that he's only a cat but he seems almost human; he's the only human that I get to speak to regularly and even then I don't say much to him. Believe it or not I would much prefer to speak to human humans..."

"You could of fooled us," said Emily.

"I beg your pardon?" said the lady.

"She means 'have'" said Melanie looking and sounding rather superior.

"I beg your pardon?" said the lady.

"You could HAVE fooled us," said Emily.

"I'm so sorry," said the lady apologetically, "But I am a little deaf. But I'm not fooling anyone. I have really lost my cat and I desperately need your help. There will be a good reward." Someone's ears immediately pricked up.

"It ain't by any chance a large tabby wiv a half-chewed ear is it?" asked Sonny cautiously as he grabbed at Horace's muddy bag for life.

"Oh my goodness yes, that's him. Have you seen him?" asked the lady as she started to shake and execute a small jig on the spot.

"Er, sort of," said Sonny guardedly. "But I have heard him meowing quite a bit," he added in order to lend credence to his split second sighting. "He's up this oak tree I think. I heard him as we walked along just a few moments ago. He sounded very distressed. But I can get him down if you want to send me into a dangerous situation. I don't mind. It won't cost much. I..."

"I can do it," said Emily firmly.

"You've done your good deed for today," Sonny hissed. "You rescued Ed."

"I want a good reward," Emily protested.

"I'll share it," said Sonny as he finally wrenched Horace's bag for life from his grasp and started up the tree without waiting for a response from the lady.

"There's some rope and a penknife in the bag," Horace called out to Sonny. "I always have rope and a penknife. I'm being prepared. You can use the rope to lower Felix down like they do people down the side of burning buildings."

"They usually run out of rope," said Charlie, who until that moment had remained silent but now wanted to be part of the action. "We need to have like a trampoline stretched out so that Sonny can drop Felix and he can bounce. I can organise it." Charlie looked around for a large piece of material and quickly arrived at Melanie's no-longer-sweetly-smiling face.

"Oh no," said Melanie, crossing her hands across her chest.

"It's an emergency," said Charlie pleadingly.

"I'm a damsel in a dress. I'm not going to be one out of a dress. Not until bedtime anyway," said Melanie defiantly as she looked away.

"What about doing a good deed?" Charlie responded almost threateningly.

"I'll wait," said Melanie nonchalantly.

"How's it going Sonny?" asked Horace to the leaves and branches on high, wishing to divert the conversation away from Melanie's dress all the while thinking that if he did nothing else that day *he* would have done a goodish deed in preventing Melanie from having her dress torn from her to satisfy Charlie's cravings for a spectacular rescue or something altogether less charitable and more sinister.

"It's quite a way up," Sonny called down breathlessly. "An' it's just climbed up further. I may be out of 'earin' range in a minute but you'll know if I've bin successful 'cos your bag will appear with an occupant. 'Opefully not me."

"So then it will be a bag of life," Edward suggested. He smiled. He thought Melanie would like that. It was clever. It was a sort of pun, a double meaning. Melanie was intelligent. She would understand. She would get the joke but no one else would. He wasn't sure what had been going on between Melanie and Horace back at the stream but something had and Edward felt that getting stuck up a tree wasn't going to help his cause. And neither was jealousy.

"I was thinking more like a bag fur life," said Melanie and the Ravens, bar Edward, laughed heartily.

"That's very funny," said Horace.

"Not that funny," said Edward.

The Ravens and the lady stood anxiously at the base of the tree for several minutes until suddenly there was a rustling of the branches and signs of movement. Horace's muddy bag suddenly appeared swinging under the tree's canopy. It continued to descend until it was a couple of feet from the ground at which point it came to an abrupt halt. "NO MORE ROPE!" came a voice from way up on high. But it was fine; Felix was in the bag, safe and well. The lady scooped him out and held him tightly to her chest.

"Well done everyone!" she exclaimed. "You are a credit to your parents! Now come across the road to my house and I will treat you all to a giant slice of cake each. I hope you do all eat cake. But please leave your spears outside the front door; they look positively lethal."

"We're Sumerians!" said Horace.

"Whatever," said the lady.

As the Ravens, all but one, diverted off the footpath for reward and refreshment, the distinct voice of a stranded scout could be heard from way up on high. "EM-I-LEEEE! 'EEEEELP! 'ORRRRR-IIIIIICE!"

"I won't be a moment," Emily said a little too quietly. "I'll be back when I've had my cake and eaten it." Horace was thinking much the same.

\*\*\*

The Ravens were in the extensive back garden in Prince Imperial Road tucking into a second slice of Victoria sponge each when Sonny suddenly appeared. They had all had a tour of the house and were listening to Mrs Thomas' fascinating life story when he finally showed up, climbing over the high fence even though the side gate was unlocked. His appearance suggested that he had been pulled through a hedge backwards and then pushed forwards through a bramble bush yet he seemed totally unconcerned. Something of much greater importance was on his mind. "Where's my bit?" he demanded.

"Oh sorry Sonny," said Emily, sounding far from apologetic, "but I was just coming to get you. I thought you might be stuck. How did you find us anyway?"

"I saw what looked like an equipment stash for a midgets' javelin convention on the drive. I was real stuck up the tree 'cos it's easier to go up than down, but only stuck for a bit 'cos then I used me initiative like we're always bein' told. I could sort of see and 'ear a man walkin' through the woods with two young kids so I called out to 'im and asked 'im if the little'uns would like a ride in my special tree-bag-for-life-lift. 'It's free and it's great fun!' I shouted. Silly old fool should've known better. The two kids climbed into Horace's bag and I shouted out, "old on tight!' Then I climbed down a bit and put the top of the rope over a bough, man 'arnessed it round me wrist, held it in me 'and and jumped. It was like jumpin' out of a 'plane I can tell ya not like I've done many planes yet but I reckon it would be the same only without the twigs. I went fast for a bit then really slow. The kids were screamin' as I went down and they came up past me missin' me by not much. One was really sobbin'. When I got to the bottom it was a perfect landing 'cos I stopped just above the ground and was swingin' like I was sky divin' so I whipped out 'Orace's penknife 'cos I 'ad that in me pocket and sliced the rope above me 'ead like I was freein' meself from a parachute up a tree 'cos I'd mistimed the jump. It was such fun an' so much quicker than climbin' down!"

"What about the two children?" asked Edward as the Ravens sat open-mouthed at hearing Sonny's adventure that had been playing out not fifty yards away in the woods. "Did you let go and did they plummet to the ground and are they now dead and are you going to prison?"

"I'm comin' to that," said Sonny. "I'm not stupid. The bloke said with crazy eyes, 'Now what?' I said, 'Take this mate,' as I 'anded 'im the end of the rope 'cos I 'ad 'eld onta it, 'and wait 'til someone my size comes along and you can do the same again like I've just done.' 'I don't think so!' 'e said all crossly but I just walked off 'cos 'e could 'ardly let go could 'e and 'e could 'ardly tie the rope up an' chase after me leavin' his precious cargo a hundred feet up an oak tree in the middle of the woods? Then I ran and I don't care 'cos I've done a good deed for today wiv Felix an' I've done another good deed what with rescuin' meself 'cos I think that counts and now we've got to stay 'ere for a bit so that the bloke doesn't find me 'an do a bad deed to me which wouldn't be very nice 'specially after 'avin' no cake."

"I don't think you can get points for doing a good deed to yourself," said Edward pompously.

"I am much obliged," said Mrs Thomas who evidently hadn't heard a word of Sonny's story but sensed that he had been drawn into an incident that required compensation. She reached into her cardigan pocket, pulled out a fifty pound note and pressed it into Sonny's hand.

"Thank you," she said. "I am so very grateful." Sonny nodded and stuffed it deep into his trouser pocket in an attempt to remove it from view as quickly as possible, remembering the old adage, "out of sight, out of mind" - but not quickly enough for Edward.

"Who said good deeds need a payment?" he asked incredulously.

"What about my bag for life?" asked Horace crossly without waiting for Sonny to answer Edward.

"I'll buy you a dozen in the supermarket an' 'ere's yer penknife back," said Sonny with a smirk, handing over Horace's blunted knife while studiously ignoring the earlier question. "An' I now 'ave my first real good deed under me belt ever... I mean for today and cat rescue 'as got t'be worth at least a month of normal good deeds even if I can't count rescuin' meself."

"Agreed," said Melanie eyeing up the last slice of cake that Sonny hadn't noticed before Archie reached across her with arm outstretched and grabbed at it greedily.

\*\*\*

"There's only one thing I don't understand," said Mrs Thomas a few minutes later as the Ravens were preparing to leave and continue on their journey once Edward had checked to see whether the coast was clear, Sonny having also been given a replacement bag for life, "and that is how Sonny could hear Felix meowing up the tree when he can't meow." Sonny shrugged his shoulders.

"I dunno," he said, "but if you go up there now you will probably find something or maybe two somethings making a similar sort of noise."

"Only human," suggested Emily.

"Only human," confirmed Sonny as the Ravens collected their spears from outside the front door and continued their journey down the road.

They walked down to the point where the road narrows and then crossed over with the intention of going for a roll down the steep slope that leads to the side of the pond but were distracted first by a fire engine that went tearing up the road with siren sounding and blue lights flashing, then a police car and then an ambulance, and second by a commotion on the pavement. Horace went over to investigate and found an elderly couple half in the road trying to shield from the cars that were passing inches away - a large, impossibly fat pigeon. It was lying in the gutter flapping one wing pathetically up and down before stopping momentarily then attempting to move before giving up and flapping its wing again. "I'm so worried," said the man clutching his wife firmly by the arm. "I'm sure it's going to fall in front of a car at any minute and be squashed."

Horace assumed that the man was talking about the pigeon but thought that he could equally be talking about his wife who was perched precariously on the kerb and who evidently hadn't been taught the first rule of first aid which was for the aider not to start a rescue by becoming another casualty. "Go and stand on the other side of the pavement," commanded Melanie as she took control of the situation. "Emily will slow the traffic down and Horace will rescue the pigeon won't you Horace? Please."

Everyone did as commanded, especially Horace who was keen to do a good deed for the old couple but mostly for Melanie even though all she had done for him so far that afternoon was get him caked in mud. With the traffic momentarily at a standstill Horace bent down and picked up the pigeon in his cupped hands. It made no effort to resist. Horace carried it across the pavement and popped it down on the grassy slope. "We're so grateful," said the man as he wiped away a tear from his wife's eye and then quickly from his. "Thank you for your help."

"It's nothing," said Horace magnanimously then added. "What I mean is, it's no great deal inasmuch as it wasn't very difficult but it was quite a big something good deed."

"Hardly," said Edward scowling.

"Not 'hardly' at all, young man," said the elderly man who had been observing Edward doing nothing to help. "Not all good deeds have to be grand or lengthy deeds. A simple act of kindness towards a sick pigeon can be a very good deed. This pigeon would certainly think so."

"Whatever," said Edward scowling some more.

Sonny meanwhile had followed Horace and the pigeon down the bank and was by now bending down carefully examining the bird that now wasn't moving at all. "I reckon it's got a broken wing mate," he said with authority as he stood back up. Horace noted that Sonny looked far more serious than he normally did. Maybe he had finally realised that a serious situation needed a serious face whatever one was actually thinking and Sonny was probably thinking - lunch.

"He's been through quite a bit already. It would be a pity for him to be caught by a fox or shimmy into the pond or back into the road. You seem to know what you're doing," said the old man to Sonny. "What would you suggest?"

"I've bin around racin' pigeons most of me life mate, although this isn't one. Too fat. He's got some unusual colourin' though. Most woodpigeons 'ave a white collar with a side that goes straight but this one don't. 'E 'as a jagged edge, somefing what I've never sin before. Personally mate, I would fink the vet's the answer. Take 'im down the road to Premier Vets and pop him in now so they can give 'im the once over." The man reached for his wallet.

"We were actually heading in the opposite direction and were waiting for the 269 bus when we spotted him. So if it's not an awful intrusion on your time, would you be able to oblige?" The man held out two twenty pound notes. "There's one for the vet's bill and one for your trouble. My wife and I would be most obliged." Sonny scrambled up the slope and relieved the man of the cash with a, "Cheers mate." He folded the notes together and popped them deep into his other trouser pocket.

"Who said good deeds need a payment?" asked Edward once more. This time Sonny did reply.

"The vet Ed," he said with a stare. "They 'ave to 'ave more trainin' than real doctors 'cos animals don't speak so's there's more t' learn. That's what's bin paid for." Edward looked away as Sonny patted the notes, scrambled once more down the slope, carefully picked up the recumbent and compliant pigeon and dropped it not so carefully into the replacement bag for life.

"Leave 'im wiv us mate. We'll soon 'ave 'im sorted," said Sonny with a smile. He then nodded down the road. "An' ere's ya bus comin', so look lively." The man and his wife slowly boarded the bus and once on Sonny opened the bag and pronounced the pigeon, "very unwell."

"Let's get him down to the vet for a second opinion Sonny," Horace gently suggested, fearing the pigeon was otherwise destined for Sonny's kitchen. Sonny didn't argue.

"C'mon then," he said and the Ravens continued their walk down to the high street. They crossed over the traffic lights and ambled on past the doctors' surgery, the big church and the almshouses. Then they crossed the side road that leads to the car park, past the post office, past The Workshed and stopped outside Premier Vets. The entrance into Mr Lillie's shop was not an easy one for the agile let alone an invalid as there was a large step from the pavement to the shop. However there was a short length of metal handrail that could be used to pull oneself up the step and into the shop if need be. Horace noticed an old lady, tall and distinguished, but who also looked particularly frail, who walked across his path and grabbed hold of the handrail. He wondered whether, even with the help of the support, she would be able to make her way into the shop. Maybe he should offer to do her a good deed? The lady saw Horace staring at her and opened her mouth as if to speak but Horace felt that he was already in the middle of doing a good deed, albeit to a pigeon whereas he probably should have made a decision there and then to attend to a bird of an altogether more ancient vintage. But he didn't. He had a couple of banknotes to keep his eye on, a pigeon to help and a Sonny to guard. He joined the Ravens whose animated conversation was in full swing outside the door into the vets'.

"Who's going in then?" asked Edward, sounding as if he were no hurry to volunteer himself.

"I don't know whether we can just go in," said Archie cautiously. "I think normally you have to have an appointment."

"Don't be daft Archie," said Melanie. "We need decisive action. This is an emergency. You can hardly go in and say, 'Excuse me but I have a pigeon that I think has a broken wing and it looks very poorly. Do you think that I could make an appointment for Tuesday next week to bring him in so that the vet can have a quick look at him? Please?' Don't be daft! It's like if you broke your leg 'cos you fell out of the oak tree or something; you're not going to limp home and get your mum to ring up the doctors' and say, 'I think that my little Archie has broken his leg and he's in great pain. Do you think that I could make him an appointment to see someone next week?' No. She's going to dial nine nine nine or whatever the other number is and when the lady answers she's going to say, 'I think my son has broken his leg, please send an ambulance quickly as he looks like he's going to die,' or if you're outside the hospital you're going to walk straight in. Well hop in. So this is the hospital for animals and it works the same way only the patients are going to bleat or something instead of talking therefore I think that we should walk straight in with our patient and demand to be seen."

"Especially if we have forty pounds to spend. We're not going to be turned down if we have money to spend," said Emily.

"Twenty," corrected Edward. "The man said twenty for the vet and twenty for Sonny. Didn't he Sonny? Sonny?" Edward looked all around. He was visibly distressed at the sudden disappearance of Sonny but more so the money. "Where's Sonny?" he asked no one in particular but hoping that someone had an answer. The other Ravens didn't so joined him in looking aimlessly around about themselves. Apart from Charlie.

"He's in the vets' already," said Charlie with a deep sigh. "Whilst you lot were arguing over what we can and can't and should and shouldn't do with Percy pigeon, Sonny's taken decisive action already and gone in all by himself to find out."

"I don't believe it!" Horace gasped, putting down his spear. He turned back round and saw the old lady still holding onto the handrail but not going anywhere, hesitated, then grabbed the door handle of the veterinary surgery, yanked it down and pushed. The door opened, a tinkly bell sounded above his head and immediately Horace stepped inside putting his hands in his pockets as he entered. His mother had once told him to keep his hands in his pockets when at the vets' because, "you never know what might try and nibble them when you're not looking," and Horace had taken her at her word even though he wasn't sure whether she had been joking or not. Sonny was standing patiently next to an extraordinarily overdressed lady in a shiny green dress with cut-glass pearls around her neck Melanie, who had followed Horace in, noted, with a cut-glass voice, Horace noted, who was speaking to the receptionist at the counter. She had a nervous-looking pedigree black cat in a very new shimmering blue pet carrier at her feet. She was in the middle of telling the receptionist a very long and laborious story about why she had changed Sooty's mealtimes recently.

"I find that if I feed him too early he then doesn't bother going outside and uses the emergency litter tray in the utility room which isn't a very satisfactory situation as that's where I dry my bedsheets. I always think that Sooty's motions add a certain unwanted odour to the linen. Now if I were to..." Horace had already heard enough. Sooty looked as though he was on his way out of the vets' whereas Percy was on his way in. As the last of the Ravens squeezed through the door Horace announced in a very loud voice,

"Stuff your Sooty. What about our Percy? We're on a very..."

It's okay," said Sonny. "It's all sorted isn't it love? I'm just waitin' patiently for the head vet to come out and have a gander."

"Are these all your friends Sonny?" asked the receptionist as she cast her gaze over the additional six pairs of eyes that had just walked in with no animal, bird or reptile in tow. She was evidently as bored as Horace sounded with Sooty's toileting arrangements. Seven youngsters, including one that called her "love" even though he was probably well under half her age, and a woodpigeon was a far more interesting proposition.

"Yes, mostly they are," he replied leaving the Ravens to try to work out not only how the receptionist already knew Sonny's name but also who amongst them was considered by Sonny not to be his friend, not that any of them would have said anything, least of all Horace. Turning to Horace he said, "Mary 'as 'ad a peep at Percy and reckons that the vet may 'ave a gander..."

"We wouldn't normally bother with a pigeon, but Sonny says that he has ten pounds to spend," she confirmed, "so we can probably give him a couple of minutes."

"Oh does he? Ten pounds you say?" said Horace, looking at Sonny with as stern a countenance as he could manage, an expression he would never usually show to his occasionally aggressive friend except at this particular moment he was in the company of sufficient witnesses for Sonny not to invoke a physical response.

"Whatever he has," the receptionist gently continued as she looked Melanie's expensive Miss Mode summer dress up and down, "we will be able to do something commensurate with the level of aggregate finance available. However, at this stage, the inducement of just ten pounds is not sufficiently high to persuade Mr Wendell to drop everything and come running."

"But it's an emergency!" cried Horace. "I don't think you understand! This is no ordinary pigeon, this is, I would imagine, one of the UK's foremost racing pigeons and is extremely valuable. Money is no object at all. We will be able to pay. We have loads more than ten pounds, don't we Sonny?" Horace dared through gritted teeth.

"He's a very busy vet, but I'm sure he'll be along shortly and...and, oh, here he is," she said as a young man dressed in a smart open necked shirt and dark chinos under a blue operating gown, and brown loafers, appeared from somewhere out the back and obsequiously asked if he might see the pigeon. At this the very well-dressed lady picked up her carrier and marched out of the surgery complaining that no one ever listened to her, but evidently someone had been listening to Horace from only a little further away albeit out of sight.

"Go through over there," said the vet pointing to a door at the side of and behind the reception desk with a NO ENTRY sign in large red letters stuck on it, "and I'll come and have a good look at your valuable cargo for you." The Ravens followed Sonny as he picked up the bag for life and headed for the door. Once inside the Ravens lined up against the wall of the consulting room that they found themselves in as Sonny plonked more than gently placed the bag for life on the table between him and the vet. Mr Wendell opened the bag far too gingerly for a supposed emergency and peered inside. He spent several seconds staring at the bird as if he were conducting a thorough examination but given that it was confined to visual Horace wondered quite how much he could deduce. Whilst he was still pondering the situation Mr Wendell, who had obviously been doing some wondering of his own, suddenly asked, "Tell me Sonny. Just how valuable?"

"Er, I don't really know," said Sonny.

"A lot," said Horace. "So although you haven't touched him yet, can you already tell us what's wrong with him?"

At this question the vet reached down into the bag, pulled out Percy and placed him on the examination table where he sat without moving. "I can tell that he's been through a fair bit of trauma poor thing. He has a broken wing to start with and much else besides. If you would like him to be as good a racing pigeon as he obviously was then he needs all the quality care that he can get." Mr Wendell looked at the Ravens who were all staring at the bag and not really taking anything much in that he was saying and certainly not disagreeing with what prognosis he had to offer - apart from Horace who detected a slight change of tone in his voice. He had lowered it slightly and then said rather too audaciously for Horace's liking, "However he's certainly not your average racing pigeon but he could still be valuable. Tell me, how much is he worth?" The vet looked at Horace and Horace looked at Sonny. Now that they were before the vet it didn't really matter how much Percy was or wasn't worth, but Sonny's brain hadn't yet caught up with the conversation; he had been elsewhere, quieting thinking about how he was going to spend the thirty pounds although he was by now feeling that it would soon be disappearing from his and into the vet's pocket, and so he absentmindedly offered,

"At least a grand." The vet looked at Sonny and raised an eyebrow. Sonny was getting further behind.

"Maybe one and a half. Just be grateful that it's only one wing 'cos two would be double."

"The thing is sir," said Horace, who was unsure how to address a veterinary surgeon so used the failsafe title from school, "we don't know how much he is worth exactly 'cos it was just found by this old couple when we were walking down the road and I don't know if it is a racing pigeon but I said that to make sure that you would see us quickly and you did and I'm sorry but the couple asked us to look after Percy and do what we could to make him better." The vet gently scratched his head and looked away from Sonny: he appeared to be deep in thought.

"I don't think that there's any doubt that he is a racing pigeon of the highest calibre. So how better do you want him to be made and what are you going to do with him once he is better?"

"I expect we'll just release him on the duck island up by the pond and he can decide what he wants to do with the rest of his life." The vet shook his head.

"I don't think that that's a good idea. The first thing he'll do is fly back home so if you like I can release him for you once he's ready."

"And I don't think that that's a good idea," said Sonny disapprovingly. "After all, if Percy isn't released near to where we found 'im then 'e won't know where 'e is 'cos 'e won't have any landmarks that 'e's expectin'."

"You seem to know quite a bit about racing pigeons."

"No," said Sonny. "I'm just guessin'." Horace looked at Sonny and frowned but Sonny didn't meet his eye; he was looking expectantly at Mr Wendell.

"In that case Horace," said Mr Wendell, "we need to take extra-special care of him. He will need quite a bit of work done to treat him and to bring him back to full health. We can x-ray his wing and bandage it up appropriately and once that's done we can do a full MOT on him. We can swab to find if canker, candidiasis, spirochaete and motile intestinal bacteria are present. We can monitor his faeces to measure worm egg counts, coccidial oocysts counts and culture for salmonella. We can provide the appropriate medication for any problems that we find plus a dose of multivitamins and electrolytes. That should set him on the right course. But it would be far better if I was to let him go from the surgery. They don't like being handled and they don't like to be caged and travel long distances."

"It's only up the road," said Sonny.

"And how much would that cost?" asked Horace warily.

"I would have to give you a full breakdown if you wanted to go ahead to be sure," said the vet but then he appeared to be fairly sure of the total for he added, "but I would expect it to be in the region of twelve hundred pounds."

"We only have forty pounds," Horace whined.

"Twenty actually," Sonny corrected. "What can we have for twenty?"

"You could save yourself a load of grief by having him put down but..."

"'Put down' what?" asked Emily looking very concerned.

"A hole," said Sonny bluntly.

"However, as your pigeon is so valuable you could pay for the work to be done and then once he is ready to fly you could release him with a small note that could be folded up and attached to a leg that Percy would take back to his owners and which would have your contact details so that they would get in touch and learn what you had done. Knowing pigeon fanciers as I do they would no doubt reimburse you with a bit on top. What do you say?"

The Ravens' expressions indicated that whatever they were going to say was not going to be very positive. "How much do we have in our pockets?" asked Archie. They pulled out what little money they had apart from Sonny who said that his fifty pound note had been earmarked. No one was quite sure what he meant but it sounded important so no one asked. The total, apart from the forty pounds, was two pounds and twenty-seven pence plus Horace's mother's chop money.

"Looks like Percy's going down a hole," said Sonny unsympathetically. The Ravens stood in silence contemplating the pigeon's imminent demise when the librareal atmosphere was broken by a sudden high-pitched wail that to Horace's young ear was similar to the sound that would be heard around the pre-pubescents of Chislehurst if word had got round that Miss Humbug's sweet shop was closing. Fortunately nothing quite so drastic had happened - it was merely Melanie having what Emily would later describe as a "meltdown." She stood up straight, pulled her shoulders back and bared her teeth at Mr Wendell in so menacing a manner that he visibly shrank back from her, possibly quite understandably concerned that he was just about to be bitten. Speaking as if her upper and lower teeth had fused together she managed to force out of her mouth the most conciliatory of statements,

"I don't care how much it costs. I will pay. We've been put in charge of Percy and we need to do a good deed for him." Melanie reached into her dress pocket, pulled out her debit card and waved it in the air. "Shall we say one thousand up front and Percy will receive the best treatment you can manage?"

Mr Wendell blinked rapidly several times but didn't say a word. It was as if he were waiting for a Raven to respond - but not one did. After all, they all knew Melanie and what she was capable of. The nearest they came to a reaction to her offer was Sonny who gently patted a trouser pocket as if seeking to reassure himself that the forty pounds that had been entrusted to him was still there, which it was.

After a minute or so of standing in silence with Mr Wendell lightly stroking his chin, he nodded almost imperceptibly, held out his hand towards Melanie and gently but firmly took hold of her debit card. He tugged just a little bit more forcefully that she would have liked. "Is this you?" he asked, staring at the gold-embossed name. "Miss Melanie Smith?"

"Yes," she said, "although mostly I'm called 'Mel.'" Mr Wendell walked over to the door. Opening it he beckoned the Ravens to come out. "Follow me," he commanded. "Mel first."

"I'll do this one," he said to Mary as he reached for the card processing machine and carefully inserted Melanie's card. He tapped in a few numbers, actually quite a few numbers, and instructed Melanie to key in her PIN.

"Hang on a minute," she said, looking at the screen and frowning, "I thought we agreed a grand."

"Plus VAT," said Mr Wendell without missing a beat. Sonny grimaced, Melanie sighed. She handed her camera back to

Emily and pressed four numbers on the keypad then ENTER. The machine beeped and spew out a receipt.

"The price of a new camera, that's all," Melanie muttered to herself.

"That's great," said the vet, taking hold of the machine and handing it back to the receptionist. "In a month's time when Percy has been nursed back to full health we will release him out the back and he can resume a long, happy and healthy life." The Ravens all nodded, apart from one.

"Oh no," said Sonny. "I think we've agreed that we'll come and pick him up, won't we Mel?"

"Yes," said Melanie as she screwed up her receipt and threw it in the bin.

"As you wish," said the vet.

"We'll be in on Saturday the seventeenth next month," said Melanie as she marched toward the surgery door with the rest of the Ravens in tow. "I hope that you live up to your name."

"Oh yes, of course my young dear," said Mr Wendell rubbing his hands. "We are most definitely premier vets."

"I wouldn't get too carried away," said Melanie under her breath as she disappeared back onto the high street, "'cos it's an anagram of 'semi pervert.'"

"That'll be your shopping for the day then Mel," said Horace once all were back outside and gathering up their spears.

"I don't think so," she replied. "That was a necessary payment for an animal in distress. There's no NHS in the animal world so it had to be done. This afternoon's purchase stroke purchases will be solely on what dad calls 'discretionary items' which is mostly what my allowance is spent on."

"'Mostly?'" queried Archie. "I would have thought discretionary purchases fitted the bill for everything that you bought.

"Not at all," said Melanie affrontedly.

"Okay," said Archie in attempt to have some ammunition in his wallet when his parents next queried him about his excessive spending habits. "So what have you bought in the last week that is not a discretionary item? In fact what is the last thing that you have bought apart from a pigeon's life?"

"My camera," said Melanie. "What about you?" Archie did not immediately reply.

"A large bag of sweets, and he's not even sharing them," Charlie complained.

"A camera is a discretionary purchase. You don't need one. You're just using it to take photos of stuff. That's not essential. That's a luxury," said Archie finally.

"Not if I'm going to be a photo or print journalist," said Melanie haughtily. "At least I know what I'm going to do with my life and I've been practising with my camera. I have a small notebook and pencil and I've even had some business cards made up. Look," she said as she pulled a colourful glossy card from another pocket and waved it in the air. "What can you practice with when all you've bought today is a large bag of unshared sweets?"

"Getting fat like my pigeon," said Sonny with a chuckle. Archie didn't respond but Charlie did.

"That's definitely your good deed done for at least a month Mel. At least an eight out of ten so you're probably the winner. So let's go and find the rest of us a good deed and if not go home 'cos there was a huge downpour forecast earlier and I don't have a coat."

"More like two months," said Edward magnanimously as they prepared to move off, "'cos if Sonny gets a month for rescuing a cat then helping to save a bird's life must be worth loads more. I reckon that if I was Mel I would think that I did enough with saving a pigeon's life to take me all the way up to Christmas."

"But only eight out of ten?" Melanie complained. "What can be a better deed than saving a pigeon's life?"

"Doing it without money? After all it's the vet that's doing all the work," suggested Emily. "What do you think Horace?" Horace had been unusually quiet since leaving the vets' and she turned to see whether he was still with them. He was, but he hadn't been taking much notice: he had moved onto someone far more in need. The old lady that he had seen earlier holding onto Mr Lillie's handrail was still there, clutching it tightly but going nowhere. Horace had some lamb chops to buy and there were plenty of people walking past her as they went in and out of the shop so he felt that a grown-up could give her hand - literally - but as he watched he noticed that no one was taking the slightest bit of notice. Then again he was in a bit of a hurry...

"C'mon Horace!" said Emily once she realised that Horace was not going to give her the benefit of his opinion for once, the truth being he hadn't even heard her ask for it. The Ravens began to walk back up the high street and to cross over for Horace to go and buy his mother's chops. Horace turned to follow them. He shot a final glance in the old lady's direction and noticed that although she was leaning into the handrail she had managed to turn round and was looking back directly at Horace, her sad, mournful eyes kept Horace's attention for just the extra second that she needed. She opened her mouth and said something. Her face seemed to be pleading with him to hear but he was too far away. Breaking away from the Ravens he wandered slowly over to her and bent his head so that his ear was as near to her mouth as he dared. He prepared for the unexpected such as having it bitten off given where he had just been, and the fanciful thoughts that had come to him whilst his hands were in his pockets. He was silent and motionless, listening for the slightest sound. After a few seconds he became aware of what the lady was whispering.

"Help me. Please. Help me. Help me."

Horace stood back up with a start. It was surreal. Usually people who needed help would be unconscious or shouting from the rooftops. The old lady needed help and had presumably been requiring some assistance for quite a while. He wondered how on earth so many people could have simply walked past without finding out if she needed any aid but then realised that if he hadn't seen her before going into the vets' then he would probably have walked straight past also. He pondered for a moment how children generally notice what's around them more than grown-ups before thinking about what he should do. "Perhaps ask what help she needs would be a start?" a little voice inside his head suggested. He quickly looked all around. He thought an adult might now stop but no one did. Everyone was going about their usual business and not giving Horace and the apparently stranded lady a second glance. Even his group of friends had wandered off although he assumed they would be back soon enough. And they were. Melanie had turned round to see where her grubby little friend was and saw him receiving what looked like a kiss on the ear.

"Looks like Horace is doing a good deed," she said to the others who then also stopped. They turned round ready to mark him out of ten.

"I thought he needed to buy chops," said Edward questioningly.

"I thought his granny was dead," said Charlie sounding more than a little confused.

"That one looks dead," said Sonny bluntly, "so I expect the only good deed that he could be doing right now is arranging her funeral."

As they gathered round Horace was asking the old lady, stretching his lips as far as they would go with every word and speaking so loudly that people across the road could hear, "HOW - CAN - I - HELP - YOU? DO - YOU - WANT - TO - GO - INTO - THE - WORKSHED?" He pinned his ear to her lips. Melanie grimaced.

"I'm not deaf," she murmured. Normally Horace would have argued the point but this was hardly the time or the place to disagree. "Please take me home," she whispered. At this precise point Mr Lillie appeared in his doorway to find out what all the commotion was about. Horace breathed a sigh of relief.

"Do you know who this lady is Mr Lillie?" asked Horace. But Mr Lillie said that he had never seen her before in his life.

"Of course you haven't. How convenient," said Horace brightly, standing up once again. "She wants to be taken home," he informed the others.

"Where's her home?" asked Melanie.

"Number twelve with a red door and I do have a name," the old lady muttered.

"This way and what is it?" asked Horace pointing in the direction that he assumed she had been walking. He liked the idea of two questions being asked both together as it would undoubtedly, in this situation at least, save a considerable amount of time.

"Yes and Peggy," she said. She let go of the handrail and grabbed Horace's wrist. Now there was no escape. Immediately Horace tried to bound back up the high street with the elderly lady clamped firmly on one arm and his spear under the other but realised that she wasn't nearly so boundy as he was. "Slow down," and "slow down some more," she ordered until he was reduced to almost literally a snail's pace.

As they shuffled along with the Ravens following on closely behind Horace asked Peggy how she had managed to get stranded outside Mr Lillie's. "Weren't you trying to get inside?" he asked.

"No," she replied. "I just thought that I would come out for a little walk but I think that I've bitten off more than I can chew."

"You haven't come from the vets' have you?" Charlie asked.

"No, number twelve." The sluggish shuffling continued and Horace began to wonder how far away number twelve was because their progress was so painfully slow.

"Are you as far as the traffic lights?" Horace asked concernedly, pointing fifty metres up the road.

"No." Horace sighed. They reached the almshouses and, glancing over the fence, Horace noted that they were at number fifty-six. He scratched his head albeit only metaphorically as he was now holding onto Peggy with his free hand lest she suddenly let go and fall.

"Peggy, what road do you live in?" he enquired gently.

"Albert Road I think."

"You think?" But Horace had no time to think for the expected downpour was on Chislehurst's doorstep. The sky had darkened with the arrival of a large, black, low altitude cumulus nimbus and the first thick telltale drops had started to fall. "Quick, in here," said Horace as the rain began to inflict a potentially serious soaking on those who had no shelter. He led Peggy into the lychgate of the high street church and sat her down on the small wooden ledge while he gathered his thoughts.

"Then why are we walking in the wrong direction?" he asked. He looked and felt slightly concerned that his unbeatable good deed was turning slowly into an extremely challenging one as well. "Albert Road is round the corner in the other direction." Reply came there none.

"You're not really dressed for a cloudburst are you?" he further suggested but Peggy had clammed up and again there was no response to his question. Horace took the opportunity surreptitiously to look Peggy up and down whilst Melanie and Emily sat either side of her and took a hand each as the rain began to hammer down on the ornate tiled roof above them.

"I've 'eard of cats an' dogs but this is more like elephants an'... whatever," Sonny exclaimed as he patted his pocket and wondered if the supermarket sold umbrellas.

Peggy was dressed in what Horace would later describe to his mother as old people's clothes - faded blouse and skirt, probably bought many years ago but still in regular use - but what did surprise him, apart from the lack of anything waterproof, was the fact that she was wearing on her feet a pair of faded pink fluffy slippers. Her footwear hadn't passed Sonny by either but unlike Horace he was going to mention it.

"D'ya normally wear yer slippers out?" asked Sonny.

"They are worn out," said the lady.

"I think what he means is," said Melanie looking down at the focus of the debate, "are they normally worn out?"

"They only get worn out once then they stay worn out until someone buys me a new pair," said Peggy irritably. Sonny raised his eyes to the lychgate roof as Melanie smiled and rephrased Sonny's question again.

"I think what Sonny is asking is, 'Are your slippers your normal choice of footwear for when you're outside your house?'" asked Melanie.

"No," said Peggy.

"Well, that's a relief," said Edward. "So why are you wearing them out today?"

"I don't know," said the lady. "I suppose because my son wouldn't put my shoes on for me." Horace's ears bristled at the mention of a relative. They were finally getting somewhere.

"And where's your son now?" Horace asked cautiously.

"At my home, I think."

"Your home?"

"Yes."

"Does he know you're out?" asked Emily, sounding grateful that they were seemingly about to solve the mystery.

"I don't know." Emily shrugged her shoulders as Horace sighed.

"I think," said Archie, putting into words what the others were thinking, "that despite the downpour, someone needs

163

to go round to number twelve Albert Road and get Peggy's son to come and collect her." Charlie pounced.

"Off you go Archie," he said decisively.

"I don't have a coat," complained Archie.

"No one has a coat," said Edward.

"But at least ya not wearin' slippers," said Sonny, "an' ya 'ave no good deeds under ya belt so scoot!" Archie immediately did as he was told. He normally did when Sonny was giving the command. He felt, although he never said anything, that he always had a choice even though the decision that he took was always the one that Sonny had suggested - or ordered. Archie trudged out into the pouring rain towards Albert Road muttering to himself.

After ten long minutes Archie returned, soaked to the skin and keen to point out that he had done not a good deed but an "exceptional" one that in his opinion was the equivalent of a month's worth of normal ones. He was ready to meet the inevitable Sonny challenge and the rain had spurred him on to respond. "No chance," said Sonny. "All you've done is walk round the corner an' back an' do a bit of detective work. That's one good deed only and one day at the most, that's all."

"It's pouring with rain," said Archie trying not to sound too confrontational - and succeeding only too well.

"Should've run then," said Sonny dismissively. "One day Arch, that's all."

"Okay," said Archie, even though he was twice Sonny's size.

"Stuff the good deed," said Charlie irritably, "did you get anyone to answer the door?"

"No, I didn't," Archie conceded, grateful for the opportunity to disengage with Sonny. "I rang the two bells and knocked on the door very loudly so if anyone was in they must've been deaf not to hear me. I even tried the house either side also but there was no answer at any of them."

"Is you son a little deaf Peggy?" asked Melanie considerately.

"No," Peggy replied, "but he may be in the bath. He sometimes has a long bath. He likes to have a bath. When I can't find him he'll probably be in the bath."

"Was he having a bath when you came out?"

"I don't know."

"Was the door red?" asked Edward.

"Yes, very," said Archie.

"Come on," said Horace finally as he looked out from under their protective shelter. "The rain is easing off and we can at least get Peggy back to her house and then decide what next to do."

"She's going to get very wet feet," said Archie peremptorily.

"Then lend her your trainers," said Charlie.

"No," said Archie before noticing that Sonny was staring at him. "Oh, okay then."

On the crawl back past the vets' to Peggy's supposed home Horace asked her what would happen when her son had finished his bath and came downstairs to find her missing. "He will probably come out in his car and drive around looking for me," she suggested.

"Okay," said Horace, thinking that he might at last be getting somewhere once more and keen to keep the momentum going. "What sort of car does he have?"

"A black Range Rover I think but I don't really know."

"No, I don't suppose you do," said Horace under his breath.

"I do know, it's just that I can't remember," Peggy assured Horace as he at last realised that she wasn't at all deaf although that was the least of his problems. He hadn't completely forgotten that he had some lamb chops to purchase and time was getting on.

Eventually the Ravens reached Albert Road, a row of large Victorian terraced houses glistening from the downpour that had coated them in warm rain and that were now bathed in sunshine after the clouds had finally moved on. As the unlikely octet made its way slowly down the road Peggy's red front door came into view. Fortunately there was a small open porch and so Horace was able to seat Peggy down once more whilst the youngsters took stock of the situation. Horace repeated Archie's action in ringing the two bells and knocking loudly but there was still no response. Whilst waiting to see if anyone would come to the door Emily told Peggy that she had a lovely front garden. It was small but full of many varieties of colourful flowers. "Do you do the gardening Peggy?" Melanie asked.

"No, that's my son," she replied and for the first time since the Ravens had made her acquaintance Peggy smiled.

"This may seem a silly question," said Horace, "But do you have a key?"

"No," said Peggy firmly.

"Or maybe you don't know?" Horace suggested.

"I do know and no I don't." said Peggy even more firmly. Horace began to think that maybe Peggy wasn't quite as batty as he had first thought.

"So how did you get out?" he queried.

"I don't know," she replied. Horace sighed yet again. Two steps forwards, one step back.

"Do you have any friends in this road?" Emily asked. Horace was not the only one beginning to wonder what to do next. He had been taught first aid and could deal with cuts, bruises, faints, hypothermia, vomiting and all manner of minor and even some major medical events apart from simply telephoning for an ambulance but where the person in need didn't appear to have a particular medical emergency no one was exactly sure what the next thing to do would be on any plan of action that they didn't have anyway.

"I have a friend at number seven," said Peggy out of the blue pointing further down the road.

"That's the wrong way," said Archie. "That way the numbers go up not down. You must mean the other direction. The way that we've just come."

"No, it's that way," Peggy insisted.

"Go and knock at number seven," Sonny instructed Archie.

"I think I will just go and try number seven to see if anyone is in," said Archie decisively without looking at Sonny as he sped off back down the road. He returned shortly with news of yet another house with no one in.

"Do you 'ave a back door?" asked Sonny all of a sudden.

"Yes, I do," said Peggy.

"I can't see it," said Edward. "All the houses are stuck together."

"They're not *all* stuck together you twot," said Sonny irritably. "Every now and then there's like an alleyway like down the road a bit so people can get round the back of their 'ouse. They don't get used much but they're useful for um..."

"How do you know that?" asked Edward disdainfully.

"Burglars," suggested Archie.

"Bin men," said Sonny.

"Did you come out of your back door Peggy?" asked Melanie gently.

"She won't know," lamented Horace.

"Yes," said Peggy.

"Thank goodness for that," said Sonny. "I'll go an' 'ave a look."

"Don't leave any fingerprints Sonny," Charlie called out after him with a grin as he shuffled off down the road, "especially near the bathroom and the body!"

No sooner had Sonny disappeared past an overgrown buddleia in a neighbouring front garden in search of a side alley than a young lady with small child in tow came staggering down the road from the opposite direction. She was laden with shopping bags. She stopped by number twelve's gate and stared at the sight of six scruffy youngsters and their charge. She put down her bags, opened the gate and walked up the short path. "Are you okay Peggy?" she asked, ignoring the Ravens. She took her hand and gave it a gentle squeeze. The Ravens sighed.

"We found her outside The Workshed," said Horace sounding a bit too much like a policeman.

"Oh Peggy!" said the lady somewhat taken aback but making eye contact with no one but Peggy. "Surely not!"

"She doesn't have a key and she thinks she may've come out of the back door," suggested Edward.

"Hayley," said the lady to her daughter, "you stay here with the children and I'll go round the back and check." As she walked off in the direction that Sonny had gone Charlie looked at Hayley and scoffed, "If we're children what does that make you?"

"We're all children 'til we're married," Hayley countered as she skipped up the path and took Peggy's hand. Peggy smiled again and for a split second Edward had the irresistible urge to run away now that an adult and a proper child appeared to be taking control. Unfortunately he knew that he had yet to do a good deed and Horace was already a long way out in front. As he stood leaning on the gate, his mind in turmoil, wondering whether to just leave on his own or try and take some of the others with him, the lady reappeared.

"The back door is locked but a tiny window is open. Too small for an old lady like you to climb out of Peggy!" she suggested.

"Hmm," murmured Horace. "But not too small for a young boy like Sonny to climb in." The lady gave Horace a puzzled look.

"Did you see another child round the back?" Horace asked. The lady hadn't.

"I do have one idea though," the lady said. "Peggy, does your friend still have a key to your house?"

"Yes," she said.

"Remind me, what number does she live at?"

"Number seven," said Peggy pointing in the wrong direction.

"Number seven's the other way," said Archie smugly.

"Yes I know," said the lady, "but I think I know which house it is." Once more Hayley was left in the company of the Ravens whilst her mother went to investigate. Again she returned after a few minutes, this time with another elderly lady who was waving a small bunch of keys in the air.

"Success!" said Hayley gently punching the air. "Here comes Mildred."

"What number are you?" asked Horace of the other elderly lady as she reached number twelve.

"Number seventeen," said Mildred.

"Ahhh!" said Horace. "Just one digit out."

"And half a street," complained Archie.

"At least I think I'm number seventeen," said Mildred.

Horace gave their and Peggy's saviour a long and laborious rundown as to how her friend and neighbour came to be sitting in her porch with six youngsters. There was much "ooing" and "oh my goodness" and a sympathetic smile each time the son was mentioned. Eventually Horace arrived at, "and now you're here fortunately," which was a cue for Mildred to work her way past the Ravens and put a key in one of the locks.

"Just one thing," said Horace. "Peggy kept talking about her son and I'm a bit concerned that he's driving around Chislehurst desperately trying to find his mother. She keeps mentioning him and she must love him very much and be quite worried as to what he's imagining has happened to her when actually she's perfectly safe at home if not exactly in it..."

Mildred left the key in the lock to put a hand gently on Horace's shoulder. She turned him gently round so that he wasn't facing his temporary charge. "I need to break some bad news to you so take a deep breath. Everything's not quite what it seems with Peggy. She's very old you know and not all there. So if you're ready for this I'm afraid to tell you..." Mildred's voice fell to barely a whisper, "... that her son died over twenty years ago. She's never got over it; it's as if he's constantly in her thoughts and her conversations." Had Mildred spoken any quieter no one would have been able to hear what she was saying, apart from one. Peggy jumped to her feet.

"He's not dead!" she protested then sat down again and began to weep. Melanie and Emily joined in more in shock than in empathy for someone whom they had just met.

"Let's get you inside," said Mildred to Peggy gently and turned the key in the lock before repeating the process with the other. She twisted the door knob and pushed.

"Oh hallo!" Mildred gasped peering into the dark and dingy hallway. "Who are you?"

"I'm Sonny the Sumerian slayer! The bathroom's free!" Sonny yelled waving his spear in the air. Mildred shrieked.

"My son!" screamed Peggy. Horace put his head in his hands.

"I think it's time to go home," Horace said eventually once Peggy and Mildred were indoors and Sonny was back out. The Ravens made their excuses and disappeared back up the road. Horace didn't even mention that he thought that he had won the good deed prize for the day due to his potentially saving the life of a human being rather than a mere cat or pigeon. The Ravens said "goodbye" to each other in the high street and went off in different directions, Horace via the supermarket. No one had a particularly warm welcome when they arrived home with the response generally being, "When I say 'a minute' I don't mean three hours!" until the story of Peggy was told and then all was well. Sonny, however, preferred to recount the pigeon adventure and the cat rescue, conveniently forgetting to mention that in repatriating Felix he had stranded two young children at the top of an oak tree. He also somehow forgot to mention that he had ninety pounds in his pocket, not all earned. Archie had to explain why he was wearing pink slippers.

Horace returned home with no chops as there were none left by the time that he finally managed to get to the butchers' counter. He didn't have a rabbit either. He thought of bringing home chips with the excuse that it was an "'artificial intelligence substitution' 'cos it's only one letter different," but didn't tell his mother that, although he did tell her about Peggy until she cried. That made him feel a lot better for it meant that he had, in his words, "an emotionally valid excuse." His mother did venture to ask him why he was caked in mud down his front. "It was Melanie," Horace said simply. He couldn't understand why his mother said, "Don't be so silly Horace. I know Melanie well enough to know that she is the last person that would be responsible for your getting in such a mess and how have you managed to come back with a different bag for life? I liked the last one: it was a present." Horace didn't argue; there was no point.

"Whatever mummy," he said quietly.

Melanie's shopping trip went better than expected. Her mother had told her it was too late until Melanie explained that Bluewater was open until nine o'clock so they went there after Melanie had showered and changed. "I was a damsel in a dress helping a dame in distress," she told her mother. The pigeon episode wasn't mentioned either although her mother did have a look at the pictures she had taken that included plenty of cats, birds and trees and as a result suggested that in her opinion her daughter had spent the afternoon on a nature trail. Melanie thought that the little pigeon saga would come out in due course and indeed it did, but not the way that anyone could have anticipated.

\*\*\*

If there had been a shortage of good deeds in the previous days, "pigeon day," as it came to be known, certainly meant that several of the Ravens were able to claim that they had fully made up any possible deficit, none more so than Horace who, in "saving an old lady's life," as he put it, although Edward told him that all he had done was walk someone home, and "even then you went the wrong way first," as if to deflect attention away from his individual lack of recent good deeds, maintained that his actions had absolved him from any further good deeds for the next year. Edward eventually went quiet. Charlie just kept quiet from the start.

The only fallout, albeit minor, was that Melanie had to explain to her father why she needed an advance on her allowance before the end of the month. Ever, mostly, truthful she told him that she had had, "an unexpected veterinary bill." Her father was satisfied with this explanation as he assumed that she had had to have Pitkin seen to until Melanie let slip that she had incurred the expense at Premier Vets.

"I thought that they did cats and other small animals," he queried.

"And pigeons," said Melanie. "They do pigeons and apparently our sick pigeon will live to a great old age once Mr Wendell has finished with him." Wincing she told her father how much Percy had cost.

"Hardly darling. Wild pigeons only live for around four years. For the amount of your veterinary bill I would have expected you to tell me that you had put down a deposit on the business whereas the only deposit that appears to have been made is by the vet who appears to have sh... deposited all over you," said her father. "Let's hope he's doing a first-class job."

\*\*\*

The Ravens congregated under the oak tree on the common several times over the next few weeks but Saturday the seventeenth was the day they were all waiting for. They had hardly sat down in its shade after lunch when Horace said, "Come on. Up we get. Let's go and see Mr Wendell and see how Percy's doing." He had George's pet carrier in one hand and was keen to fill it with a pigeon that had been restored to full health. "If only George knew," Horace thought to himself. "Gosh," he said absentmindedly out aloud. The Ravens looked at him. Horace couldn't believe it! When he wanted attention he didn't get it yet when something accidently slipped from his lips everyone stared at him. He felt obliged to explain.

"I was just thinking a great idea that people have so much trouble getting their pets, especially cats but probably dogs and rabbits and things, into a pet carrier when going to the vets' and sometimes we have to push George quite hard but imagine if you had a picture of a pigeon at the back of the carrier. They would launch themselves in with no fuss at all."

"An' bash their 'ead an' knock themselves out then ya would 'ave to go to the vets' and say that not only are ya there 'cos of whatever reason ya are but also 'cos ya pet is unconscious so not so great an idea 'Orace," said Sonny.

They chose not to walk through the woods lest they chanced upon more potential good deeds situations and they had mostly had their fill for the time being. The walk down the pavement was relatively short and executed in something of a rush, certainly at a pace that Peggy would never have been able to match. Arriving at Premier Vets Horace took a deep breath and opened the door. The Ravens filed in. It wasn't until Sonny appeared that the receptionist acknowledged them although she did throw Melanie a nervous glance. "If you would like to pass that over," she said, spying Horace's pet carrier, "I'll go and find your pigeon."

"How is he? Can we see Mr Wendell?" asked Horace nervously.

"He's been a model patient," said the receptionist taking hold of the carrier. "I wish they could all be like him. Now if you would excuse me for a moment I'll go and pop him in this for you."

When she returned she apologised that Mr Wendell was rather busy and so unable to see them. Horace said that it was fine if Percy was fine and Mary assured him that he was. Horace took hold of the carrier, glanced inside then passed it to Sonny who looked a little more intensely. "Mr Wendell says that you're to take Percy immediately to where you found him and release him. Pigeons hate being kept in confinement and want to be free. Er, now?" she said sounding ever so slightly as if she were in a bit of a rush.

"That's funny," said Sonny in no rush at all, "'cos mostly that's where racing pigeons are. In confinement. In a cage and quite 'appy. So much so that when you take 'em off somewhere an' release 'em they fly straight home to their cage. So what does Mr Wendell say to that?"

"Er I don't know Sonny," the receptionist stammered.

"Then why don't you go and ask him?" Sonny suggested in a way that was more of a command than a request.

"Er, because he's um very busy," said the receptionist all the while wishing that Sonny would stop staring at her.

"Or is he listening behind that wall?" Sonny suggested as he jabbed his finger over the receptionist's shoulder.

"Come on," said Edward tugging at Sonny's sleeve, alarmed at his friend's rather aggressive questioning. "Let's go and release Percy so that he can go back to his friends. He's probably missing them." But Sonny was going nowhere.

"Too busy counting his money I expect," said Sonny with a tone of voice that had changed from relatively benign to cross to threatening. The Ravens began to wriggle uncomfortably.

"I...I don't know what you mean," the receptionist spluttered. "Now if you would excuse me..." She stood up and made to go through the door behind her.

"I'll tell you what I mean," said Sonny slamming the pet carrier on the counter harder than was expedient for a recovering feathered friend occupant. "Your boss is a connivin' thievin' git and do you know why?"

"N...no... er... why?" the receptionist mumbled.

"'Cos this 'ere in 'Orace's carrier," growled Sonny stabbing at the grill, "ain't Percy." At this suggestion the receptionist turned round and disappeared, running, into the back of the surgery.

"I'll see if Mr Wendell is free," she said over her shoulder.

Just as the Ravens were readying themselves for a bit of a wait Mr Wendell appeared - in far less time than it would have taken for the receptionist to go out to the back, interrupt Mr Wendell from his busyness, tell Mr Wendell what the problem was for him to decide whether to show his face or not and finally to emerge. He leant across the receptionist's desk and gripped the counter top with both hands. Smiling obsequiously and looking at Horace he asked him what the matter was. "I'm pleased to say that Percy has made a full and speedy recovery. If you like I will release him for you now. He really doesn't like to be caged. Or. Er. Carriered. Er, ha, ha?"

"Tell me Mr Wendell," said Melanie the aspiring journalist taking her cue from Sonny as she pulled out her notepad and pencil, "how many pigeons have you cared for over the last month or so?"

"I'm not sure if that's any business of yours young lady," said Mr Wendell firmly.

"You see, I don't expect you see many and you certainly won't have had many being admitted. It's just that there is a problem with Percy not being who you think he is and for that reason I would like to get to the bottom of who we have in the carrier. After all, we wouldn't want someone to think that the pigeon that you have given them back is the one that we have and instead they have taken Percy home. Getting pigeons muddled up can't be that easy I presume? In any event..."

"YOU HAVE PERCY, UNDERSTAND," growled Mr Wendell.

"No mate," said Sonny with a wag of his finger. "You 'ave Percy and we 'ave someone else."

"No you don't," said Mr Wendell. "You are obviously mistaken."

"I am NOT mistaken!" Sonny shouted across the counter. "I don't forget a bird. Percy 'ad a jagged white collar which was most unusual but this one 'as a more normal collar. And what's more you owe Mel 'ere a few quid for losing 'er bird. AND compensation. AND, um, other stuff." Mr Wendell did not reply to Sonny. He watched Melanie not look up, so intent was she to get everything down in writing.

"What are you doing Melanie?" he asked finally.

"I'm writing a report about a dodgy vet who lost a much loved pigeon that was injured or, more likely, had him for his tea having fleeced a young girl of over one thousand pounds and then substituted another pigeon that he trapped on the common and took back to his surgery." Mr Wendell scowled.

"Who do you think you are, chief reporter for *Chislehurst Village News*?" asked Mr Wendell now glaring fixatedly at Melanie.

"Something like that," she said as she produced one of her glossy colourful business cards from a pocket and placed it on the counter. Mr Wendell inspected it without picking it up. He tapped his head gently with his fingers as if he were trying to encourage his brain into formulating a speedy response.

"I suppose," he said slowly, "there's always the possibility of a mix up, albeit remote. Still, I did the work on Percy so he's back to tiptop condition wherever he is." Melanie closed up her notepad and made for the door.

"I'm pleased that we don't have a misunderstanding on our hands. Good bye Melanie," Mr Wendell said cheerily.

"I won't be gone long Mr Wendell," said Melanie without turning round as she opened the door. "Just long enough to 'phone my report through to *Village News* and to inform the police of a huge fraud that has just taken place involving a substantial amount of money."

"You stupid little girl," Mr Wendell snarled aggressively. "What are you going to do? How are you going to prove that this pigeon isn't Percy? You'll be laughed out of the police station. No one's going to believe your stupid little friend here who's probably going to suggest that we put on a pigeon identity parade. How are you going to describe your Percy to the police? 'Er, greyish feathers mostly with a beak and that goes 'coo roo-c'too-coo?'"

"No," said Melanie calmly patting her camera. "I'm going to show them the photos that I took of him from the moment that we helped him out of the gutter until the moment we brought him in here. Then I'll take some photos of what we have now. Either Percy isn't Percy or you've been performing some sort of advanced avian cosmetic surgery."

"Just a moment," said Mr Wendell now in a more conciliatory tone. He came round to the other side of the counter, walked over to the door and pushed it shut. "What about if I give you a small amount of compensation as a result of a little misunderstanding? Shall we say a large box of sweets?"

"What about my money?" asked Melanie who noticed that that the vet was sweating profusely. "I paid you a huge amount of money and you said that you would nurse Percy back to full health."

"I did nurse him back to full health," Mr Wendell protested. "I still had all the costs even though he seems to have been released by mistake."

"No mistake mate," said Sonny walking over to the door. "You owe Mel 'ere a grand plus VAT, plus compensation, plus an apology plus other stuff that I don't know about or your name's in the papers."

"Compensation for what?" asked Mr Wendell frowning.

"For losing a prize racing pigeon," said Sonny accusingly.

"Sounds to me like blackmail." Sonny was momentarily silenced until Edward came to his aid.

"You can't legally blackmail if you're under eighteen," he said with authority.

"And h... how much would this compensation be?" asked Mr Wendell meekly.

"Another grand," said Sonny menacingly.

"I think that's a bit over the top," complained the vet.

"You're right," agreed Sonny. "But if we go to the papers we'll be able to get well over the top and you'll be locked up." Mr Wendell scowled.

"I'll get my cheque book."

"Cash," said Sonny. "The Post Office is open. And you can keep your pigeon and 'ave 'im for ya supper like ya probably 'ave already wiv poor Percy."

\*\*\*

Outside the vets' the Ravens were in joyant mood. "Well done Edward," said Melanie who couldn't stop smiling. Her bank card had been recredited in full even though she hadn't taken a single Percy photo and Sonny had another large bulge in his trousers which he patted satisfyingly.

"Edward the lawyer," said Archie grinning.

"Edward the liar," said Sonny. "You can blackmail at any age. And it's very serious."

"Edward the bluffer," said Edward as he momentarily basked in the adulation from at least two of his pals. He felt that he had joined the "good deed done" side of the Ravens.

"But Mr Wendell wasn't going to know," he continued. "Mostly it's how you say stuff. 'He speaks as one who has authority.' That's what it's about. I can't remember who said that. Some dodgy blackmailer probably. But it's quite true."

"Jesus," said Archie. "It was Jesus."

"Near enough Ed," said Sonny. But Edward had moved on.

"Let's go up to the common and divide this money up. Anybody know what a grand divided by seven is?"

"'Ang on a moment," said Sonny. "I got this extra under me own steam. Why do I have to divide it up?"

"'Cos you do," said Edward.

"A not very even amount," suggested Emily. "It's a pity there aren't six of us 'cos then it would be, um, easier. But what are we going to do with it all? Why don't we do a good deed and give it to someone?"

"What like buying indulgences?" suggested Melanie but no one knew what she was talking about so didn't respond.

"Plenty of sweets," suggested Archie.

"I might go into Mr Lillie's and buy another penknife," said Horace, "after the hacking that Sonny did with my last one on the rope up the oak tree." However the others were still in shock from what Sonny had just pulled off that they were unable to think of anything in particular - which was just as well...

Sonny made to walk back up the high street knowing that the Ravens would be following very closely behind until Melanie stopped in her tracks and said - a little too loudly for one who was an accomplice to a sizeable quantity of cash just a matter of a few feet in front of her,

"Sonny put the money in the pet carrier where we can all see it and I will carry it."

"B...but."

"No 'b...but.' If it wasn't for me and my debit card we wouldn't be in this fortunate position." Sonny looked all round at his friends and quickly realised that no one was on his b... but side. He reached into his pocket and slowly and carefully pulled out the wodge and grudgingly put it in the carrier that Horace then locked shut and handed to Melanie. Horace turned to walk off when he suddenly halted and asked, as much to himself as his friends, in an almost surreal tone,

"Am I dreaming?"

"What's the matter Horace?" asked Melanie who felt a cold shiver running down her back as her body literally responded to Horace's spine-chilling stare.

"Look," he said, pointing towards The Workshed. "Who's that holding onto the handrail?"

"Oh no," sighed Archie as he rather dramatically drooped his shoulders. "It's Peggy. Again!"

"At least she has some shoes on this time," commented Sonny staring at her feet. "And presumably 'er own."

"At least we know where she lives and where we can find a key," said Horace casting off the macabre physiognomy and breaking into a smile as he ambled over to her with a much more animated spring in his step than he had on the previous occasion.

"Hi Peggy!" he called out as he drew near.

As the Ravens followed on behind she raised one hand to wave but then her legs started to wobble. Horace felt that he should run but then his legs started to wobble as well. "It's okay Horace," she said once he reached her. His arms were waving in sympathy but also because he didn't know quite where to put them - certainly nowhere near Peggy's grabbing hand.

"But Peggy, I thought that you were supposed to be staying indoors. I can't believe you've escaped again. The problem is we really don't have time to walk you all the way home," Horace lamented all the while wondering whether Peggy had had a bit of a sore throat the first time that they had met such was the near normal volume that she was now speaking at.

"Oh, it's okay Horace. I don't need any help today. You see my son is with me. He's in The Workshed buying me a lawnmower so that he can cut the grass. My existing one is past it, a bit like me, and so I have come out with him to get a new one but I'm waiting here whilst he sorts it all out." Horace turned to look at the Ravens and exhaled deeply.

"What are we going to do?" he mouthed to his friends. He turned back to Peggy who was still holding on to the rail, smiling benignly.

"Peggy, about your son. Do you mind if I just pop into The Workshed and speak to him?" said Horace turning detective.

"No, not at all," she replied. "In fact there's no need to because here he comes."

Emerging out through the door of The Workshed was a smartly dressed middle-aged man with two young children in tow. "This should be interesting," thought Horace. He walked up to the man, and pointing at Peggy, asked before she could say anything, "Excuse me but do you know this lady?"

The man looked Horace up and down and then looked at Peggy. He chuckled to himself more than Horace thought was necessary then said with an authority that took him somewhat aback,

"Actually I've known her all my life. And how come? Because she's my mother. Why?" Horace went immediately and more than he had done on the beach in Bournemouth on the occasion when his mother had forgotten to apply any suncream, very, very red.

"Oh, it's n...nothing," he stammered. "It's just that we rescued her the other day when it was pouring with rain and..." But the man was no longer taking any notice for his attention had been demanded by his sons who were staring at Sonny. One suddenly lifted both his hands and, pointing, shouted, "Daddy! Naughty boy!" and daddy looked and frowned then said, more firmly than was normal for most fathers,

"COME HERE YOU!" Sonny turned and made as if to run but then thought better of it, not because of any altruistic desire to accept his punishment but because of the thought of his leaving his financial share behind which he would probably never see again were he to scarper.

"What's the matter Sonny?" Edward asked. "Do you know this man?"

"I'm afraid I do, sort of," admitted Sonny lamely, by now assuming an all-too-regular Horace stance and staring at his feet. "The last time I saw 'im which in fact was also the first time I saw 'im, I was giving 'is two kids a rather excitin' ride up an oak tree.

"Oh," said Archie.

"Yes, indeed, 'oh,'" said the man. "And would you like to know what happened?"

"No," said Sonny hastily knowing full well that he was about to find out anyway.

"With one hand holding the rope I had to somehow, with my other hand, get my 'phone out of my pocket and dial nine nine nine. When the operator who answered asked me whether I wanted fire, police or ambulance I said, 'I think I need all three and you might as well send mountain rescue as well.' Fortunately the first three came very quickly. The fire brigade sent up the largest ladder you have ever seen in your short lives and the police went off on an unsuccessful hunt for you whilst the paramedics checked Peter and Paul over. Fortunately they were unharmed but my wallet wasn't and do you know why?" No one said a word. "Because if it's anything other than a fire then the fire brigade charge and do you know how much they charged? Just under one thousand pounds."

The man suddenly made an unexpected lurch towards Sonny and grabbed his arm. "So do you know what I'm going to do now?" he growled. "I'm going to march you home and I'm going to tell your father what you've been up to and he's not going to be very impressed when I tell him and he's going to be even less impressed when I tell him how much he's going to have to reimburse me to keep me from going back to the police." The man looked at Sonny and frowned. Sonny was still looking at his feet.

"You don't seem very bothered. I would be bothered if I were you. When I see your father..."

"Well you ain't goin' see my father."

"Why not?"

"'Cos 'e's... away," said Sonny finally.

"Then let's go straight to the police station." The man tugged at Sonny's arm.

"What yer goin' do with yer kids? Leave 'em on the pavement wiv yer batty mother?"

"If I have to," he replied. Such was the conviction with which he spoke that Sonny believed that he actually meant what he said.

"If you want t' get me to the police station then you'll 'ave to drag me there, " said Sonny menacingly.

"I'm not letting you go," the man said. Melanie had heard enough.

"I think that I speak for all here present in saying that we would rather you didn't take Sonny to the police station," she said gently, "however you intend to get him there, and that it would probably save a load of argument if you take what's inside the pet carrier."

"I don't want a cat! I want reimbursing!" the man exclaimed.

"If you care to look inside the pet carrier I think that you will find what you're looking for," said Edward holding out the palm of one hand in the direction of the carrier. The man went over to Melanie, took the carrier from her and peered in through the grill. Then he frowned.

"Do you normally wander around the streets with a load of cash in a cat carrier?" he asked incredulously.

"Only when we've been repaid for a poorly pigeon," said Melanie. The man sighed as he reached inside the carrier and pulled out the wodge before letting go of Sonny's arm.

"That should do it," he exclaimed.

"In that case, can I have my bag for life back please?" asked Horace chirpily.

\*\*\*

The Ravens made their way once more slowly back up the hill, avoiding the woods that had recently been the source of so much drama and anguish. "So where are we with the good deeds?" Horace asked finally. The others groaned.

"It's just too much of an effort sometimes," complained Archie. "I think that we should just stick to doing our best and that's that. If nothing comes along for us to do our best at then that's that." By their silence it was assumed by all that everyone was in agreement.

The Ravens started to split off as they neared the top of the hill. Their conversation had ended with a discussion about curry and it was making them feel peckish. Sonny continued alongside the woods. He was feeling particularly aggrieved at how the day had gone. He didn't mind not having much money but he did mind having it and then losing it, however just the circumstances. The afternoon was drawing to a close and his thoughts were also turning to dinner but not curry. He was feeling quite hungry after the day's exertions but he knew that there wasn't much back at home to eat and no chance of being able to afford a curry. His mother wasn't working at present despite her best efforts. He stopped outside Mrs Thomas' house and sat on her low wall. He sniffed and stifled a tear.

Suddenly there was a loud scream behind him. He stood up, turned round and instinctively ran up Mrs Thomas' path. The scream was so clear that it could not have come from inside the house Sonny surmised. He clambered over the side gate and into the back garden where he found Mrs Thomas standing by her back door with her hands to her mouth. He hardly recognised her. Gone were the cardigan and slacks - replaced by an elegant purple silk dress with matching shoes in places of wellies. Her hair had been tidied up into a stylish bun with hanging ringlets. At the end of the garden Felix lying flat in the grass looking ready to pounce. Between them lay a great big fat - motionless - pigeon. "Oh Sonny! Do something!" she cried. "Felix has caught a pigeon! Oh he's so naughty! Oh poor pigeon! Poor, poor pigeon! I told him to drop it but he's going to attack again at any moment. Oh Sonny! I hope it's not dead! Can you do something?" Sonny walked over to the pigeon and knelt down beside it on the grass.

"Come an' 'ave a look Mrs Thomas," he said. "It looks like Felix has caught a very expensive racing pigeon. You can tell 'cos of the tag..."

"I'm not coming near it!" Mrs Thomas sobbed. "I hate flappy things! Can you do something? Please Sonny."

"Of course I can," said Sonny calmly as he inspected the fat pigeon with its jagged white collar, unusual colouring and broken wing all of which Sonny noted he had seen not long ago. Contrary to Mrs Thomas' comment there was no "flappy" to be seen. In fact there was absolutely no movement of any description to be witnessed. "It'll be worth someone's while getting 'im fixed. You don't want t'be caught with an injured racing pigeon in yer garden especially if yer cat is the culprit. I can whip 'im down to the vets' down the road if ya like. Anonymously of course. They're very good with pigeons..."

"Oh yes, if you could please," said Mrs Thomas without hesitating as she continued to blub. "How much do you think it will be?" Sonny took a deep intake of breath. He could hardly believe his luck!

"It'll be around a grand I'ld say."

"Er, how much?"

"A grand. A thousand. Just be grateful that it's only one wing 'cos two would be double." Horace looked more purposefully at Mrs Thomas than she realised. "You see, the fing is, birds are a bit more, um, complicated. It's not like a cat with a bite, it's far more..."

"Yes, yes. I realise that. Felix costs enough for his jabs. I'll just go and find some cash. Can you look keep an eye on Felix while I pop upstairs and find some money and a box?"

"Plus VAT." Mrs Thomas turned and looked at Sonny.

"I'm sorry. I missed that."

"The vet. He'll charge VAT on the bill."

"Oh yes, of course."

Mrs Thomas returned a few minutes later with a shoe box and a large envelope stuffed full of notes which she handed over to Sonny. "I think you'll find that's enough in there," she said uncertainly, "I'm a bit short of ready cash at the moment. You will be pleased to know that I've just taken on a new daily. She came round today and we got on like a house on fire. The thing is, I gave her a cash "hello." A bit odd I know but I didn't want to fail to secure her services. She starts on Monday." Sonny peeked inside at the jumble of notes.

"Oh, that looks fine Mrs Thomas. Leave it to me. Now let me have the box and once I've poked a small hole in it for air I'll pop Per... the pigeon in it and go straight back down... I mean straight down to the vets'."

"Oh Sonny, you are such a good boy. Does your mother always tell you what a good boy you are? I hope she does. Rescuing cats and now pigeons." But Sonny wasn't paying much attention. He was busy putting Percy in his coffin.

"It's okay Mrs Thomas, he's still breathing," said Sonny once he had replaced the lid. "Would you like to have a last look at him before I go down the road?"

"No I most certainly do not!" Mrs Thomas exclaimed. "Take him away and make sure that he's nursed, or whatever vets do, back to health and then go and release him as far away from my back garden as you are able." Sonny nodded his compliance although he had no intention of doing anything of the sort. His dinner was assured. He was also going to have curry now. Or pigeon. Maybe both; he hadn't yet decided. What he had decided was that he was going to leave Mrs Thomas' house, start to walk in the direction of the vets' but once out of sight he would cross over into the woods and resume his journey home with over a thousand pounds back in his pocket and no one to share it with.

Mrs Thomas saw him round to the front of the house where she even gave him a quick hug and thanked him once more. "You are a little star Sonny. Thank you. Thank you for your help. I wish more children could be like you."

"No, thank you Mrs Thomas," said Sonny with a cheesy grin all the while wondering what the world would be like if it comprised mostly Sonnys.

"Now off you go as my brother is about to turn up. He's taking me on a rare trip out to dinner this evening with our mother. She's very old you know. He's also bringing his two sons, my nephews. I haven't seen him for a few weeks. The boys have suffered some sort of trauma and he's going to tell me all about it. Oh look, here he is now. You might as well say 'Hello.'"

Sonny looked up and saw a black Range Rover come to a halt at the side of the road. Horace could vaguely make out an old lady in the front and a man driving. As for the two boys in the back, they were already staring at Sonny and poking their father in the back. "An' yer nephews' names?" Sonny enquired.

"'Peter' and 'Paul,' after the founders of Christianity in Rome. They're a couple of lovely boys, just like their father. I hope they haven't been through too much. They... Sonny! Wait! Come back! Wait! You're going the wrong way! Sonny! SONNY! What ever's the matter?"

But Sonny was not going to wait. He was not going to come back. He was not going the wrong way. He was going straight home and he wasn't going to stop running until he arrived, vaulted the garden gate, rushed up the path, opened the back door, gone inside and double locked it, dumped the coffin on the kitchen table, ran upstairs and hidden under his bed. For Mrs Thomas would far too soon be finding out exactly what the matter was without his input.

***

Sonny's mother's pigeon pie that evening was delicious even though the pie was a bit short on pigeon. As she put her knife and fork down, having ingested the evidence, she enquired of Sonny as to the circumstances that lead to a pigeon appearing on her kitchen table in a shoe box.

"It's a bit of a long story mum," said Sonny in all truthfulness. "Would you like to 'ear it?"

"Not really," said his mother.

"As you wish," said Sonny with a grin. "Maybe I'll tell you tomorrow over a curry."

"Curry?" repeated Sonny's little sister Misty. "I love curry. Can we afford curry? I want king prawn butterfly, a chicken lashslick, a darka tal and a lemonade. Then I'll have a..." Sonny opened his mouth to confirm that the family was temporarily solvent but his mother beat him to it.

"Yes Misty, we can I'm pleased to say," she replied with a huge smile on her face. After all it was a long time since she had had good news to impart. "I managed to secure an almost full-time job today. I'll be working as a daily. I'll be cleaning and doing household duties. But it's more than that. I'll be shopping, running errands. That sort of thing. It's very well paid. It's with a delightful lady in Prince

Imperial Road called Mrs Thomas. I can see us now having lovely chats together, telling each other about our families. I'm always going to have plenty to say about my family aren't I Sonny? She said that she was very particular who she employs and so I am... what's the matter Sonny? You've gone as white as a sheet?"

## Introduction to Horace Horrise goes to Portugal

*Horace has signed up to go on an international trip with his local scout district. In the meantime he has much to do including generating some extra income so that he can build up his collection of penknives. He thinks that he has found the ideal solution but, as usual, things do not go as planned.*

*Once the trip is underway, Horace decides that he is going to pay a visit to Portugal's premier music event which just happens to be on his campsite's doorstep. Once again, events do not go as expected and Horace finds himself in a situation that even he could not have ever imagined in his wildest dreams.*

*Matters go from bad to worse, but when he throws the campsite into a nocturnal meltdown it looks as though an early bath is the least of his worries, but eventually Horace, in having tried to do his best, ends up somewhere which even he would never have expected.*

Whilst writing "The Adventures of Horace Horrise" I went with a load of scouts from my local district to Portugal. Usually a weekend camp with a dozen young people will throw up one or two ideas so a week in the summer sun with two hundred young people and leaders was going to mean that my notebook was nearly always in use. From the boy who brought his pet rabbit along in his rucksack without anyone knowing to the girl who wondered what sun cream tasted like so decided to find out, passing on the way the individual who pulled out a plug to covertly charge up their 'phone overnight not realising that the plug belonged to the main camp freezer so we all had to have burgers and ice cream for breakfast and then cook everything else before refreezing, the trip was a source of enough material to fill several stories and not just this one with tales, tall tales and even a few true tales starting with this introduction.

After I returned from Portugal I went on a family holiday and sat and wrote "Horace Horrise goes to Portugal." The music festival, O Sol da Caparica, was real enough. We were camping next door and the music went on every night for four nights until the early hours. Some of the older scouts went and sat by our campsite's perimeter fence and with their eyes shut could have been in the midst of it.

The Workshed has featured in earlier stories in this book. It is now closed but as The Workshop it was an Aladdin's cave of anything that could possibly fall under the heading of hardware. I remember one day asking if they stocked carpet gripper rod and going on an exploration of the cellar where a few ancient lengths were located. Everything was stocked from a washer (you could buy such items in units of one) to a ride-on lawn mower.

Sonny doesn't appear in this story as I wrote it before he appeared (for the first time in "The Very Secret Diary of Horace Horrise"). Given what the six Ravens got up to in Portugal without him it's probably just as well.

"Horace Horrise. Household Account." We've all been there.

## Horace Horrise goes to Portugal

"Notices" at 3rd Chislehurst Scouts was normally the signal for much shuffling of feet (without trainers moving) and witty asides (without lips moving) as their scout leader, John, informed the attentive ears (that weren't even really listening) what would be happening over the course of the coming few weeks. Whilst five of the Ravens stood in their patrol finishing off the evening's earlier conversations with only one ear each listening out for any mention of food or drink or adventure, Horace was "all ears" although two was usually the maximum. His attentiveness was amply rewarded. Just as any vestiges of attention was almost completely gone with none of the other scouts even looking at John, preferring instead to plan the straightest route from where they were standing to the scout hut door, he suddenly announced,

"District will shortly be inviting scouts to apply for a place on a trip that is being planned to go to Portugal. There will be just two hundred places available - first come - first served." There was no time to waste. Horace shot his hand into the air.

"Count me in Skip!" he cried. The other scouts stopped their shuffling, whispering and plotting and looked at John then Horace then John once more, wondering, "What have I missed?" as Horace continued,

"So that's one place sorted Skip. Just another one hundred and ninety-nine to go!" he expertly calculated. Maths had always been one of Horace's stronger subjects.

"What's eighty-seven minus forty-three?" one of his teachers had once asked him.

"Less," he had confidently replied.

"Well, thank you Horace," said John who was secretly very pleased that 3rd Chislehurst would be represented on the trip even if it was only going to be by the one boy that they could probably do without.

"However, there's plenty of time. District hasn't even started to think about exactly where we're going to stay yet. They just picked on Portugal because there's a strong scout presence out there."

"Typical, in my opinion Skip. These days it should be easy to find somewhere to stay. I can sort that out for you Skip," said Horace confidently. "I'm sure that with two hundred of us we can take over a huge hotel or something. Shall I start finding out?"

"No Horace," said John firmly. "There's nothing for you to do except wait for the parents' meeting by which time everything will be sorted. They will be told all they need to know and how to apply for those scouts who want to go on the trip."

Horace sighed. He wondered why Skip would mention something before it was time to apply. Normally things happened on a day that had past. It would be like, "Apply now for something that's so just about to happen that it happened yesterday" and then people wonder why no one's turned up and if they have turned up they wouldn't have the permission form because they hadn't yet been given it because they probably hadn't yet been printed or emailed. No, Horace was not going to miss this trip of a young person's lifetime.

The rest of the scouts, meanwhile, had stopped their whispered asides and were listening intently to this John / Horace exchange. The Ravens were particularly desperate to ascertain what Horace had signed up for but not one was going to ask John to repeat himself for they knew what his answer would be,

"A wise man looks, listens and learns, but
A foolish man shuts, shuffles and spurns."

As John announced "To the right, dismissed," instead of the usual exodus through the hut door the Ravens crowded round Horace to find out what they had missed.

"Nothing yet," said Horace magnanimously, "but we need to get our skates on 'cos next year the District is going to Portugal and there's only space for one hundred and ninety-nine and as you know there are thousands of us in this area."

"Where's Portugal?" asked Edward carelessly, knowing full well where it was approximately, but not exactly. However Emily quickly took all the heat from any other response that might have been forthcoming by saying,

"Durhhh! Dimwit! Don't you know where Portugal is?"

"No, not exactly. Near enough but not exactly like I could walk there without a map but I could point you in the direction sort of roughly. Anyway, smarty-pants, if you're so clever, where is it?" Emily looked around and found the other Ravens all looking at her expectantly. There was nowhere for her to hide. Why did she have to open her big mouth? She was going to have to try slowly to talk her way out of the corner that she had just put herself in and hope that in the meantime someone would come to her rescue, not that it was looking very likely at that particular moment.

"It's, well, um, warm in summer and um, well it's on the sea like it's a port..."

"Yeah, yeah," said Edward irritably. "I could've told you that. But where exactly is it, like, what's it near?" There was no hope of escape for Emily. She blurted out as authoritatively as she could,

"It's sort of near Brighton."

"Brighton!" exclaimed Edward, knowing at that moment that he himself was not the biggest dimwit by a long chalk.

"Portugal's nowhere near Brighton. It's sort of attached to Spain somehow, but it's nowhere near Brighton. In any case Portugal's a country, Brighton isn't. Brighton's a place full of men. And a pier."

"I must've been thinking of the wrong Brighton," said Emily lamely.

"The thing is Ravings," said Horace, not wishing to prolong Emily's agony, "I think Skip would like me to find some accommodation and that's what I'm going to do - tomorrow."

\*\*\*

Saturday morning and Horace lost no time in researching a suitable place for the two hundred scouts to stay during the following year's trip. His parents had gone out for a mid-morning coffee at one of twenty or so such establishments in Chislehurst. There were so many coffee shops to choose from that each time they went out they used to play "coffee bingo," the idea being that they would work round and round through the alphabet and go somewhere that had the letter that they were on in its name. Today they were on "F" and, there being no Fs in any of the names, had reverted to Horace's father's "F"avourite which was, oddly enough, the pub. "Oh, I might as well have a pint whilst I'm in here, dear," he would say once he had ordered one at the bar, lest his wife tried to talk him out of it. Nevertheless she still told him that it wasn't coffee to which Mr Horrise explained that Horace had told him that apparently scout leaders refer to beer as "leaders' coffee" although he had no idea neither how Horace would know this nor whether it was even true or not.

As his parents sat together in contented wedded bliss, him with a pint of bitter, her with a glass of Sauvignon Blanc and, so as to maintain the high ground if only by a couple of centimetres, a small coffee, back at home Horace sat at his father's desk and typed "Scouts Portugal" into his laptop. He scrolled down past the sponsored adverts thinking that if they needed to advertise then they probably weren't any good and alighted upon "PNIC - looking after travelling scouts for many years". Horace clicked on the electronic map beside the entry and found himself staring at a long beach south of Lisbon with "PNIC" pinpointed as a large wooded area just behind the beach. He zoomed in a little further and discovered that a short distance away there was a cake shop. "That will do us just fine," he thought to himself and dialled the number next to the PNIC description. After a couple of clicks and a short pause he could hear a ringing sound, not the same as at home, but something was happening. Then there were a couple more clicks and he heard,

"Bom dia." Horace was not sure why someone was calling him a "bombardier".

"No," he replied, "just 'master.'"

"'Master,'" the foreign voice replied. "Where are you telephoning vom?"

"Chislehurst. Where the caves are."

"'Caves?' Like for storing wine?"

"No, not really. They were used in the war for people to hide when bombs were dropping and they had a hospital down there and..."

"Yes. Zis is very interesting but vat do you vant?"

"I live in Holbrook Road, do you know it?"

"No."

"I would like to know whether you have space for two hundred scouts for next summer." The voice laughed.

"'Two hundred?' Is zat all? We 'ave space for two thousand!"

"You have a very big hotel." The voice chuckled.

"Yes, we 'ave very big indeed. Scout 'otel! All ground floor!" and the voice chuckled again. Horace wondered what sort of hotel had space for two thousand, on the ground floor, when he could see only trees on the satellite images. He thought maybe it was an old photo.

"Is your hotel underground?" Horace asked.

"Yes, on the ground. Zat is right!" and the voice chuckled even more. It then asked,

"Are you a scout?"

"Yes," said Horace. "I'm an invested one."

"You're in a vest? Zat is good. It's very cold in the caves?"

Whilst Horace pondered this answer the voice continued, "We 'ave plenty of space for next August. Normally very busy but August is quiet."

"In that case I would like to reserve two hundred rooms. My name is Horace. And one more thing, how far is the cake shop from your hotel?"

Having satisfied himself that he had found the ideal venue for the trip to Portugal, made contact with someone and "done his best," Horace felt that he needed to pass on his findings to whoever was in charge. He opened up his District's webpage and clicked on "Contact Us." Under "Enquiry" Horace typed, "Yesterday Skip told us that we are going to Portugal next year and I said that I would find a suitable place to stay. I've found a large hotel near Lisbon and it's for scouts and it's called 'PNIC' and the person in charge is a Bombardier and there are no stairs and it's on the ground floor and it's by the beach and it's near a cake shop." "Send." Horace didn't receive a reply but in due course John handed out a letter that advised the scouts that District was organising a summer camp to Lisbon in Portugal the following year and if parents would like their child to go then they needed to complete the booking form below, sign it and return it to their scout leader having paid a small deposit. Once that was done their scout would be officially booked in unless they heard otherwise.

The Ravens gathered together at the end of the troop meeting and all agreed that they would be going to Portugal whatever their parents said. Melanie said that she wasn't too sure whether her parents would agree so Horace told her that she needed to take matters into her own hands and "This is what you have to do..." Horace ran home, went straight up into his bedroom, shut the door and sat at his desk. He pulled the letter from his pocket, flattened it out on the desktop and reached for a pen. The information requested was very straightforward: name, contact number, emergency number - Horace simply repeated the contact number - medical and dietary requirements. His wrote slowly and very, very neatly. Then it was a case of ticking a few boxes to agree to the repayment schedule and to pay the required deposit which Horace ignored. "That was easy enough," thought Horace before realising that the form needed to be signed. This would normally have spelt the end to such a fraud but not when Horace was around. He knew that whenever his father signed anything he didn't sign "David Horrise." To be more accurate, he did sign "David Horrise" it was just that it didn't look like "David Horrise" and no one who didn't know his name would be any the wiser once he had signed. To Horace his signature looked like a "D" followed by a wiggly tadpole then an "H" followed by another wiggly tadpole. Horace did the same.

The following Friday Horace arrived at the scout meeting but didn't hand his form in immediately. When John asked for them Horace merely watched as his scout leader put the small pile on a chair beside him. "Not going to Portugal, Horace?" he asked as the rest of the Ravens took a step forward and waved their forms in the air.

"The thing is," Horace explained unconvincingly, "I have quite a bit of stuff in my pockets and I'll have to sort through to find the right piece of paper." During the course of the evening when John was distracted, Horace slipped his form into the pile which he later observed John put into a card document wallet with PORTUGAL written on the front in large letters. "Sorted!" thought Horace.

The summer holidays came and went and nothing was said about Portugal by either John or parent or scout; the more time that was put between Horace's handing in of his form and his parents' raising of the issue of Horace's apparent booking the better as far as he was concerned. However, once the scouts were back at school and meetings had resumed, Portugal was again on the agenda. Over breakfast one morning in early September, whilst she was washing up some dishes, Horace's mother suddenly said, "Horace?" all the while looking out of the window.

As usual, Horace didn't quite know whether his mother was about to speak further to ask him something - generally or specifically, or whether she was just attracting his attention before accusing him, admonishing him or maybe even praising him. Horace thought it odd that she appeared to have deliberately waited until he had a mouthful of cereal before speaking. As far as his mother was concerned she had picked her moment carefully as she wanted Horace to look up and no more which would indicate that he was ready to listen without launching into an impassioned defence of something that may have happened of which she might not even have been aware. Horace did indeed look up as she turned her head round and then back again.

"Your father received an email yesterday. It was from Tim Linehan. He's someone in the District and he's organising a Portugal trip next summer. Apparently..." She paused for a moment. "Apparently your father has signed you up." She turned round again and looked at Horace suspiciously, lowering her eyebrows but with her hands still in the washing-up bowl.

"Would you happen to know anything about it by any slim chance?" she asked sarcastically.

Horace wasn't going to lie, but he wanted to break his mother in gently. Of course he knew about the trip, but he knew very little about the country and so it was to this understanding, although he perfectly well knew that this was not what his mother was meaning by "it," that he responded.

"No, mummy." Then he added lest his father came in and shouted, "Cancelled!"

"But I think that I would really like to go if it's at all possible."

"I thought that you didn't know about it?" his mother asked distrustfully.

"I didn't know about the email, but I did know about the trip," said Horace, moving "it" from Portugal to the email. Had Mrs Horrise been slightly more awake she would have picked up on the fact that she had not even been referring to the email but to its contents, however she wasn't so she didn't.

"I really can't understand it. Your father is usually so methodical about his 'paperwork' but this one seems to have slipped completely through the net. He says that he has no recollection of it at all."

"Okay mummy," said Horace acceptingly and there he could have left the matter apart from the fact that he wanted to go, he needed to go, and now was probably a good time to push the matter forward a little.

"But if I decided that I definitely wanted to go, could I please mummy?" His mother had momentarily stopped washing up, even though she still had her hands in the bowl, and was once more looking out of the window; she appeared deep in thought. Horace didn't like the silence. Silence often implied something beyond anger so he decided to bring the silent period to an end.

"It's okay, mummy, I don't need to go. I'll be just as happy at home in the summer holidays for all those long weeks, indoors, with you, looking after you and not getting in your way very much. In fact," Horace started to turn the screw, "I don't think that I really want to go after all. It would be quite nice having a whole summer holiday at home with you."

Horace was playing for the highest stakes. His mother could have just said, "Okay then," and that would have been that. But whenever he returned home from his first day back at school after the summer holidays, Horace always thought that the house looked as though his mother had been having a great big party with glasses everywhere and the recycling box full of empty wine bottles.

"Your mother's in bed," his father would say, who appeared to have arrived home from work before even Horace had from school.

"She has a bit of a headache."

"Funny that, daddy," Horace had said the previous year. "It's odd that mummy always gets a headache around the beginning of September."

"It's probably something to do with the change of season," his father would suggest with a straight face.

"Yeah, the wine season," thought Horace but said nothing.

Finally Horace's mother spoke, ignoring his offer to stay at home. She said, "Your father and I have spoken about this trip already and if, after careful consideration, you feel that you would like to go then you may. So off you go and have a quiet think about it and when you are ready come and find me and let me know. I'm around for most of the day."

Horace quickly finished off his cereal and went upstairs to his bedroom. The scrambled eggs and toast could wait for a bit. He opened his bedroom door then closed it again without going in. He went back downstairs and found his mother still at the sink and still washing the same plate. Without announcing his arrival he sat back down, picked up his knife and fork and announced,

"I am pleased to confirm that I, Horace Horrise, after careful consideration think that I would like to go to Portugal with the scouts."

"Well, blow me down with a feather Horace," said his mother without turning round. "'Careful consideration' of thirty seconds' duration would seem to some to be a case of a decision having already been taken before the offer had even been made." She turned round, held out her hands that were covered in soap suds and raised an eyebrow at her son. Horace merely shrugged his shoulders and said not a word. He felt that words were unnecessary. Inside his organs were dancing a merry jig but he just calmly cut into his eggs on toast. He sensed that he had momentarily entered the world of the mute, where speech was superfluous as communication was by mime. His mother had made an offer and Horace had accepted it. Words may mollify the situation but they may also make a tense situation far worse.

"The funny thing is, Horace," said his mother turning back to the washing up and speaking to the window once more, "I was talking to Charlie's mother a few days ago and she asked me if you were going to be going to Portugal with the scouts and I told her that I had absolutely no idea what she was talking about. Now I'm going to look really stupid when I suddenly remember, "Ah, yes, of course Horace is going to Portugal, how could I forget?"

Horace shrugged his shoulders again. It wasn't his fault that his mother had been so unequivocal in her response. Had she said, "Oooh, I'm not too sure - we'll be making a decision shortly," then she would have been able to play for a bit of time whilst she checked up with him. But oh no, mummy had to rush straight in and now she was going to be paying the price. There wasn't much for Horace to say. He put down his knife and fork just as Olivia came into the kitchen; he picked up his plate and took it over to the sink. Now was as good a time as any to creep out and go and tell Charlie the good news.

\*\*\*

The next few months were witness to the usual Horace adventures, punctuated by various Portugal meetings, letters and emails. Mr Horrise had been asked to set up a standing order for Horace's payments, including the outstanding deposit, which amounted to several hundred pounds. "Cheap at twice the price," thought Horace's father as he pinged off the first payment from his account. Mrs Horrise had asked Sam if he would like to go to Portugal but he said, "I would rather have the money, thank you," not realising that family finances "don't work like that."

As the suggestion had been made at the breakfast table Mrs Horrise had hoped that Sam would be encouraged to go in order not to be left out, egged on by Horace's inevitable gloating but it wasn't to be. In fact this apparently spontaneous question led to an outcome which was to cost Mr Horrise almost as much as Sam's (non) trip.

Horace's ears had pricked up at his brother's obtuse proposition. A trip to Portugal was something that Horace certainly wasn't going to pass up on even if he could have had the money instead. In any case, staying at home would still involve a small element of expense on the part of his parents and so the net income would not be particularly great. However, a seed had been sown and Horace spent the next few evenings in his room thinking of all the things that he cost his parents although he only came up with four: food, drink, clothes and school trips.

One evening over dinner Horace took a deep breath and asked, "Daddy?" Horace's father put down his knife and fork and looked Horace in the eye. Normally Horace would make any proposal to his wife first but as she had not yet told her husband of any such conversation recently either it had been declined and so Horace was moving the request "up the chain" or it was of such great importance that Horace felt that he needed to go straight to the top. Either way Horace was given his father's undivided attention, for a few seconds at least.

"Daddy, how much do I cost?" Mr Horrise was undaunted by his younger son's question.

"In terms of what?" he asked by way of reply. "Grey hairs, shattered nerves, poor neighbourly relations...?"

"No, none of that," said Horace brightly, pleased to have been given his father's ear and hoping to keep it for a further short while. "I mean food, drink, clothes and school trips. The thing is daddy, that whatever it costs you to feed me, if I started eating less, let's say half as much then the money that you save could be...well...err...given to me as umm...well...money then we would all be winners. I would eat less and so I would be fitter, mummy would be able to do less shopping and so have more time and if I gave you a small discount then you would be richer as would I. So what do you think daddy? Daddy?"

Mr Horrise picked up his glass and took a small sip. Horace decided that his father was deep in thought, probably doing the calculations in his head, checking and double checking before telling Horace that it was an excellent idea. His father placed his glass back on the table, picked up his knife and fork and continued eating. Horace did not want to interrupt his father's thought process but the longer the silence went on the more discomforting it became. At least he hadn't simply said "No," and that was that. Horace began to think that maybe he had pushed his father a little too far, maybe beyond "No," maybe Horace's idea was just too radical for even his father, maybe he had to consult with Horace's mother - in which case, "consult, she's sitting next to you" - although so far she had said nothing. That was not to say that she wasn't the power behind the throne. Horace was confused. Eventually Mr Horrise pushed the last potato to the edge of his plate, took a final sip of his wine and smiled a faint smile as if he were recalling a mildly amusing incident from long ago. Sam, however, could stand it no longer.

"We wouldn't be winners, Olivia and I. In any case we already have less thank you very much, so we're already losers. For all I know you could've been planning this for months, slowly upping your food intake on the pretext that you were growing. I know you are growing, but I mean growing more than is normal. So now you could be eating twice much as normal then you could say to dad, 'Guess what, I have an idea that can make us all winners' - except dad who's been getting quite a lot poorer recently thanks to hoggy Horace here!"

"It's okay Sam," said Mr Horrise who evidently felt that he needed to respond before matters got out of hand.

"Let's give it a try and see what happens. We'll start tomorrow with Horace on half rations. At the end of the week. I'll do a tot up and see who the winners are and if there are in fact any losers."

"Result!" thought Horace with a big smile on his face. He was right to have let Sam have his say; in fact Sam's negative intervention might well have helped his father make up his mind. Horace felt that he was definitely going to be a winner and a very rich one at that. Roll on next Saturday!

The following weekend could not have come quickly enough for Horace. He had had much less cereal in his bowl each morning and had also cut down considerably on his milk intake. He had not asked to go on any school trips, not that any were planned, and he had not asked for any new clothes, not that he needed any.

On returning home from school each afternoon he had not gone near the biscuit tin and had consumed water instead of squash. A similar approach had been taken towards his evening meal. On Tuesday Horace had popped into Waitrose to ascertain the price of a three hundred and seventy-five gram pack of Cheerios and from that had calculated that the saving on that item alone over the course of just one week would amount to several pounds. In short, Horace approached the coming Saturday expecting one thing and one thing alone - a windfall.

Unsurprisingly he was the first down to breakfast. This was not a particularly common occurrence, especially on a non-school day, but today Horace had to be prepared. He found himself a cereal bowl and spoon, the box of Cheerios and some milk from the fridge. He then rummaged around for an egg-cup before placing all the items on the kitchen table and sitting down. He opened the pack of Cheerios and scooped out an egg-cupful which he put down in front of him before helping himself to a couple of the oaty rounds and popping them in his mouth. He had becoming increasingly hungry as the week had worn on but it was all going to be worth it. In advance of his anticipated windfall Horace had been into The Workshed during the week to look at the Swiss army knife display. Starting with the smallest he had taken each one down from the display and caressed it in his hands before opening the blades and inspecting all of its features then returning it to its place and moving onto the next.

The Workshed was a haven for little boys that never quite grew up so was frequented by a number of quite old little boys also. It was possible to buy a single nut, bolt or screw of almost any shape or size. It was considered by many of the "little boys" to be their personal shed, apart from the fact that it was closed on Sundays and had its own special resident. There was an ancient old sofa in one corner and a very relaxed atmosphere all around, helped by the fact that most products never seemed to have a price on them so looked more like one's shed than a shop. Items were not generally stored in boxes on the shelves; normally one of each item would be on display and, "I'll see if I have one out the back" was the usual response to anyone who appeared close to making a purchase. If a customer seemed as if they were going to be in "The Shed" for more than an "In, buy, out" then it was likely that they would be offered a mug of tea or coffee and a biscuit, or even a mince pie from late September to Christmas. This would mean than a five-minute trip could turn into at least a twenty-minute one which in turn meant that there always seemed to be several customers in The Shed at any one time, not necessarily in the actual process of buying something. Authentic little boys were particularly welcome and with a jug of squash on the counter at all times often the young people would leave with full bladders. They would inevitably then have to run home to the consternation of the new Chislehurst resident who, on passing "The Shed," would see a young person come out with a wave before taking to their heels and wondering, as a result, whether they should run off themself or call the police.

The proprietor of The Workshed was a Mr Lillie. Not one single Chislehurst local could remember a time before Mr Lillie. Word had it that Mr Lillie's father had somehow morphed into his son without anyone noticing. There were those of advanced years in the village who sometimes made mention of there having been two Mr Lillies at various times long ago but no one was too sure. Neither could anyone recall there ever having been a Mrs Lillie although presumably there would have been such a person, if not title, at some point in the past.

Dressed in white open-necked shirt and brown trousers under a brown but oil-stained full-length brown warehouse coat, with brown lace-up boots he was comfortably at home with hand-drills, work-benches, clamps, files, rasps, hammers, screwdrivers and, fortunately for Horace, penknives. Mr Lillie did also sell equipment that needed to be plugged into an electricity supply but whenever such an item was sold he behaved as if he was glad to see the back of it and not just because it was a sale. Lawn mowers were a prime example. Petrol versions he could happily accept but electric versions were beyond the pale. "It will cut quickly enough," he would tell each customer once the transaction had been completed, "but it won't cut particularly well. Grass needs to be cajoled and coaxed to give up its length - a bit like a small child in the barber's chair, not hacked by a high-pitched guillotine screeching its way down the grooves to its victim. With a hand-push lawnmower you are at one with the land. As you walk up and down your lawn with the cutter reel spinning you feel that you could name each blade of grass as it throws up its heady scent of summer."

Customer satisfaction was definitely not always Mr Lillie's priority.

Horace had worked his way through half of Mr Lillie's penknife display when the proprietor sidled up to him, puffing on his pipe with a beaker of apple and blackberry squash in his hand. "No Smoking" clearly didn't apply to Mr Lillie's shop. "It's my shop and I can smoke in it if I want to, and if someone doesn't like it they can go to the DIY shed on the by-pass - but they'll be ripped off, there's nowhere to sit down and if they want a tea they'll be poisoned by Steamin' Hotties in the caravan in the car park."

Mr Lillie had once received a warning letter from the local authority reminding him that under existing legislation smoking was not permitted in any enclosed public space. He did think at first that he would make his shop a "private space" with access granted by invitation, "Like at the jewellers where they have a look at you first before letting you in." Then he considered making the shop unenclosed by taking the roof off - then he had an even better idea. He screwed up the letter and left it on the counter top for all of his customers to have a go at seeing if they could make the ball even smaller and more compact. At the end of the week on a Saturday morning he clamped the ball in a vice before attacking it with a rasp. It took him over an hour, and customers during that period had to more or less serve themselves, but by the time that he had finished, just before elevenses (which, to all intents and purposes, went on all day), the letter had been reduced to a pile of white refined sawdust whereupon he quite literally put it in his pipe and smoked it.

The second warning had come in the form of a visit. The shop door opened and the tinkly bell sounded to warn of customers. Mr Lillie sensed trouble in the embodiment of a tie, a slip case and a moustache. Individually they might not have posed a threat but all three together were a concern, especially as they were sniffing the air and gazing up at the ceiling. Mr Lillie took his pipe from his mouth and placed it, still smouldering, on its own custom-made stand beneath the counter. Formalities over (the "customer" introduced himself as Mr Fagg, much to the amusement of Mr Lillie, from the local authority) Mr Fagg informed Mr Lillie that he understood that the existing legislation regarding smoking in public places was not being enforced in his shop, neither did he have any smoke detectors nor fire sprinklers fitted.

"Been a complaint has there?" asked Mr Lillie somewhat abruptly.

"Er, no, not as such," replied Mr Fagg. "However we have reason to believe that..." At this point Mr Fagg thought that he saw a plume of smoke coming up from behind the counter. He stopped what he was saying, forgetting his official-speak and asked,

"Good Lord and don't panic but are we on fire?! Where's your fire extinguisher, I assume you have one? Quick!"

"Yes I do, thank you Mr Butt," said Mr Lillie absentmindedly, "and I have quite a few out the back. But 'no', we're not on fire, I was just engaged in a little soldering before you rudely interrupted without an appointment, but if you keep me from my work we might soon be."

"In that case," said Mr Fagg, "I'll be quick." There was no way that he was going to be accused of being responsible for a premises that he was visiting burning down, one that he was being paid to protect.

"Can I take a look behind the counter?" he asked solicitously. In his experience those who were asked something politely normally responded in the affirmative.

"No," said Mr Lillie curtly. "I'm afraid that you can't. Health and safety regulations, that are in force in the establishment, do not permit me to allow access to this side of the counter to unauthorised persons. You are an unauthorised person and so access is denied."

"So how do I become an authorised person?" asked Mr Fagg, not at all intimidated by Mr Lillie's response.

"You have to apply."

"To whom?"

"The proprietor."

"Who is the proprietor?"

"Me."

"How do I apply?"

"In person, in writing or over the 'phone."

"Can I apply now?"

"If you like."

"Okay, quickly. So what do you need from me?"

"Just say that you apply to be an authorised person." Mr Fagg thought that despite the simplicity of the application, a little more formality was required. He put his slip case on the counter, put his hands down by his sides and said,

"I, Mr Fuller Fagg of the local authority hereby solemnly and soberly apply to be an authorised person of The Workshed, High Street, Chislehurst." Not knowing how neatly to complete this oral request, which otherwise would have ended "Yours sincerely," and with a signature, Mr Fagg said, "Amen."

Mr Lillie gazed quizzically at his unwanted interlocutor but said nothing. "Well," said Mr Fagg eventually, aware that the "fire" wasn't getter any smaller, "Have I been authorised?"

"No," said Mr Lillie. "Permission refused. Good day."

Knowing that he was beaten and that he would have to go back to base and consult, Mr Fagg turned to leave and took several steps towards the door. As he did so Mr Lillie bent down behind the counter from where he hadn't strayed during the whole of his encounter with Mr Fagg, and took a huge drag on his pipe. As he was preparing to exhale this vast chamber of smoke that was swilling around inside his mouth Mr Fagg stopped, turned round and informed Mr Lillie that, "I will be back. Meantime you'd better sort out your fire." When he saw that Mr Lillie's visage had changed from one of composure to that of a pumped-up chipmunk with bulging pink cheeks and with smoke trickling from his nostrils and ears he did consider standing his ground for a minute but he was aware that he had already started to take his leave and so to then postpone it could render him liable to a complaint of bullying. As Mr Fagg was extremely risk adverse he turned back round and left the shop leaving Mr Lillie to blow such a monstrous amount of smoke out of his mouth and in the direction of his ceiling that he was glad he didn't have any smoke detectors installed otherwise the alarms would have been heard all the way to London and unless he had got to the door in time the fire sprinklers would have been going at such a rate that he probably would have drowned. Up to the time of Horace's latest visit on his penknife research Mr Fagg had yet to return and Mr Lillie was back to his bad old ways puffing away happily on his pipe even though the tinkly bell had been temporarily silenced after Mr Lillie had accidently pared it whilst over-enthusiastically demonstrating the reach of a set of telescopic tree loppers.

Once Horace had worked his way through half of the penknife display he had been in The Workshed for over an hour. Mr Lillie put his hand gently on Horace's shoulder and passed him the beaker of squash. Horace could have been forgiven for jumping in surprise but even though he was deep in concentration he subconsciously knew that Mr Lillie was approaching as the smell of "Three Nuns" was growing stronger.

"That's my favourite of the lot, young Horace," said Mr Lillie as he watched Horace open the next penknife from the display.

"Tell me, are you adding to or replacing? I know what you scouts are like with your penknives. Put them down and forget where you put them, give them to someone to try out then forget who you've given them to, had them confiscated..."

"No, nothing like that, Mr Lillie," said Horace cheerfully. "I'm adding to although I'm only adding to one at present. It's a Spartan Red and it even has a reamer though I don't know exactly what that is."

"A reamer is used for widening holes, Horace. Let me help you. What do you want your new knife to do that your present one can't?"

"It's not quite that easy, Mr Lillie. You see there are things that I can do with my knife that it's supposed to do. Then there are things that I can do with it even though it's not supposed to do them. What I would like is a knife that can do things even though I may not need it to. It's a case of being prepared you see," Horace sighed.

"Really, Mr Lillie, I could do with all of them as they all do different things and I can then have a different knife for a different day and activity. However, now that I'm shortly going to be much better off, due to an extremely loo-creative idea of mine, that's what Sam said anyway, I expect to be adding to my penknife collection on a weekly basis for a whole year until I have fifty-two. That will be enough."

"In that case, Horace," said Mr Lillie, who was keen to see at least a little of Horace's forthcoming windfall, "you'ld better get your skates on. I can't hold these prices much longer as they're due to all go up next month."

"The trouble is," said Horace, looking slightly puzzled, "I don't know what the prices are 'cos none of the knives have any amounts on them."

"It's quite simple really," said Mr Lillie, totally unfazed. "Whatever they are at the moment they will be more next month. So the fact is you need to buy them now rather than in the coming weeks as they are less expensive at the moment."

"But I can't buy them all now," said Horace despairingly. "I said I was going to be much better off, not have a lottery win."

"I'll tell you what I can do for you Horace," said Mr Lillie benevolently but with a more selfish ulterior motive, "seeing as how I know you. How about if you take one of each type of penknife home with you now and you can pay me at the rate of one penknife a week? That way you avoid the price rise and you get all the penknives straightaway. I'll see if I have one of each out the back."

As with the deal that Horace had struck with his father he could see only winners and very soon he was walking home laden down by fifty-two penknives in his school rucksack and a verbal agreement to pay Mr Lillie for one penknife each Saturday starting immediately.

Horace heard the stairs creak, just a little but enough to know that someone was on their way down. He picked up the egg-cup and as the kitchen door opened he started to pour the Cheerios into his cereal bowl. "Oh, hi Olivia," said Horace somewhat disappointedly as his sister sat down with her cereal bowl and filled it to the brim. Horace carefully poured his few Cheerios back into the egg-cup.

"What are you doing?" she asked contemptuously, frowning at her brother's antics.

"It's all about timing, Olivia," said Horace with conviction. "I want mummy and daddy to see just how little I am eating and therefore how much I am saving them."

"More for me then," said Olivia, filling her bowl with milk until the Cheerios at the top started to float.

"It doesn't work like that," said Horace wondering where he had heard that same expression himself recently, but Olivia wasn't listening - Horace's loss was her gain so far as food was concerned and she would wait and see what happened on the finance front before passing comment.

After a couple of minutes there was another creak on the stairs and Horace started his egg-cup antics for a second time. However, now it was Sam who also filled his bowl full of Cheerios and milk before asking Horace exactly the same question as his sister.

Horace knew that the next creak would signal the arrival of one of the people his egg-cup shenanigans were aimed at but he was caught unawares by his father coming in not from upstairs but from his study. "Morning children," said their father as he walked straight over to the kettle thus completely missing Horace tipping his egg-cupful of Cheerios into his cereal bowl for the third time. He popped two slices of bread into the toaster before helping himself to some orange juice from the fridge. Only then did he sit down at the table - just as Horace finished his second, and last, mouthful.

Horace could contain himself no longer; he couldn't even wait for his father's toast to ping out. He had a financial negotiation to conclude and debt to settle before the shops closed.

"Big day daddy," Horace cautiously advanced.

"Correct Horace," said his father, as if expecting an approach from Horace. "Your mother is just finishing off your account for this first week."

"'Mummy?' daddy?" Horace wasn't sure whether he liked the sound of this. However it may be a good sign but then again it could be a very good sign. Good because his parents were obviously taking the matter seriously enough to share the responsibility, or very good because the calculation was going to be very exact. He didn't haven't to wait long. Once again there was no creak and his mother appeared at the door. She was still in her dressing gown as she smiled at Horace and handed him a large envelope.

"Hot off the press, Horace," she said, still smiling.

Horace took the envelope and read what was on the front. It said,

"Horace Horrise. Household Account. Week One."

He opened the envelope and pulled out a sheet of paper. He was feeling very grown up. He looked at all the writing and figures. Up and down his eyes darted trying to make sense of it all. He thought that the more he looked at what was written the more the calculations would go in his favour, but they didn't. What he read didn't look very good, not very good at all. In fact it was bad, very bad, for on the sheet was written,

"Horace Horrise. Household Account. Week One.
(This account <u>excludes</u> all material purchases apart from food.)
Being on call for Horace Horrise twenty-four hours a day including: driving, conversing with, washing (clothes and dishes) and drying (clothes and dishes) and putting away, ironing, cooking, cleaning, shopping, tidying-up, correspondence and calls, problem solving, doctor and dentist appointments, remembering important dates for parties etc., helping with homework, lying to teachers (occasional), getting-up, tucking-in, reading to, playing with, dealing with sick(ness) and above all - loving unreservedly:
£10 per hour (discounted rate) x 24 hours x 7 days ÷ 3 children = £560
Less
Saving due to reduction in food intake = £20
Sub-total owed by Horace = £540"

Horace was open-mouthed with shock. More than shock. This was a catastrophe of the highest order. When you're not expecting something it can come as a shock. But when you're expecting the opposite...

Horace read through the account again. "Even if I eat nothing I cost mummy and daddy five hundred and twenty pounds," thought Horace. "What am I going to do? And that's not even the total total."

Horace looked up at his parents. "I'm sorry, but I don't know what to do. I am, well, was I think only trying to do my best."

Horace put the sheet of paper carefully down on the breakfast table. Any less delicately and he thought it would bite. Maybe he would just have a few more Cheerios. It was Saturday after all. As he reached for the cereal box his mother smiled at him gently. "Horace, there is a little bit more on the other side."

"I don't know if I want to look, mummy," said Horace as a tear trickled down his face. "I didn't realise that I cost so much. I'm really sorry, but I don't know how I can be any cheaper and I'm probably even more expensive so if you don't mind I won't look at the other side. If I don't look I won't know and that's probably the best thing right now." Horace shook the packet of Cheerios and was perturbed to find that it was empty.

"I'll just have a small biscuit," he said pathetically and stood up from the table. "Maybe one without chocolate."

"Well I'm going to find out how much he costs," said Olivia picking up the sheet of paper and turning it over before muttering a quiet, "Oh!"

"What does it say Olivia?" asked Sam who realised that he was partially complicit in this exercise and was as eager as his sister to know what else Horace cost.

She read out, "It says, 'For the love, joy, happiness, fun and laughter that you - one of our precious gifts from God - bring to the family = Priceless
Total owed by Horace = Nothing'"

Olivia put down the sheet of paper as Horace took four of the special double chocolate titans out of the biscuit tin. He turned and faced his mother. "I love you mummy."

"I love you too, Horace," she replied gently. "Enjoy your trip to Portugal."

"I will mummy," Horace assured her. "But in the meantime do you have a few pounds for Mr Lillie?"

\*\*\*

As the months became weeks, 'plane times were sent out and kit lists issued. Throughout the district there were many young people and not a few grown ups that were getting more and more excited. The Ravens were no exception. The six of them were going, all having secured parental agreement through a combination of pleading, blackmail, stealth, and straightforward request in addition to Horace's forgery.

The departure day finally arrived and two hundred scouts and leaders assembled at Heathrow Airport to board an early morning flight to Lisbon. It was recommended that each scout take no more than enough Euros to see them through a few extra ice creams and drinks during the holiday as everything else would be provided. However, let loose in the airport "duty free" shop with more money in their pockets than they had ever had before in their lives proved too much of a temptation for some of the Ravens. As they all met back up at the boarding gate Charlie confided in Horace that he had bought a tin of caviar and had spent all of his money.

"What did you do that for, stupid?" asked Horace, glaring angrily at his friend as Charlie showed him the tiny tin. Horace realised that a friend with no money would mean that Horace would unquestionably be called upon at some stage to lend him (because it was nearly always a male, the girls being far too sensible to waste their money) a few pounds.

"'Cos I like sardines, that why, and I don't think you can get them in Portugal," said Charlie defensively.

"Of course you can get sardines in Portugal," scoffed Horace. "That's where all our sardines come from. But caviar isn't sardines, it's fish innards."

"Well, I didn't know that..."

"And it's only eaten by Russian people."

"They didn't tell me that when I bought it."

"Well how would they know that you weren't Russian?"

"I was speaking in English and I have an English passport."

"You could be an English Russian. Anyway they're still going to sell it to you 'cos a sale's a sale. But I don't reckon you'll like it 'cos we have different plates to the Russians and..."

"Different what?"

"'Plates', like what you taste with your mouth. So you won't like it. Anyway it says 'Caviar' on the tin."

"I know that. I can read. It's just that the tin looked like a sardine tin..."

"A tin of dog food looks like a tin of mince. Ask my grandad sometime. But you wouldn't want to eat dog food would you?"

"But why was it so expensive?" Charlie asked, trying to steer the conversation onto less confrontational grounds.

"I don't know. Maybe it's posh innards. After all, fish is fish although mummy normally takes the innards out and throws them in the bin. Maybe she should try selling them."

"Maybe there's posh bits of the ocean like with Chislehurst and, well, other places," said Charlie as they boarded the 'plane.

\*\*\*

The first coach from Lisbon airport drew into the campsite and the weary travellers disembarked. They looked around and took in the sandy ground and the plentiful tall pine trees that were all over. Apart from these two features, and the fact that there wasn't a cloud in the sky, they could easily have been back home. As they took in the surroundings of their new home for the next few days they were suddenly and enthusiastically greeted by the campsite manager who introduced himself as Bagheera. "Welcome to PNIC," he cried to the gathered scouts.

"I 'ope you 'ave a wonderfuw time. I must zay a big 'ello to my friend 'Orace! Iz 'e 'ere?"

"Blimey," said Charlie, "he sounds just like he comes from south London!" Horace ignored his best friend and put his hand up.

"Ah, 'Orace, my friend from Chislehurst! Welcome! Do you like our 'otel?! Ha, ha! It's 'cos of 'Orace that you are all 'ere as 'e told Tim about us! 'Ave you any questions? You can put your 'and down now 'Orace."

"I h-ave my h-and hup Bagheera 'cos I h-ave a question," Horace said, slightly piqued at his new friend's response.

"Fire away, H-orace," said Bagheera in a manner that sounded far too contrived.

"You said on the 'phone that August was usually a very quiet month but I don't understand what with all the holidays and stuff. I mean, children in Portugal have holidays and all of England is on holiday so why aren't you really busy? If we want to go camping in August at home Skip has to usually squeeze us in somewhere. Once we had to..."

"Yes, thank you Horace," said Tim eager to show the scouts to their camping area. "I think Bagheera understands."

"You are correct 'Orace," said Bagheera, quite happy to take the question having, like Mr Lillie, already made the sale. "Zere is one good reason. Starting on Thursday zere is a huge festival in zis area. It's called 'Viva em Caparica'. It's zee biggest public festival in zee whole of Portugal with bands and DJs and it's for four days and it's very, very busy."

"So why are you not busy?"

"Because my little friend, zee busy people are outside PNIC at zee festival and not in 'ere."

"So where exactly is it?"

"Opposite. When you come off zee main road and go down zee side road we are 'ere on zee right. The festival will be on zee left."

"Cool, will we hear it?"

""Ear it'? Yes, you will 'ear it. You will be lying in your tent and you will be able to 'ear ever-y word. It will be like you are at Glastonbury festival only 'cos you are in 'ere and not over zee road you 'ave even better time 'cos to you it iz free!"

"And what time is this festival?" asked Melanie who was suddenly starting to look forward to her stay in Lisbon even more than she already had been.

"It starts in zee evening and it finishes at about four o'clock in zee morning. After zat all is quiet and you can all go to sleep for three hours."

"No difference to the usual scout camp there then," said John sarcastically.

\*\*\*

"As you can zee, you are zum more scouts at zis campsite this week." The Ravens had joined not only the scouts on their trip but also all the others from the campsite, mainly from parts of Portugal although relatively small in number due to the festival, having formed a large circle for the first morning's flag break; Bagheera was welcoming everyone.

"We 'ave about twenty scouts from zee north of our country and zey would like to give you a traditional Portuguese welcome," he said encouragingly.

The English scouts, who were uniformly wearing their scout shirts and international scarves but apart from that could have come straight from a St Trinian's own clothes day, turned towards their Portuguese counterparts. The 1st Porto scouts were standing side by side in height order. They were immaculately turned out with Baden-Powell style hats, beautifully ironed shirts, clean folded scarves, badges sewn on neatly and not a single sign of any stitching, shorts with straight creases down the front, knee-length socks with red garters, and highly-polished shoes. Bagheera turned to them and nodded.

"Allllllllll! FOOM-hah! FOOM-hah!" shouted the tallest Portuguese pair as they bent down patted their knees and raised their hats in unison.

"Sooooom-HAH! Sooooom-HAH!" the next pair screeched in response. They clapped their hands, one, two, three, then a double clap - clap clap, clap clap. The others in their group all clapped together.

The chanting worked its way through the ten pairs. Each chant was slightly different, each set of actions also. Furthermore, the responses were unique to each pair. Occasionally the shortest pair would throw in a well-timed "A-ha! A-Ha!" clap clap. When it was the turn of the shortest pair they threw themselves almost literally into their actions and then chanted, "Bustier - rustier, all zooooo-MAH!" Then this little group all took off their hats and bowed. The English contingent started to applaud but the Portuguese hadn't yet finished. The shortest pair restarted but with the tallest pair's chant and actions and this continued back up the line with only the middle pair repeating themselves. Horace and the Ravens were mesmerised. As the group started to take their hats off and bow for the second time Bagheera began clapping enthusiastically; the rest of the scouts followed. As the clapping subsided Bagheera turned to Tim who was standing next to him. "You 'ave anything?" he asked.

"Errr, let's just see." Tim put out his hands and started to pat the air down to bring an end to the applause.

"Scouts, I think that you'll agree that that was magnificent. Fantastic. Now let's see what we can do. If your group has something like that we'ld all love to see it. Just raise a hand or call out." No one moved. Silence. This was quickly becoming very embarrassing - for Tim who should have just let be, for 1st Porto who felt that they may have excelled themselves just a bit too much and for the rest of the scouts who had no idea what to offer - apart from Horace who slowly raised his hand.

"Yes Horace?" Tim didn't want an answer, he wanted a group response as Horace opened his mouth. He didn't ask "What do you have?" he just said, "Off you go."

Horace took an ostentatious step forward and brought his feet together in the manner of the Queen's Guard coming to attention. He pumped up his chest, clenched his right fist, pushed it up into the air in front of him and shouted,

"'Ere we go, 'ere we go, 'ere we goooo!" as the other English scouts all joined in.

"'Ere we go, 'ere we go, 'ere we go - ah!
'Ere we go, 'ere we go, 'ere we goooo!
'Ere we go-ah, 'ere we goooo!"

Then, instead of any taking off of non-existent hats and a sober bow the English scouts to a boy and girl almost fell to their knees laughing.

"All riiiiiight!" shouted Horace and the laughing continued accompanied by much whooping, once they had caught their breath, and cheering. 1st Porto looked totally bemused. Bagheera turned to Tim.

"Is zat it?" he asked looking genuinely puzzled.

"Yes, I'm afraid that it probably is," confirmed Tim, feeling more embarrassed than he had in a long time.

"So what happens now Tim?" asked Bagheera.

"Er, well normally there's a punch-up."

\*\*\*

"Gosh! Just imagine going to a real festival with DJs and bands in a huge arena," said Melanie gloomily as they stood outside the campsite gawping at the enormous billboard beside the main road, "and not a pretend one where the climax is 'Kumbuya' or Cecil the frigging caterpillar round a poxy camp fire". The Ravens were on their way to the beach for a game of wet sand rounders but had been distracted by the Viva em Caparica poster which appeared to be boasting

238

twelve hours of music a night with over thirty performers on two stages. Thursday had arrived and the place was beginning to get markedly busier with people and equipment passing in and out of the venue's "stage door" that the scouts had to walk past to get to and from the beach.

"You can't go and that's that," said John as the Ravens read through the list of bands and DJs wondering aloud if any of them were English.

"One, you're too young; two, you need to be accompanied by an adult and three, you don't have a ticket. Now let's get down to the beach. Tim will be waiting."

"Skip," asked Emily, ignoring his injunction, "What does 'Termos e condições' mean at the bottom of the poster?"

"It means 'no scouts allowed,' now come on," said John irritably. A visit to Viva em Caparica one evening would have been right up his street but no one from the campsite was going so he was trying to forget all about it.

As John marched off down to the beach, commanding the Ravens to "Follow!", Bagheera appeared from the other side of the road. "'Ello 'Orace!" he called out, smiling at the group. "'Ow 'ave you been enjoying your camp?"

"It's been exceptionally fine, Bagheera," said Horace with a grin. "We've been having a great time and now we're off to the beach with Skip."

John turned round and beckoned the Ravens but when he saw Bagheera he waved before continuing down the road.

"The scouts can catch me up," he thought. "I will now be able to grab a quick espresso before then."

"Bagheera, I have a question," said Emily. "Can you tell me what that means at the bottom of the poster?" she asked, pointing at the Portuguese phrase.

"'Termos e condições' means zings zat you can and can't do."

"And what can and can't we do?"

"It says zat you cannot bring zings into zee festival like guns and knives and..."

"Okay, what else?"

"You 'ave to be at least zix years old and you need to be with a responsible person, zings like zat, zat's all."

"Thank you Bagheera," said Melanie, "you've been very helpful."

"So," said Charlie as they went off to catch John up, "one, we're not too young; two, you don't need to be accompanied by an adult and three, we don't have a ticket."

"And I bet they sold out months ago," said Melanie woefully. "If only we'd known before we came out." The Ravens walked dejectedly down to the beach, found Tim leaping around on the sand with his sidekick, who for some reason was called "Moto," and made the most of the rounders game. The festival was just going to have to wait until they were older.

The Ravens had spent several days speculating on the reason for Moto's name. No one had thought to ask him, instead they guessed that it was an acronym for something. Being somewhat bossy, Emily decided that it stood for "Man Of Tremendous Authority" but couldn't work out why the others simply laughed when she told them.

The Ravens took the long way back to the campsite in order to buy some "Pasteis de Nata" from Horace's cake shop, delicacies known to most English people as "custard tarts", only the Portuguese versions were a whole lot better. John had said that he had done enough walking for one day and would meet the Ravens by the campsite gate which gave them a few minutes of leaderless freedom. The long way back also took the Ravens past the main entrance to the festival where they stopped and stared, munching on their pasteis. "Oh my goodness, look at that!" exclaimed Emily.

There on the side of the main entrance was what looked suspiciously like a ticket office with a small queue of people outside.

"It has 'Ten Euros' stuck on the front by that grill," said Emily pointing at a piece of paper stuck precariously to the front of the ticket office. "How much money do we have left in total?" The Ravens pooled the Euros that they had on them and it came to just over fifty once Archie had guessed how much he had.

"That's simple then," said Melanie brightly. "One can't go and five of us can go and have no drinks or chocolate."

"Okay," said Charlie. "So now we have everything sorted out apart from we're locked in so escape's impossible with that wire fence all around the perimeter and we'll have to go back 'cos Skip's waiting for us."

"There is one other thing," said Archie who had stood listening to the conversation but who was otherwise distracted by the fact that he appeared to have left his purse on the beach. "I think we need to go and have a hunt for my cash."

"Come on," said Horace, "we'll all go and have a look. We'll go back the quick way and tell Skip as we go past."

\*\*\*

"I knew we'ld find it, we're scouts," said Archie, once his money had been found exactly where they had been sitting, slightly buried in the fine golden sand. "I hid it so that no one would see it," he explained. "Including you," said Emily, "and as scouts we should be able to get out of Camp Confined if we put our minds to it. Here's my cash Horace, you look after it and if we all escape we can worry about who will be sent straight back to camp at that point but my opinion is last out, first back in."

The other Ravens handed in their cash to Horace. "I have twenty Euros," said Emily, "so if I'm last out I think that I should still be guaranteed a place." The other Ravens didn't say a word, especially the one who had no Euros, having spent them all on "posh sardines" at the airport.

The Ravens walked slowly back to camp. Much of their usual banter was absent; they were too busy plotting their individual escapes. Their route took them back up past the "stage door" which was also the entrance for the staging, lighting and sound equipment, stallholders' equipment and other items as well as personnel needed to showcase Portugal's finest contemporary musicians and DJs. With only a few hours to go before the festival opened, the Ravens could clearly see the back of the stage through the wide metal gates that had just been opened by two thickset security guards in order to allow a huge juggernaut lorry out. The stage now had a roof on it and it looked as though it was just the finishing touches that were now being applied. Beside the gates were six Portaloos. They appeared to be brand new and instead of being the usual green or blue in colour they were black. They looked larger than the normal mobile toilets. Each one had thousands of silver stars stuck to it with the exception of one which had gold stars instead. Taped to the door of each Portaloo was a sheet of paper on which had been printed, in English,

"STAR PERFORMERS ONLY"

"Hang on a moment," said Horace. "'Star performers' beware, I am desperate to go to the toilet." In truth, Horace was not exactly bursting to go, but even by scout campsite standards the Portuguese versions were fairly poor. Every morning at flag break Tim had reminded the scouts that all used toilet paper had to be placed in the bucket beside the toilet in each cubicle and, "Do not flush paper down the pan as you will block up the whole of the camp sewage system." Then the scouts had to chant, "If you want a poo, the paper in the bucket - you just have to suck it!" "Not literally," Emily had to be told, "It just means that you have to put up with it," John explained, noticing her grimace.

The optimum time to go to the toilet was just after flag break which was when the cubicles were being cleaned and while most of the scouts were rushing off to their morning activities. Otherwise the later in the day that a visit was needed the worse the smell and the bigger the pile of toilet paper, culminating in a very late evening or early morning visit whereupon one would bear witness to a what resembled a model snowy alpine mountain that had been sprayed with finest Swiss chocolate. By midnight a gas mask wouldn't have been a bad idea and scouts could be seen taking deep breaths before entering. They would do their business, wash their hands and exit, exhaling rapidly. Most scouts didn't even dare put their cubicle light on knowing what a singularly grim sight was there to greet them if they did. They would sit on the toilet and, once it had been used for what it was intended, the toilet paper would be held over the left or right shoulder and dropped, hoping that they had guessed the correct side.

"Any toilets but the camp toilets," was agreed by all and every trip away from the campsite became an opportunity to catch up on toileting duties in usually more salubrious surroundings. Soon the various off-site activities were being marked out of ten, not for the quality of the activity but for the standard of the local toilets. Stand-up paddle boarding, that took place in a delightful, secluded cove to the south of Lisbon, down a long winding track, should have scored a ten as an activity. Instead Horace marked it a one as the nearby toilet not only had a smaller bucket but also it had no toilet seat. Horace was looking forward to some quality time in the toilet but instead found himself hovering above the porcelain as if he were about to take part in a Haka and hoping that the hit would be a direct one. So desperate had the situation become that Tim had to remind the scouts that anyone who appeared to removing the bottom half of their swimming costume or trunks in the sea would be accused of engaging in an extremely anti-social activity and dealt with accordingly. The tour of Benfica's football stadium, an activity that even Emily would have scored a seven, was given ten by all of the Ravens. When the Ravens were being shown round the stadium in a group of twenty, when the guide pointed out the visitor toilets and asked if anyone would like to make use of the facilities, he was bemused to see all twenty scouts disappear to return five minutes later having toileted, washed, dried and hand-creamed. Melanie had somehow even managed to have squeezed in a shower.

The Ravens stopped and watched as Horace picked out the gold star Portaloo and turned the handle. While the security guards were distracted by the juggernaut's manoeuvrings, Horace opened the door and jumped inside. However, he had not been inside the Portaloo for more than a matter of seconds when a fork-lift truck appeared from inside the compound round the side of the juggernaut. It deftly poked its prongs into some grooves under the toilet and lifted it up off the ground. It reversed and then headed straight back into the compound with the security guards shutting the gates behind. It was all over in less than a minute. Charlie thought of shouting "Stop!" and blocking the truck's progress but quickly decided that getting out of the festival wasn't going to be particularly difficult. In any event Horace had just saved the Ravens ten Euros.

"Actually," said Emily finally, as the other Ravens stood open-mouthed at Horace's sudden Portaloo kidnapping, "we could all get free entry if we're quick!"

Without thinking through the consequences of six scouts not turning up for dinner, Charlie, Emily, Archie, Melanie and Edward picked a Portaloo each and in a flash stepped inside their respective conveniences. After all, "missing" wasn't much fun and not worth the hassle but "missing in the festival" probably was worthwhile. Unfortunately they weren't as "lucky" as Horace as one of the security guards turned round just in time to see five Portaloo doors shutting. The wide metal gates were reopened and the fork-lift truck appeared and then stopped by the Portaloos as the guard walked over to the nearest one and shouted something in Portuguese then tried the handle. The fact that it was locked was of no hindrance to him. He pulled out a penknife and inserted the flat-head screwdriver into the middle of the handle mechanism and turned. The door popped open and there stood, or rather sat, Charlie. The guard said something to Charlie which he understood to mean, "Out you get sonny and tell your friends to do the same if they know what's good for them." As the remaining Ravens emerged the fork lift repeated the exercise with the silver Portaloos as it had done with the gold only this time devoid of any precious content. The only slight embarrassment was on Edward's part who, being the last to be ejected, had had more time to go about his business. As he wasn't responding to Charlie's pleas to "get out" the guard penknifed the door to find Edward hastily pulling up his shorts.

"Any toilet but the camp toilet," Edward muttered feebly as he joined the other Ravens on the side of the road.

"Never mind," said Emily as they walked back to the campsite. "At least we can now all join Horace later with the fifty Euros."

"Err, yes Emily, that's right," said Charlie sarcastically, "apart from the fact that it's Horace who has our fifty Euros." The remainder of the short walk back to the campsite was completed in silence.

During dinner the camp nurse came over to where the Ravens were sitting and asked after Horace. Anne-Marie -

tall and slender and always wearing bright red lipstick - was every teenage boy's dream date, a vision that was only partially shattered by her sticking up a poster on the sub-camp mess tent wall with the heading, "What Colour Is Your Urine?" "One" was "clear, almost like water" whereas "Ten" was "golden orange, like liquid marmalade." Rather than encourage the scouts to drink more water, the poster immediately led to a competition to see who could produce and display in the plastic water bottles, of which the catering team had bought no fewer than five thousand, one of every colour of urine from one to ten. In the Raven's sub-camp Charlie had managed all ten inside three days, something Anne-Marie viewed with such deep suspicion that she brought into service her secret weapon, some pH paper, which was used to test the acidity or alkalinity of a liquid. Together with a degree of conjecture, Anne-Marie concluded that Charlie's "one" was in fact water, "ten" was peach tea (which Anne-Marie told Tim later that she was relieved to have ascertained as she was on the verge of recommending Charlie's hospitalisation) and "five" was lager although no one did ever find out how Charlie had managed that particular trick. He even had his and Horace's tent searched - twice. Unsurprisingly Charlie was disqualified and the eventual winner was, in due course, Melanie. Her trick was to not drink for a whole day which she realised was foolish, but on the following day produced a "ten" which she divided up into separate bottles and then simply watered the contents down by varying degrees.

"He's in the toilet Anne-Marie," said Melanie, who never knowingly told a lie. It was not down to her to explain exactly which toilet he was in, nor where it was.

"Oh my goodness," said Anne-Marie looking slightly worried, "I hope he's okay. How long has he been in there now?" Charlie thought that, "several hours" would be about right but Emily "ummed" and "ahhed" and eventually Anne-Marie moved onto her next patient.

"We might as well try to escape," said Emily over pudding. "You never know, Horace might have escaped and be waiting with the money."

"Spending it, more like," said Archie gloomily, "but you're right and it'll be dark soon so no one will miss us then. Skip will just think that we've gone to bed. Let's agree to meet up by the wide gates at ten o'clock. Then we can plan our next move. Until then everyone's on their own, we can't risk all being caught together."

\*\*\*

Emily was the first to taste freedom. She had brought industrial-size nail clippers with her, which Melanie had said were big enough to clip hooves, and she had disappeared into the far reaches of the campsite with them. Emily scrambled through some fairly dense undergrowth and eventually came to the wire perimeter fence. She walked alongside it until she found an area that was thick with shrubbery on the other side. Using a technique that she had learned at scouts during an evening of origami, she cut through the fence in a vertical line up from the ground for thirty centimetres. Then she folded up the two corners which gave her more than enough space to crawl through. Once on the other side she folded the corners back down and tied them together with a piece of string that she had brought along specifically for the purpose.

Archie's means of escape was also via the fence, but he wasn't going under it, he was going over it. Earlier in the week one of the activities had been pioneering and the Ravens had learnt how to make an A-frame using long, thick wooden poles and a length of rope. The result resembled an outsize easel with one leg at the back and two at the front. Archie liberated some rope from the stores and dragged three large poles from the wood pile to the perimeter fence. There he expertly lashed the poles together before lifting one of the legs over the fence and securing the remainder of the rope to the other two legs to make a makeshift ladder. Precariously he climbed the structure before sliding down the pole on the other side praying that there weren't any splinters. He left the poles in place as they were well hidden and went in search of the others; he found Emily who was looking very pleased with herself.

"What kept you Archie?" she asked gloatingly. Archie didn't answer. He was just relieved to have successfully escaped and come second.

Edward and Melanie weren't at all sure how they were going to break out to begin with. Disconsolately they wandered up to the main gate where they found Bagheera standing at the front of his car with the engine running, talking to Charlie. Their countenance changed in the blink of an eye. They knew exactly what they had to do. They didn't need to say anything to each other, they didn't even need to look at each other. Bagheera was facing away from the car so they walked slowly up to the back of it, opened the boot and climbed in. Fortunately it was the type of car that was built with space in mind so the pair were actually quite comfortable. Edward reached up and pulled down the boot lid leaving a small gap, holding onto it all the while. Soon they were on their way. They looked through the gap as Bagheera turned left and then stopped at the junction with the busy main road. Taking their chance they lifted the boot lid a few centimetres and slid out. As they let go of the lid it sprung up into the air so the pair walked calmly back down the side road with the lid shielding them from Bagheera in the driver's seat, and mingled with the crowd. They didn't dare turn round; had they done so they would have seen Bagheera climb out of his car, scratch his head and close the boot.

As the pair walked down the road they met Charlie coming up. "Nice work, you two!" he exclaimed.

"Thanks Charlie, but how come you're out?" asked Edward quizzically. "Last time we saw you you were chatting to Bagheera."

"That is indeed correct, but what was I chatting to Bagheera about? I was explaining to him that I had a couple of bags of rubbish that I was told to put in the bins outside. Normally I would have just left them and Bagheera would've done it but he was in a bit of a rush to go home so he said that he would let me do it. He then asked if I would shut the gate and set the combination lock behind him as he left. He then said, 'I'm sure zat you won't be vanting to escape on your own, not with you going 'ome tomorrow!' So now I have escaped aaaaand I have the combination code aaaand I have twenty-five Euros!"

"Twenty-five Euros!" exclaimed Emily, "That's two and a half tickets. How did you manage that?"

"Apparently Horace mentioned my caviar purchase to Bagheera who told him that the one that I had bought was one of the best that money could buy, although I hadn't bought very much, and offered me twenty-five Euros which I have accepted 'cos it didn't even cost me that much just about. So come on, let's go and see if anyone else has escaped."

The five Ravens met back up outside the wide gates that were firmly shut, now with four security guards, and so they wandered back up to the main road and the ticket office by the entrance.

"What we can do is buy two tickets and then we'll just have to play some sort of game and the two winners can have them with five Euros to spend," said Charlie. He walked up to the window and asked for two tickets to the festival.

"Ten Euro," demanded the woman behind the glass.

"I need TWO tickets," said Charlie, sticking two fingers in the air.

"And I vant TEN Euro," demanded the woman once more, waving both hands in the air. "Ten Euro man, five Euro child," she explained. "You are not man. Ten Euro." Charlie thought fast.

"Here, you have twenty-five Euros. I would like five tickets please." The response wasn't what he was expecting.

"You ticket touting. You are the worst!" screamed the woman pulling down a little black blind over the window in front of her.

"No, no, no! No ticket tout! Look, there are five of us! Look!" Charlie pleaded with the blind. Slowly the blind rose halfway and the woman peered out over Charlie's shoulder whereupon she saw the other four Ravens standing in a rather pathetic huddle looking back at her.

"Okay, five ticket. Twenty-five Euro." The woman looked over Charlie's shoulder at the four Ravens again, took the money and passed through five tickets. "You 'ave a good time. No drugs, no guns."

"No drugs, no guns," repeated Charlie. "No money."

Charlie walked over to the Ravens waving the tickets. "Half price for children! Result!" he declared as he handed out the tickets. "Now let's go and have some fun."

"And find Horace," said Melanie benevolently.

The Ravens joined the queue at the entrance and slowly made their way to the front. Once inside they stood and soaked in the heady night-time atmosphere. It was very bright, as if they had suddenly walked in on a solar eclipse. It felt as if there were thousands of people inside already. There was noise and lights and unusual smells all around with an array of stalls selling all manner of food and drink but, unsurprisingly, no Horace. They wandered down the main path towards the stage. The further they walked the thicker the crowd became until they were reduced to shuffling and pushing through. To one side there was a roped off area with thick red rope with a backdrop on which was printed in large gold letters, "VIP". On the ground was a plush deep pile red carpet and it seemed to the Ravens as though there were dozens of security men on the carpet, almost as many as there were supposed VIPs milling about. The VIPs were almost all immaculately turned out, "all bangles and jangles," Emily suggested. As they walked alongside the rope they could just see tucked away at the back of the VIP area, sideways on, the black Portaloos. The

Ravens were all very quiet, taking everything in. They had never seen anything like it before.

"Duck!" Charlie said suddenly. The Ravens instinctively did as commanded before slowly turning round to face the same way as Charlie was looking. Through the crowd they saw, not two metres away, Anne-Marie! She appeared to be by herself but had a bright-red drink in her hand and a huge grin on her face.

"Blimey," said Archie. "if she drinks all that her urine will be off the scale in the morning!" and the Ravens laughed heartily - except Emily. She had been looking along the VIP carpet and her eyes had taken her to a bar at the far end. It was decorated in the same manner as the Portaloos except that each small star was twinkling brightly, perfectly at one with the jangles and bangles that the bar staff were serving. Above the bar, slightly set back, there was a raised platform. It was also mostly black but was furnished with several red sofas around the edges accessorised by a number of large multi-coloured cushions. In the middle there was a huge rectangular glass table on which several enormous bottles of Champagne had been placed, in even more enormous ice buckets.

"This is obviously the VIP plus area," thought Emily as she surveyed the ten or so people standing or sitting, chatting or simply posing above the mere VIPs who were below them as well as the Ravens and the rest of the great unwashed on the far side of the rope. There was one woman in particular on the raised platform that stood out. Everyone seemed to be looking at her. She was tanned with long straight blond hair, dressed in a shimmering gold cat suit. Emily concluded that she was definitely an A-list VIP plus celebrity someone although she had no idea who this woman actually was. Mystery woman was sipping on a glass of Champagne and appeared to be listening intently to her animated younger male companion - not saying much at all. She didn't need to as he was in full flow - a perfect foil to her relative silence. His clothes were also a contrast to her stunning attire - he was dressed in more of a beach grunge style comprising flip-flops, khaki shorts and "Chief Scout in Training" t-shirt. "Hang on a moment," thought Emily.

"Hor-aaaaace!"

\*\*\*

Horace quickly and purposefully shut the Portaloo door and turned the lock. Straightaway he noticed the carpet. Black carpet. He had never seen carpet inside a Portaloo before but that wasn't the only novelty. There was a toilet, unsurprisingly, but unusually the aroma was perfectly pleasant without a hint of pong or rancid disinfectant as if someone had tried too hard to disguise a particularly bad odour. There was a sink with, amazingly, a plug (that fitted) and a large mirror on the wall behind the sink. There were several small posters that were stuck to the wall behind the toilet, almost like wallpaper. They were of an extremely glamorous woman wearing professional headphones and who looked as though she was bending over some turntables. In front of the "wallpaper", hanging in a large metal frame - was a gold record. Despite the fact that this was a special Portaloo, one in which one could easily spend some quality time, Horace knew that he had a job to do. However, his plan came to a sudden halt before it had even got going. The Portaloo shuddered as if it were caught up in a mini earth tremor. Horace slumped down on the toilet lid and grabbed his thighs - there was nothing else to hold onto - as the Portaloo felt like it was moving. Horace thought that maybe he was in the toilet equivalent of a flight simulator but then the shuddering stopped and so he stood back up, steadied himself and looked out of the small window in the wall opposite the mirror. He smiled to himself as he realised that somehow he was being transported into the festival compound. Before long the shuddering started again and Horace sat back down before the Portaloo came to a rest. Now was the time to make his escape. He stood back up and unlocked the door. He pushed the door slowly open but he only managed a couple of centimetres. All he could make out was a length of fairly thick cable that appeared to be running across the front of the door. He shut the door and looked back out of the window. He could see all manner of coming and going as what he imagined to be back-stage staff, administrators, security assistants, PR people and various hangers-on rushed hither and thither. As he continued to look out of the window another Portaloo hove into view and Horace finally realised how he had been transported into the festival. The Portaloo kept coming and coming towards him and then, just as he thought that he was going to be hit, it swung round ninety degrees and came to a halt. It was positioned so close to his Portaloo that his view out of the window was almost completely obscured. He pressed his cheek against the wall next to the window whereupon he could just about see past the front of his neighbour, but it was an awkward position to hold. He sat down on the toilet lid again and pondered his next move. He could hardly shout out, that would result in immediate ejection. Escape, of the furtive variety, was rapidly becoming impossible. The door was barred, the window was too small, below his feet was the sewage tank. "What would Charlie do?" Horace thought to himself as he raised his eyes Heavenwards to a greater power and instantly forgot about his best friend.

"That could be interesting," he thought as he spied a small hatch in the ceiling. Horace climbed onto the toilet and stretched but he could only just about touch the ceiling and no more. However, from the toilet he was able to climb onto the sink and now he could not only touch the hatch door, he could push it open and reach inside - which he did. Horace reckoned that he could easily fit inside as there seemed to be plenty of room above but was in no hurry to find out - until suddenly the door handle rattled! Now he had to, and quickly. Horace's legs thrashed wildly in the air as he hauled himself clumsily into the roof space just as the door opened. He manoeuvred himself so that he could see out of the hatch and from the darkness of his plastic loft he gazed down on a smartly-dressed man who had entered carrying a day sack on his back and holding a small vase of flowers which he immediately placed beside the sink before adjusting it fastidiously. Then, from his day sack, he produced a bottle of liquid soap and a jar of hand-cream which he positioned side by side in front of the flowers. He then pulled a pure white hand towel through the rail in front of the sink. He put a diffuser next to the toilet before leaning out and hanging a framed picture onto the back of the door. Horace pulled his head back in order to get a better look at what the picture was - it appeared to be another gold disc! Finally he placed a roll of white toilet paper in the holder before smiling to himself and pulling shut and locking the door. Suddenly it went quite dark apart from a ray of light streaming in through the little window. Then the man pressed a button on the wall and a small lamp came on above the mirror. He pumped a button on the floor and water flowed from the tap. He pressed a button beside the toilet which then flushed. Horace wondered what the man was about to do now the door was locked but given the primary purpose of a Portaloo he had quite a good idea. Horace felt around him; there appeared to be no escape through the roof and even if he could push the roof off it couldn't be done without being seen and so the only option was to quietly close the little hatch door and leave the man to finish his business, apart from the fact that he was once more reaching into his day sack. Horace couldn't think what more the man could produce that would enhance this smallest room but this time the item appeared to be a little more sinister. The man flicked a switch on the object before lifting it up to the ceiling. Horace shrank back as much as he was able into the darkness as the hand came up through the hatch and deposited the item to the side, right next to Horace's elbow! Then the hand reached for the hatch door and pulled it shut. The man muttered "Adeus minha querida" and kissed the gold discs gently before unlocking the door, exiting, closing the door and disappearing into the festival leaving Horace prisoner in a Portaloo with a make-over and something decidedly dodgy with a red blinking light. He waited in his molded cell for a few minutes before he could stand the heat no more whereupon he pulled open the hatch door and blinked at the light from above the mirror and several chunky candles that the man had also installed in any remaining space and which were giving off a fair amount of light themselves as well as a not inconsiderable amount of heat. Horace was now able to take a better look at his surprise gift. It comprised a block of something the size of a small book that was wrapped in duct tape and strapped to an old mobile 'phone with the battery exposed and an aerial extended. There were some wires coming from the "book" and going into the side of the 'phone and then there was the matter of the little red light.

"Whatever it is," thought Horace, "it is not a wifi router and if it's what I think it is, my departure from this Portaloo is actually going to be through the roof after all, but swift and with me in several pieces. Oh Tintin, what would you do?"

Horace was confused. He couldn't begin to think why someone would want to plant such a device in a toilet of all places. Nevertheless this someone was definitely up to no good and so, rather than break out of the front door and frighten off the man, Horace decided that the best thing to do would be somehow to stop the device working. He knew that "it" needed a power supply and so, with one hand on the device to steady it, tugged gently at the battery until it came out. The little red light went off and Horace sighed. He could now plan his next move. But just as Horace had decided what to do the door opened again. "Maybe the toilet's in service now," he thought as he moved away from the hatch opening again. "I'll wait here until the coast is clear and then make my escape. Maybe the man's come back for his explosive thing or whatever it is," he wondered as he slipped the battery into his pocket.

Horace kept his head well away from the hatch as he gazed down below. A beautiful tanned youngish woman entered wearing a white silk dressing gown and not much else as far as Horace could make out. Humming to herself she put down her glass of Champagne that she was holding, locked the door and arched her back as if doing some stretching exercises. She gazed into the small mirror then flicked up her long blond hair before reaching for the cord of her dressing gown. Now there were things in Horace's short life that he had seen that he hadn't wanted to see, and there were things that he wanted to see that he hadn't yet seen and this particular situation was definitely in the latter category. But Horace was a gentleman, and an honourable one at that; he knew right from wrong and this singular situation was about to be very wrong. The only problem was, what could he do? What would a gentleman do? Would a gentleman know what to do? How often would a gentleman find himself curled up in the roof of a Portaloo with a Miss World below? Horace decided that he had two options, to "sit" it out or announce his presence. He quickly decided that the only realistic option, however difficult the inevitable result - immediate and probably violent expulsion at least but maybe prison or do they have executions in Portugal? - was to announce himself which he did in as gentlemanly a way as he could think - he coughed softly. Of course there really was no way that Horace could have made himself known without scaring the life out of the poor woman. The bronzed beauty arched her back some more and then her neck until she was, deliberately or otherwise, looking up at the hatch. Then she froze. All she could see were two small eyes peering out from the gloom and so she did what any sensible woman would do in a similar situation. She screamed. "Aaaaaargh! Aaaaaargh! Aaaaaargh!" However, fortunately for Horace, the sound checks were in full swing and so no one was taking any notice, imagining that the noise, even if they had heard it, was one of the performers giving their larynx a bit of a warm-up and not the A-lister who had just come eye to eye with a Portaloo prowler. The woman might simply have unlocked the door and ran back into the VIP area to summon help but such was her self-conscious déshabillé that she had decided to put herself back together again first even if it did mean having to share several extra seconds with her toilet trespasser. When she failed to move a further muscle Horace poked his head through the hatch and announced, "I'm sorry but I'm lost."

"'Lost?' 'Lost?'" The woman was thinking fast. This was just a boy. Maybe he had been playing hide and seek, and evidently he didn't appear to be posing much of a threat.

Even so, the situation was a bit weird. "'Lost?'" she gasped a third time, "How do you get lost in a mobile toilet, English boy?"

The woman gained her composure as Horace wondered how he could respond to this perfectly reasonable question without causing her any further alarm. Eventually he decided that a bit more time was ideally what was needed therefore he asked quietly, "If it's okay with you, do you think that I could come down so that I can explain?"

"Where are you from?" asked the woman also not answering the question. This was becoming infectious but as far as she was concerned she was keen to keep Horace at arm's length for the time being, certainly until she was satisfied as to the reason for the stripling squatter in her own personal Portaloo.

"Chislehurst," replied Horace. "It's very hot up here."

"'Chislehurst?'" the woman replied, evidently unsure as to where Chislehurst was.

"Yes, it's in Kent. Do you know it?" asked Horace expectantly, rather in the manner that Americans think that anyone who lives in or near London is related to the monarch or is a personal friend.

"No," said the woman.

"It's the bottom bit of England on the right. We have caves there."

"'Caves?' Like for storing wine?"

"No," said Horace patiently. Then he added, "Cor dear, you sound just like Bagheera. Like the Flintstones."

"'Bagheera?' 'Flintstones?'" asked the woman who had decided that maybe escape was the best option after all. "I tell you what, crazy boy. You come down and I'll go out."

"No, no, no," said Horace sounding very serious and frowning. "I really don't think that that would be a very good idea."

"Why not?" asked the woman reaching for the door lock. Horace wanted to tell the woman that he had possibly just disabled a bomb but he knew that if he said that then not only would the woman definitely open the door but also that she would run out screaming and screaming and screaming so loud that this time everyone would hear.

"I need you just to think for a minute," said Horace, wondering how on earth he was going to tell the woman not so much the reason for why he was in the roof-space but what had happened while he was up there.

"What would be quite useful to think about would be something like is there anything odd going on in your life with someone who maybe doesn't like you?" The woman did think she could indeed name several people who didn't like her but given who she was that was hardly surprising. Jealousy was something that the victim could not always do very much about. However Horace had asked about anything odd going on in her life and, combining the two, there was only one person - her beloved fiancé. He had been behaving very strangely recently and she hadn't needed Horace's comments to lead her to this conclusion. In view of their forthcoming nuptials he had recently made her the sole beneficiary of his not very much at all whilst she had made him the sole beneficiary of her considerable wealth and since then he had been acting very, very oddly. One minute he was buying her a very expensive present, the next he was being extremely spiteful towards her. She had latterly decided that she had to do something about the situation but wasn't at all too sure what. Now it appeared that, bizarrely, this eleven-year old ruffian in her Portaloo roof may possibly, unbelievably, unfathomably hold the key.

"Descend," she said beckoning up at Horace, "and quickly tell me your story."

Horace clambered back down once the woman had put the towel on the edge of the sink, "Mind the flowers!" and sat down on the closed toilet lid whilst she remained standing, perched against the sink. Horace thought that it was all rather cosy although he would have preferred somewhere slightly more salubrious for their introductory meeting - such as round a campfire with a pile of s'mores - but at least the toilet had a seat.

Horace told the woman everything, firstly about how he had managed inadvertently to get into the festival grounds and then how he was trying to plot an exit in as unobtrusive a way as his entrance when a man came into the toilet and...

"Wait a moment," said the woman, much to Horace's relief as he was unsure how to move onto the next part of this little episode without her screaming the place down again. "You said 'a man'. What did he look like exactly?"

Horace had only had a bird's eye view but he tried his best. "He was quite smart and he had a day sack and he put loads of things all around like flowers..."

"Okay, I know who that is. That's fine," said the woman sighing heavily. "Continue."

"But it's not fine," said Horace desperately. "But it's okay 'cos I defused it."

"'Defused?' What do you mean?"

"It means 'to stop something from exploding.' Look." Horace reached into his pocket and pulled out the battery.

"I can't see that that's going to do much damage," she said dismissively.

"No, not on its own. But it's what it was attached to that could do the harm. The man put it into the roof space when I was hiding up there. I'll climb up and get it." Even though this meant Horace clambering onto the sink again the woman was in no mood to remonstrate this time. There was no way that she was going to put her hand up there. Horace reached in and pulled out the device.

"There!" he said triumphantly, shoving it in the woman's face, "What d'you think of that?!" The woman was transfixed, presumably thinking about what the consequences might have been and for whom - her very self. So much was now making sense. She recalled that only the previous day, during a heated argument, her fiancé had told her that one day she would regret having ever met him. But an explosive situation was not what she would ever have anticipated. It was almost unbelievable but Horace's minimal description matched him and he did have plenty to gain even at the expense of something far more valuable or so she imagined. A cold shiver ran down her back. Somewhere on the other side of the Portaloo door there was a man who was shortly to attempt to execute a dastardly deed. It was just by chance that the woman had made an early, unplanned visit to the toilet and so time was just about still on their side.

"He's probably going to try to remotely detonate the device at some point, hence the 'phone, but not yet as he doesn't know I'm in here. I normally use the toilet just before I'm about to go on stage. You stay in here and lock yourself in now that the device is safe and I'll go and get help."

"Okay," said Horace obligingly, yet he was desperate to find out who his new companion was. Despite their personal meeting he had no idea but she was obviously someone sufficiently well-known to be appearing on stage as well as having her own toilet and a flushing one at that.

"But can I ask you a question? I don't want to sound rude, but there is something that I would like to know."

"Of course."

"Who exactly are you?" The woman laughed.

"Oh, I'm sorry. My name is Catarina Lawrence. I'm known to my adoring fans as 'Cata L'. I'm Portugal's leading dance DJ apparently. Everyone knows me over here which is often a good thing but it looks as though it also has its downside and a quite considerable one at that. I'm the Portuguese Pete Tong. I'm acknowledged throughout the dance world. My father is English and I was educated in England although I have lived mainly in Portugal. I've played all over the world, from the smallest pubs to the biggest clubs and parties. I've been in some good places and I've been in some bad places so I know how to look after myself. Now I'm here at the best place in the world, 'Viva em Caparica', where I'm going to be doing a warm-up shortly and then headlining on the main stage and you're in my toilet! Now let me go and get some help."

"Just one more question?"

"Yes?"

"Please can I go to the toilet? Your toilet? I'm bursting."

\*\*\*

Horace excused himself from his raised position and joined the Ravens out in the crowd, stopping for a few selfies on the way. No one else knew who he was but he had come from somewhere important and had been chatting to "Cata L" and he now had a security guard in tow so he must be a somebody. The noise volume from the band that was playing nearby was deafening but the Ravens thought that they understood what Horace was telling them: that he had saved someone from being blown up and that someone else had been arrested. "Yeah, sure," said Emily scornfully and the others nodded in agreement with what they thought that they had heard but weren't too certain.

"Come on," said Horace beckoning. "I'll get you all a pomegranate juice. It's a deep red colour like wine so we can look all grown-up. It's a Lisbon speciality according to Catarina."

"That's probably what we saw Anne-Marie drinking," said Melanie, "but how are we going to get served? We've no chance."

"That is why Catarina has assigned me my own minder. This is 'Dur-man' or something like that. I don't know if that's her first name or what but because I could be in danger she's looking after me this evening and I was told that she will do anything we need."

"Blimey," said Emily. "Can she get us vodka?"

"Then," said Horace, ignoring the request, "we can get some chocolate churros. It's like doughnut only it's a stick shape and they squirt hot creamy chocolate down the middle. It's really yummy. Then we can go to the custard tart stall and have some of them each. Once we've done that we can go and watch Catarina on the main stage as she's just about to do her first set."

Through Horace's newly-elevated temporary status and with the help of Dur-man the Ravens managed to secure a small space at the front of the crowd to one side. Emily thought that it was only because they were children that they were allowed up the front but didn't say anything. Then an electronic keyboard sound started to waft from the stage and through the air. Catarina walked onto the stage and waved. She hadn't even reached her decks and the crowd was already going wild. She set up the first deafening beat track of the night and with one hand on the controls she waved the other at the crowd some more. "Cata L!" they shouted. "Cata L! Cata L! Cata L!" The new beat grew faster and the music was off and running - and getting even louder.

"Anyone for some more pomegranate and chocolate churros?" asked Horace and Dur-man disappeared shortly to return with a large tray of both and more custard tarts. The Ravens all cheered. Maybe Horace was telling the truth after all.

Halfway through the set their suspicions were confirmed. Catarina turned down the volume by a couple of notches and shouted breathlessly, speaking alternately in Portuguese and English, "This evening I would like to thank my new friend from Chislehurst, England where there are some caves! He is someone who, quite literally, 'saved my life tonight!'"

She then turned the volume back up two notches to Elton John's song, "Someone Saved my Life Tonight" with a remix-dance-electro-beat. As John launched into the second verse Catarina shouted, "Give it up for my own sugar bear, Horace Horrise!" The crowd went wild some more as Emily stood open mouthed.

"Or-a-see o-he-see! Or-a-see o-he-see! Or-a-see o-he-see!" the crowd chanted. Coloured lights perforated the night sky, strobing rained over the crowd.

"We want Or-a-see o-he-see! We want Or-a-see o-he-see!" the crowd shrieked. Catarina gestured down at Horace and he smiled back before he felt Dur-man take him by the hand and pull him to one side.

"You famous now Or-a-see!" she affirmed before leading him up the side steps.

"More churros," thought Horace but the reality was even more satisfying. Before he realised where Dur-man was leading him he found himself at the edge of the stage.

"Go and beware of wires!" she commanded and pushed Horace towards Catarina, still holding his pomegranate juice and chocolate churros. The crowd was leaping and dancing as out from the front of the stage huge jets of foam were being sprayed over the masses as the volume of the music increased even more. Horace waved and the chanting got even louder. Then Catarina gave Horace a kiss on the cheek as fireworks exploded behind the stage and enormous rockets shot up into the sky before exploding and showering the crowd with bright gold stars.

And not fifty metres away, towards the back of the crowd, stood one solitary English scout leader and camp nurse who

268

couldn't even see the stage through the foam and smoke, but as she sipped on her glass of Cerejeiras wondered to herself how funny it was that the Portuguese were calling out a name that sounded just like one of her scouts whom she was sure was in her camp and probably still in the toilet.

And not three hundred metres away over the perimeter fence, across a road and over another perimeter fence, two hundred scouts and leaders - less seven - were sleeping fitfully in their tents each thinking the same thing: that possibly they were dreaming but whatever it was that the DJ was shouting, it sounded just like the name of one of their fellow scouts that funnily enough they hadn't seen around at all that evening.

\*\*\*

Two o'clock in the morning and despite the first night of the festival having two more hours to run the Ravens decided it was time to go back to camp. "I would like to say, 'call it a day,'" said Charlie, "but it's going to be more like calling it a night." The crowd was still growing in size, the music was off the scale loud and still getting louder and all six Ravens had been granted special access to the silver star Portaloos, the gold one having been covered in police "NÃO ENTRE" tape.

"We'd better not go through the main entrance," said Charlie, "in case anyone sees us," without realising that most of the scouts would be tucked up in their sleeping bags and those that weren't would not be the ones likely to tell. Emily led them to her hole then, once all were through, she closed it up again before they dismantled Archie's pioneering which was, somewhat ironically, only about three metres away from Emily's opening.

Horace felt that he hadn't been asleep for very long, and indeed he hadn't, when he suddenly awoke with a severe stomach ache and a tickly feeling in his throat. Several glasses of pomegranate juice and a large quantity of chocolate churros on an empty stomach plus the custard tarts plus the added excitement of the evening was a very potent mix. Horace shook Charlie until he awoke, or at least made a groaning sound, and then announced what never fails to make a scout leader sigh resignedly, "I think I'm going to be sick."

Charlie did not need telling twice. From lying supine he sat straight up in his sleeping bag and immediately went into a forward roll without even attempting to get to his feet. Fortunately the drowsy duo hadn't zipped up the tent flaps so in two rolls Charlie was outside, still in his sleeping bag, having grabbed his rucksack on the way out, just as Horace started to retch. Charlie wasn't sure what to do once outside but so long as he could hear Horace he knew that he was okay so he just sat looking at the moon until eventually Horace crawled out and said rather pathetically, "I think I've made a bit of a mess, but at least it's all in the tent."

"For that we should be extremely grateful." said Charlie wearily, imagining having otherwise to pick his way through a sandy minefield of illness. All he wanted was a few hours sleep but now Horace was okayish he wasn't sure what to do once more.

"How much of a mess have you actually made?" he asked reticently.

"If you can imagine someone putting loads of mud in the tie-dye before shaking it all up and then throwing it everywhere, that's what it now looks like in our tent - with bits of carrot. There's always bits of carrot!" said Horace, far too cheerfully for Charlie's liking.

"And the smell?"

"Well, if you think of what the toilets here smell like by bedtime and then multiply by one hundred, that's what it now smells like."

"So now what are you going to do?" asked Charlie despairingly.

"What are we going to do, Charlie," corrected Horace. "It's not just me."

"As far as I'm concerned it is. It's you that got us into this mess. I mean mess as in mess mess. Oh, never mind. I can't think. My words are coming out but I'm not even sure what words they are." Charlie was feeling very tired and even a little weepy. He also didn't feel particularly well. He wasn't sure if it had been just the talk of sick or maybe he was going to be ill also.

"Actually I got you out of the mess mess, but I'll suggest what to do. I can sort our tent out. You can go in Anne-Marie's sick bay tent. I don't think that there's anyone in it 'cos it looks like the flaps are, well, flapping and in the morning you can tell her that you're in there due to sickness. You don't have to tell her that it's my sickness. Off you go - quietly, I have a tent to clean."

Charlie didn't need telling twice. He reached into his rucksack and pulled out his torch. The entrance to the sick bay tent was about ten metres away across the sand and with no obstacles. He shone his torch at the entrance and positioned himself so that he was facing the tent head on. There was no way that he was going to get out of his sleeping bag unless he really, really had to. Holding onto his rucksack he rocked himself into another forward roll. Over he went, one, two, three, four, five and he was in! He zipped up the flaps and immediately went back to sleep.

Once he had seen Charlie disappear back under "canvas" Horace sat down on a large log and considered how he was going to get his and Charlie's tent clean by breakfast. The usual "slop and mop" routine was out of the question as Horace would have to find a broom, a bucket, a mop, several cloths, some disinfectant and a clothes peg for his nose. No, he had just thought of a better idea. The toilets stank and there shouldn't be many people in them at this time of night. He dragged out his rucksack from the tent, he would have to deal with that later, then unpegged the ground sheet and guy ropes. He would drag the tent up to the shower block for it was his intention to turn it inside out and then take it into the shower with him so that they could both be cleaned. He would then turn the tent outside in and repeg it before putting on his wetsuit and retiring for what was left of the night. Hopefully the tent would dry out before breakfast. The only other problem was his sleeping bag. He had thought of taking that into the shower with him also but didn't know if they were allowed to get wet. He couldn't recall his mother ever having put it in the washing machine. Maybe they just had to be replaced each time they got a bit smelly? Horace decided that as he didn't really need his sleeping bag anymore on this trip he would just have to tell his mother that it had become too smelly to bring home, "'cos it was covered in pomegranate juice and chocolate churros and custard tart"; he would conveniently forget to tell her that this heady cocktail had covered his sleeping bag via his stomach. So he buried it. He rolled it into a tight cylindrical shape before forcing it into its stuff sack. Getting down onto his hands and knees he scraped back enough sand to make a shallow grave in order to entomb his evil-smelling evidence. "That's the first bit sorted," he thought to himself.

Horace picked up one corner of the tent and started to drag it up the path to the showers. He was glad that he and Charlie were sharing a polyester three-man and not one of the large canvas patrol tents. Even so it was becoming quite a struggle especially as it had the contents of half his stomach slopping about inside.

Normally the route from Horace's sub-camp to the shower block would be rather circuitous as the scouts were not allowed to go the most direct route because it would take them through the outbuilding area including the reception, a workshop, the food store and leaders' rest area, all of which surrounded a small quadrangle and which were out of bounds for several perfectly sound reasons. Nevertheless Horace's load was burdensome and surely no scout leader would be prowling around at early in the morning a.m? In any event, Horace was prepared. He would feign sleepwalking and if that failed he would claim sickness. Maybe he would try both together although he realised that that might incur some extra difficulties. He took a deep breath and walked past the leaders' rest area and into the quad pulling his tent wearily behind him. All of a sudden he decided that he needed a brief rest and this was a good place to stop, hidden from the other tents and the occasional wanderer. As for the leaders they were obviously fast asleep. He looked around at the towels strewn across the ground, boxes everywhere, various bits of games equipment, folders left open on chairs, half-finished drinks. There was even a laptop sitting on one of the tables. Horace couldn't believe his eyes. "They make enough fuss over our tents, but look at this lot! It's just as well it never rains, it would be a complete disaster if it did. At least I suppose no one's going to break in and steal anything," he thought, "unless they find Emily's hole."

"Once I've sorted out my tent I might come back at breakfast time and offer to Tim to clear up, that'll give me Brownie points to hold in reserve." As Horace continued surveying the disaster area, aided by the light of the moon and a few lamps that had been left on inside the buildings, he espied what looked like a fire hydrant with a large "button" on top and four hose connectors coming out of the sides, but he couldn't be certain of their purpose. However Horace had been thinking through dragging his tent into the shower - how it might not be as easy as he had first envisaged and now he stood before a much quicker and easier solution. All he probably needed was a bit of hose to plug in. Looking around Horace concluded that hose was about the only thing that didn't seem to be available.

"I don't know which way the water will come out but if I just put the tent completely over the hydrant and press the button the water will just come out and wash the tent on the inside without going everywhere, a bit like a car wash for the inside of a car," thought Horace. "That'll work."

He hauled the stinking material over the hydrant and pushed on the button through the tent. Nothing happened so he bashed it with his fist. Still nothing. So he pressed then bashed the four connectors then started to kick it.

Horace was getting desperate. "I - am - not - leaving - here - without - cleaning - my - tent!" he shouted at the hydrant under his breath, literally through gritted teeth, as he kicked the hydrant after each word. All of a sudden there was a low whooshing noise like a toilet being flushed that crescendoed into the sound of a very angry waterfall - only the water wasn't coming down it was going up! It came flying straight out of the top of the hydrant like a liquid rocket. Horace put his hand in the vertical torrent as if to calm it but it nearly took his fingers off. He didn't even know where his tent had gone. Horace knew about Isaac Newton and his quote about, "What goes up must come down," and now he was having first-hand experience of what he meant. For the thousands of litres of water that were being pumped up into the night sky were now falling, as if someone had turned the Atlantic Ocean upside down, he thought.

Horace half-heartedly jabbed at the now uncovered hydrant but he knew that it was useless. He knew how much effort it had taken to get it going and he didn't even know how he managed to succeed in that endeavour so stopping it was going to be impossible. He was completely drenched and although on another day he might have enjoyed the experience of standing at the bottom of a waterfall in his trunks, the fact was that he was standing in his sicky t-shirt and sicky shorts feeling cold, very wet and undoubtedly in humongous trouble so right now all he wanted, he decided, was to be at home amongst his family in a nice warm bed with Tintin. The outbuildings' concrete floors were slightly raised and Horace realised that he was standing in a couple of centimetres of water that was starting to resemble an industrial-size paddling pool. The towels were soaked, the boxes were disintegrating, the various bits of games equipment were floating and the folders were giving up their contents. At least the drinks had been topped up. As for the laptop, Horace hoped that there was nothing too important stored on it. It was, by now, time to take decisive action. Therefore Horace did what any sensible person would do in the circumstances - he ran. He ran as fast as he was able. He ran back to where Charlie and his tent were, at least where the tent had been for most of the trip. He pulled over a beach chair and grabbed a towel off the string line. It had been a long day. Soon he was also asleep, as asleep as one could be given the situation - which was actually very asleep.

\*\*\*

"Horace. HORACE!" Horace woke with a start and opened one eye before shutting it again, blinded by the morning sun and the fact that Emily was staring at him.

"What d'you want Emily? I've just gone to sleep." he drowsily complained.

"It's seven o'clock. I just got up for a wee and saw you sitting there with a towel on your head. Where's your tent? Where's Charlie?" she demanded. "Have you heard?"

"Don't know and in the sick bay tent and no I haven't and I don't want to either," Horace not very patiently explained.

"Oh dear, what's made him sick?" she asked, seemingly totally nonplussed that Horace should have lost his tent and not be at all concerned.

"Me, sort of," said Horace trying to explain but then realising that it might take a bit longer to fully satisfy Emily's curiosity.

"I'll tell you later. Right now I need to sleep."

"It's a bit late for that. You might as well be getting up, not that that means doing much more that just standing up, as far as you're concerned," she said, trying to sound positive.

"Skip said we had to get up at seven today so he'll be on the prowl soon followed by Tim followed by the one with the funny name."

"They all have funny names, Emily," complained Horace. "Sometimes I think I'm speaking to a load of characters from out of the Tweenies."

"If I were you I'ld be getting ahead of the game. Pack up your kit, find your tent and then go and have a wash..."

"'A wash?' That's the last thing I need Em." Emily looked at him suspiciously.

"Oh, look Horace," she said brightly. "Here comes Charlie. He doesn't look very sick. Maybe he's feeling better already."

"Charlie," said Horace forlornly, once Charlie had forward rolled back over to the pair, even though he was now out of his sleeping bag. "Can I borrow a towel and some of your clothes?" Of course he could. Horace sneaked into the sick bay tent to dry himself fully and get changed. When he emerged he saw to his horror Charlie talking to John.

"Good morning Horace," John called over. "Can I have a word? Where's your tent? Charlie says he doesn't know."

"All packed up and by the lorry ready to go back with all the other stuff," Horace lied. Lying wasn't something that he wanted to do but desperate times called for desperate measures. "In any event," thought Horace, "it's only a lie if John goes and checks and finds that the tent isn't by the lorry. Which even if he does could take a bit of time what with all the other bits of kit that will be starting to pile up."

"You can go and check if you like," Horace suggested.

"No, that's fine Horace," said John smiling. "Well done. I wish everyone was as prepared as you were. But tell me one thing. How did you manage to pack it up with Charlie still in it and without his knowing what you had done?"

"Oh I don't know Skip," said Horace feeling very confused at John's line of questioning. "Maybe he was dreaming."

\*\*\*

"Scouts alert!" The scouts had all gathered in a large circle around the Union Jack as Tim had an important announcement to make.

"I'm sorry to you all because, as you will all no doubt be aware and if you're not you should be, as you will all have been for a wash or shower and or flush this morning, that the campsite at present has no water. Unfortunately, during the night the water hydrant that is situated in the leaders' compound suffered a catastrophic malfunction and, as is usual, after a few minutes the mains valve - the one that regulates the water into the campsite - kicked in and cut off our water supply. Regrettably this was not before the leaders' restroom and stores were flooded. So if any of you

278

would like to volunteer to help clear up the mess?" Horace put his hand straight up into the air.

"Thank you Horace, I must say you are an example to us all. I didn't see you around at all last night and so scouts you can see of what benefit this is to the common cause. It was Benjamin Franklin, one of America's founding fathers who said, 'Early to bed and early to rise makes a man healthy, wealthy and wise.' So 'well done Horace' although goodness knows how you slept through all that racket last night!"

"That was no racket Tim, that was Catarina Lawrence," said Horace, somewhat affronted by Tim's description. "She's known to her adoring fans as 'Cata L'. She's Portugal's leading dance DJ. Everyone knows her over here. She's the Portuguese Pete Tong. She's known throughout the dance world. Her father is English and she was educated in England although she's mainly lived in Portugal. She's played all over the world, from the smallest pubs to the biggest clubs and parties..."

"Okay Horace, thank you. You've obviously been doing your homework," Tim joked. "Is she a relation of yours?"

"No, just a very good friend," and all the scouts laughed - all apart from six.

\*\*\*

A few hours later and the scouts had once more formed a large circle for the final flag-down of the camp.

"As you know we 'ave about twenty scouts from zee north of our country and zey would like to give you a traditional Portuguese 'bon voyage.'"

279

The English scouts turned once more toward their Portuguese counterparts. The eldest one spoke in perfect English, "We have a goodbye song that you all know. It's 'So long, Farewell' from 'The Sound of Music.'"

With the clearance of intonation, in tune and with even more actions they sang first all together, then in pairs as they turned and left the circle, complete with the "cuckoo"s in the correct places.

By the time that the last "Auf Weidersehen, goodbye" was sung Horace and the Ravens were, once more, mesmerised. The group returned and took off their hats and bowed. All was calm. The scouts clapped politely and Bagheera turned to Tim but said nothing. "It's okay," said Tim. "We're prepared."

Tim had prepared his sidekick Moto to read out a letter of thanks for Bagheera that had been signed by all the leaders, to present a card to him signed by all the scouts and to give him a memento in the form of a presentation wall plaque and a tie-dye t-shirt in the district colours. But Moto was nowhere to be seen. Tim put his head to his hands.

"Please Tim." It was Horace with his hand raised again.

"I don't think I can take it a second time Horace," he said despairingly.

"It's okay Tim, we've been practising."

"I don't doubt it Horace."

Horace took one step forward and opened his mouth as the rest of the scouts joined in.

"Oggy Oggy Oggy!
Oi Oi Oi!
Oggy Oggy Oggy!
Oi Oi Oi!
Oggy!
Oi!
Oggy!
Oi!
Oggy Oggy Oggy!
Oi Oi Oi!"

"Am I to dare to ask what 'appens now Tim?" asked Bagheera cautiously.

"You mustn't be surprised if a Welshman appears dressed as a leek," said Tim with a smile. "At least no one gets hurt."

\*\*\*

The scouts had gathered in the car park by a small fleet of coaches ready to take them back to the airport. Bagheera had appeared to say goodbye and to wave everybody off.

"You 'ave been fantastic guys. Some of zee best. And I 'ave good news. If you vant to go to zee toilet, it's too late for shower but if you vant a vee zen zee water is back!" and the scouts all cheered.

"But if you vant a poo, the paper in zee bucket..."

"You just 'ave to suck it!" the scouts all squealed back and then cheered some more.

"Anyway," he continued, "you all 'ave a safe journey 'ome. You should 'ave an easy flight. You know, zee planes take off out over zee ocean. You look up 'ere at the blue sky and...and..."

Bagheera was looking and pointing up and over the outbuildings when he stopped speaking and started to frown, apparently at what he saw, before putting his hand slowly back down. "What's the matter Bagheera?" asked Tim. Their convivial host had stopped mid-sentence. Was he overcome with emotion; had he suddenly taken ill? Bagheera looked at Tim and then back to the heavens as if trying to erase what he had just seen. He blinked. But it was still there.

"Tim," he said finally. "What on earth is zat tent doing on top of zat huge pine tree?"

\*\*\*

Once inside the airport and through security the Ravens had more than an hour to kill which was rather a long time with only a few Euros left between them. They wandered round trying all the samples that they could find and by the time that they had slumped back down together, still with half an hour to go before boarding, they had spent the Euros; they all reeked of a combination of several perfumes and after-shaves - one on top of the other - and had nibbled at everything from chocolate to chorizo. As they sat in a line on the airport chairs playing "I spy", Emily, who had been looking at the front page of the newspaper that a passenger opposite her was reading, shouted out "I spy Horace!"

"No you numpty," said Melanie. "You have to just give the letter."

"Alright," she said obligingly. "I spy with my little eye something beginning with 'H'".

"Horace!" the Ravens cried.

"Yes!" she confirmed. "Where?"

"Here!" they cried, all pointing at him, including Horace who was pointing at himself.

"No!" cried Emily triumphantly, "Over there! Look!"

The Ravens looked at where she was pointing which led them to the front page of the newspaper, "24 Horas em Lisboa" opposite. Underneath the headline was a picture of Cata L at the festival, microphone in one hand and holding up someone's hand with the other. It was Horace! Horace smirked. "What does the headline say?" he wondered aloud.

"I don't know," said Charlie, "Let's ask."

Charlie stood up and wandered across to the passenger. "Excuse me," he said politely. The passenger put down his paper and looked up to see six young people staring at him.

"Can I help you?" he asked.

"Yes, you can," said Horace before Charlie could open his mouth. "What does that say in English please?" he asked, pointing at the headline above the picture.

"That? Oh that's Cata L, she's Portugal's top DJ. She's famous, she..."

"Yes, we know all that," Charlie interrupted. "We just want to know what it says."

"Well there's quite a bit about it. Apparently last night Cata L was nearly..."

"Yes, yes, we know," said Emily impatiently. "The headline?"

"It says, 'Someone saved my life tonight.'"

"Thank you," said Horace. "And when you've finished with the newspaper do you think I could have it?"

The man neatly folded the paper up and handed it to him. "Well done Horace!" he exclaimed. "You're famous! Nearly as famous as Cata L, for a while at least."

\*\*\*

Mr and Mrs Horrise had been enjoying a few days of relative peace at home in Chislehurst without too much drama from the remaining two offspring who had spent much of their time out and about. Olivia had even had a few days on cub camp. Until Horace returned the only low point had been when Olivia had returned and announced as she walked in through the front door, "Akela is a cow!" and then stomped off to her room refusing to give an explanation for her rather uncharacteristic outburst. The reason became clear several days later when Akela herself rang the Horrise household and told Mrs Horrise that her daughter had been disciplined for answering back. Akela had told Olivia off for having an extremely untidy tent with clothes and accessories strewn all over the ground sheet. She said that she had expected Olivia just to say "sorry" but instead Olivia curtly informed Akela that it was her "floordrobe" and what did she expect if they weren't given hangers? Mrs Horrise had tried not to giggle.

In fact, even with Horace back at home all was peaceful among the children. They seemed to have missed each other and all Saturday afternoon and all day Sunday they had played perfectly happily together. This harmony was only shattered by their mother, of all people, when she went into the children's bathroom on Sunday evening to find it in not too dissimilar a state to Olivia's floordrobe but with a far more unsavoury addition. "Hor-ace!" she hollered from the door even though he was only a few feet away in his bedroom. Horace came out and found his mother on the landing with one hand on the bathroom doorknob with the door wide open and her staring inside.

"Yes mummy?" Horace asked, not too sure what on earth could be the matter with the bathroom when it was a place that he didn't frequent too often; certainly he was the least likely of the three to be found in it.

"Why in the name of goodness," she asked, "is there loads of stinky used toilet paper all over the floor? Have you forgotten where it goes? It looks like a bomb's hit it!"

Horace's mother turned round and looked at him suspiciously. "Is that the sort of thing that went on in Lisbon?"

"Very nearly mummy, yes."

"Horace, what are you talking about?"

"Just wait there a moment mummy whilst I go and fetch you a certain newspaper that a man gave me at the airport. Do you have an English / Portuguese dictionary? Or maybe, like your magazines, you will get the idea from the photo."

\*\*\*

If you've enjoyed "The Further Adventures of Horace Horrise" please check out my website www.johnhemmingclark.com or www.amazon.co.uk for details of my other Horace Horrise books.

Please also leave an Amazon review. I would be very grateful. On Amazon - find "The Further Adventures of Horace Horrise" at www.amazon.co.uk and scroll down to and click on "Write a customer review" then "Submit".

**www.johnhemmingclark.com**

# ALSO AVAILABLE BY JOHN HEMMING-CLARK

## In You Go!
## A Year or Two in the Life of a Scout Leader
Paperback: £9.99 ISBN: 9781897864265
*"...this is one of the funniest books I have ever read." Amazon review*

## Sleeping Bags & Tortures. The Private Diaries of an Adventurous Scout & his Scout Leader
Paperback £9.99 ISBN 9781897864326
Hardback £16.99 ISBN 9781897864302
*A brilliant book, I couldn't put it down. By presenting the story through the eyes of both a Scout and their Leader you get a great insight into the crazy adventures of the 3rd Chislehurst Scout Troop..."*
*Amazon review*

## 1000 Fantastic Scout Games
Paperback £9.99 ISBN 9781897864296
*"Great book, fantastic to have so many games to hand ..."*
*"A lot of new ideas covering indoor and outdoor games with easy to follow instructions. I highly recommend this to any Scout or play groups and is suitable for all sections and ages." Amazon reviews*

## 250 No Equipment Games
Paperback: £6.99 ISBN 9781897864388
*"Perfect for the times when you go to get a ball and the cubs have taken them all to camp, or you haven't planned a game and it needs a new one. Some in, some out, some noisy, some quiet, something for everyone." Amazon review*

## Letters Home from Scout and Guide Camp
Paperback £1.99 ISBN 9781897864364
*"I took this book to our cub camp and the children as well as the adults really enjoyed it. Very funny - a lot of fun. This book is "very enjoyable" by all ages. It made an evening of excellent entertainment."*
*Amazon review*
Available online from www.johnhemmingclark.com or (inc. download)
www.amazon.co.uk. Cards: Tel: 020 8468 7945.
Cheques: ("Searchline Publishing") Searchline House, 1A Holbrook Lane, Chislehurst, BR7 6PE